Karen Tapia

CATHLEEN SCHINE is the author of *The Three Weiss-manns of Westport, The New Yorkers,* and *The Love Letter,* among other novels. She has contributed to *The New Yorker, The New York Review of Books, The New York Times Magazine,* and *The New York Times Book Review.* She lives in Los Angeles, California.

D0167657

Additional Praise for *Fin & Lady*

"Much more than a simple coming-of-age story—Schine animates the turbulent sixties through the tension of two siblings left to fend for themselves."
—*Vogue*

"A sparkling comic cocktail."
—*More*

"Schine knows that laughter isn't just an escape from life's sorrows but also a recognition of them. . . . She conveys the rapidly shifting mores of the '60s, as well as the slowly unfolding understanding of these appealingly vulnerable characters."
—*The Washington Post*

"Schine is a wonderful storyteller with a sensational ability to marry the comic with the bittersweet, and she is adept at re-creating tricky family dynamics spoken and unspoken. . . . Smart [and] entertaining."
—*The Miami Herald*

"A clever, lively story (does Schine write any other kind?)."
—*Minneapolis Star Tribune*

"[Lady] shares more than a few traits with Truman Capote's iconic heroine. . . . Quirky [and] engaging . . . A charming novel, ideal for summer."
—*The Christian Science Monitor*

"An enchanting novel about enchanting things . . . [*Fin & Lady*] is a historical novel through and through, and it provides the reader with the particular gift of the genre: an exhilarating sense of how it felt to live, talk, read, and love during another, seemingly more glorious time."
—*San Francisco Chronicle*

fin & lady

Cathleen Schine

Picador

A Sarah Crichton Book
Farrar, Straus and Giroux
New York

FIN & LADY. Copyright © 2013 by Cathleen Schine. All rights reserved. Printed in the United States of America. For information, address Picador, 175 Fifth Avenue, New York, N.Y. 10010.

www.picadorusa.com
www.twitter.com/picadorusa • www.facebook.com/picadorusa
picadorbookroom.tumblr.com

Picador® is a U.S. registered trademark and is used by Farrar, Straus and Giroux under license from Pan Books Limited.

For book club information, please visit www.facebook.com/picadorbookclub or e-mail marketing@picadorusa.com.

Designed by Abby Kagan

The Library of Congress has cataloged the Farrar, Straus and Giroux edition as follows:

Schine, Cathleen.
    Fin & Lady / Cathleen Schine. —First Edition.
       p. cm.
    ISBN 978-0-374-15490-5 (hardcover)
    ISBN 978-1-4668-3708-9 (e-book)
    1. Brothers and sisters—Fiction.   2. Guardian and ward—Fiction.
    3. Greenwhich Village (New York, N.Y.)—Fiction.   I. Title.
    II. Title: Fin and Lady.
    PS3569.C497 F56 2013
    813'.54—dc23

2013005510

Picador ISBN 978-1-250-05005-2

Picador books may be purchased for educational, business, or promotional use. For information on bulk purchases, please contact Macmillan Corporate and Premium Sales Department at 1-800-221-7945, extension 5442, or write specialmarkets@macmillan.com.

First published in the United States by Sarah Crichton Books, an imprint of Farrar, Straus and Giroux

First Picador Edition: May 2014

10 9 8 7 6 5 4 3 2 1

To

my sister,

Jennifer Schine

Fin & Lady

"Let's go home"

Fin's funeral suit was a year old, worn three times, already too small.

He knew his mother was sick. He knew she went to the hospital to get treatments. He saw the dark blue lines and dots on her chest.

"My tattoos," she said.

She sang "Popeye the Sailor Man" and raised her skinny arms as if to flex her Popeye muscles, to make him laugh.

He knew she was sick. He knew people died. But he never thought she would die. Not his mother. Not really.

Lady came to the funeral, an unmistakably foreign presence in the bare, white Congregational church: she wore large sunglasses and wept audibly.

Fin's neighbors, the Pounds, who raised big, thick Morgan horses, had been looking after Fin since his mother was taken to the hospital.

"I'm sure your mother knew what she was doing," Mr. Pound said doubtfully when he saw Lady Hadley approach, her arms open wide, a lighted cigarette dangling from her lips.

"I don't think she had much choice, dear," Mrs. Pound whispered to him. "There was no one else, was there?"

"I like Lady," Fin said loyally. But she was terrifying, coming at him like some mad bird with a squawk of "*Fratello mio! It's all so dreadful!*"

Lady put her arms around him and held him close. She was all he had, as Mrs. Pound had pointed out. All he had. He barely knew her. Unfamiliar arms. A stranger's cheek, wet with tears leaking from beneath her dark glasses. He wanted to cry, too, for so many reasons that they seemed to cancel one another out. He stood there like a statue, nauseated and faint.

The other mourners stared at Lady. Why wouldn't they? She stood out. She vibrated, almost, in that quiet church. She was beautiful. Fin liked her hair, which was long. He liked her teeth. She thought they were too big, but she was wrong. She was like a horse. Not one of the Pounds' heavy Morgan horses with short sturdy necks and thick clomping legs. She was like a racehorse. Jittery. Majestic. Her long neck and long legs—and her face, too. She had a horsey face, in a beautiful way. And bangs, like a forelock. He'd told her that, the last time he'd seen her. He had been five. "You look like a horse," he'd said. "Charming," said Lady. "Me and Eleanor Roosevelt." He had not meant that at all. Eleanor Roosevelt, whose picture he'd seen in the newspaper, did not look like a horse. More like his grandmother. Big, sloping breast. Important face. He meant that Lady's eyes were huge and dark, that her cheekbones were high and pronounced, that her face was aristocratic and long, that her hair flew in the wind like a mane, that she was coltish even in her movements of tentative wildness and reckless dignity. He didn't know that he meant all that when he was five. He just knew that she reminded him of a horse. He was eleven now. He had not seen her for six years. She still reminded him of a horse. "A racehorse," he had added when he was five, and Lady had smiled and said, "Oh, that's all right, then."

When the funeral was over, Lady would not allow him to go to the grave site.

"It's barbaric," she said to Mr. and Mrs. Pound.

They looked at her with shocked faces, pinched by hurt at what they, rightly, took to be Lady's dismissal of every aspect of almost two thousand years of religious tradition.

"The kid is hanging on by his eyelids," she said.

"I saw Daddy buried," Fin said. "And Grandma and Grandpa."

"I rest my case," said Lady.

"You're the boss," Mr. Pound said. He heaved a sigh, then he shook Fin's hand and wished him luck in his new life.

Mrs. Pound hugged him and said he'd make his mother proud in heaven, and then he did start to cry and ran outside.

Humiliating, to cry at his age. Babies cried. The Pounds had a baby, a bald sticky one that screamed for no reason, out of the blue. Mrs. Pound would pick it up and hug it. Fin wanted to shake it, although, really, he could not imagine even touching it. It was an obnoxious baby. "I'll give you something to cry about," Fin's father used to say. Then he died. The Pounds' baby had its parents. Stuart was its name. Fin had taken one of its toys and given it to the dog. The baby didn't even notice.

Lady found him outside, pressed against the side of the church, still crying like Stuart, who didn't even know enough to realize his toy had been stolen.

"Go away," he said.

"Fat chance."

"Leave me alone."

"Come on, pal." She took his hand, gently.

"Just please go away."

He tried to pull his hand back. Lady did not let go. Instead, she gave a violent pull.

"Hey!" he said. "Quit it." She had almost yanked him off his feet.

"See?" she said. "Nothing like a good shock. No more tears! Poof! Just like hiccups."

They walked toward the parking lot. He kept what he hoped was a safe distance. His father had called Lady a loose cannon. Among other things.

"Come on, Finino," she said, reaching out, taking his hand. Her voice was so gentle.

Finino. That's what she'd called him the first time he saw her.

"Come on, Finino," she said again. "Let's go home."

Lady's car was a turquoise convertible, a Karmann Ghia, and driving in the tiny sports car with the sky above him diverted Fin for the ten-minute trip back to the house.

When they got there, Fin and Lady stood for a moment on the porch.

"Now, Fin," she said, a hand on each shoulder, surveying him, "this has been a tragedy of monstrous proportions."

Monstrous proportions. Fin remembered how much he loved the way Lady spoke. Sometimes she sounded like the ladies in slinky dresses in old movies on TV. Sometimes she sounded like a cowboy. Monstrous proportions. It was a tragedy, it was monstrous, a monster so big he would never get past it.

"So. Of course you'll want a nice bath and then a nap."

"No thank you." He looked down at the worn boards of the porch. They needed paint. He had helped his grandfather paint them just two years ago, holding the brushes mostly, cleaning them with turpentine and a rag.

"No? Really? That's what I do, you know, when tragedy strikes. A nice stiff drink, a soak in the tub, a nap . . ."

A stiff drink. That's a good one, Fin thought.

"I'm eleven," he said.

"Ah," she said. "Too old for a nap, too young for a drink. Is that what you're saying?"

He felt shy in front of Lady. She was so vivid. Everything about her. Her dress was inches shorter than any dress he'd ever seen, and though it was a good sober navy blue like his suit, it had incongruous bright white piping along the edges that seemed to be made of plastic. When she smiled, her head tilted back and her teeth emerged, white and straight except for one.

He heard the cows in the distance. They were in the upper pasture. Who would bring them down? Who would milk them?

"What about the cows?" he asked. "I can't just leave them." It was a sweltering day, and he stood in his heavy wool suit on his own porch in the heat, in the dull cushion of sadness he realized he must now carry with him every minute of every day. He wiped his eyes and his nose on his navy wool sleeve, leaving it stained and wet. He imagined the cows, abandoned, bony, and weak. "The cows," he said, looking at Lady. "What about the cows?"

"Is that them? Mooing?" Lady took him by the hand. "Come on, Fin, let's go see what they want. Cows!" she called out. "Oh, cows!"

Fin gave her a sideways glance to see if she was making fun of him, but she looked quite earnest. He led her past the manure pile, through the gate, over the hill in the lower pasture and into the green hills of the upper. The cows were gathered, flicking their tails, beneath a tree, two of them lying down, two standing facing the approaching humans.

Fin patted the two standing cows, Daisy and Darlington. They had been his mother's favorites. Guernseys.

He looked back at Lady, who had kept her distance from the animals. Lady's shoes—flat, not like his mother's high heels, and white—were covered with mud and manure and grass stains.

"You ruined your shoes, I guess," Fin said, a little guiltily.

"Are they okay? The cows?"

"I guess they are."

"You do a lot of guessing, don't you, Fin?"

He grinned. "I guess."

They went back toward the house. Fin herded the cows through the gate with clucks and slaps on their rumps, determined not to cry again as he thought of leaving them. The cows would remain on the farm in their own barn awaiting his return when he was old enough to take care of them himself. Jim Cornelius was moving in and would look after the farm, Lady said. Fin liked plump, smiling Mr. Cornelius. He was the music teacher at school. But Mr. Cornelius did not belong on his grandparents' farm, in his grandparents' house. He belonged behind the upright piano in school, pounding out the notes and overenunciating the words of cheerful songs that made no sense:

Have *you ever*
Seen *Quebec?*
Don-*key riding* . . .

When they got back to the house, Fin's suit was filthy, covered by a film of dust. He stood inside the door, leaning against the screen, weary and low. He wished Lady would offer him a glass of lemonade. His mother often made lemonade for him in the summer. But his mother was gone. She had died of cancer, a word that was whispered fearfully, as if even its enunciation might be deadly. The thought of her holding a glass out to him in those last weeks before she was moved to the hospital, her emaciated arm trembling, her face drawn and purposefully cheerful, made him miss her in a way he had not yet had time to do. How could he, with all the sympathetic fussing of neighbors interrupting him every time he sat down to think? They meant well. But sometimes you need to be alone. He felt alone, even surrounded by neighbors and pie. But sometimes you need to really be alone. He glanced at Lady and got the feeling that would be no problem in the future.

More than anything he had ever wanted before, he wanted at that moment to bury his face in his mother's shoulder one more time. But there was only Lady. She tilted her head and gazed back at him curiously until he finally found the courage to ask her if he could get a glass of water.

"Water is for washing," she said gaily. But she followed him into his grandmother's kitchen, watched him get a glass out of the cupboard and hold it under the tap, then lighted a cigarette and watched him drink.

"What about Gus?" he asked when he'd finished.

"Gus?"

"Our dog." He paused. Then: "My dog."

"Oh God. A mutt, too?"

"He's not a mutt. He's a collie."

"Shouldn't it stay here with its flock of cows? Won't it be sad without them?"

"He would be sad without me." What Fin didn't say was that he would be sad without Gus, but Lady didn't need him to, it appeared.

"Oh God," she said again. "Well, where is Rin Tin Tin hiding, anyway?"

He was at the Pounds'.

"He's at the pound? Good grief, they couldn't wait until after the funeral?"

"No," Fin said. "The Pounds, the people you met, the people who took care of me."

"Thank God," she said. "I do not approve of euthanasia, Fin. Remember that. If it ever comes up."

"What's euthanasia?"

"Come on," she said.

Fin had packed his clothes in a large suitcase. A pair of blue jeans, two pairs of cotton slacks for school, his shirts. His sneakers. Two sweaters. His winter jacket. He hadn't been sure what to pack, really. He had never packed for himself. His toothbrush. He had almost forgotten it. In a box he'd put his baseball glove, toy soldiers, comics, models, books, and records. He wondered if Lady had a record player.

"The rest will be put in storage, Finny. So don't worry."

"This is all I have," he said. "There is no other stuff. No stuff that's mine."

"I'm afraid it's all yours now." Lady pointed to his grandmother's collection of little Delft houses, to the needlepoint pillows, to the cranberry glass and the wooden rocking chair—to everything in the house. And then she pointed out the windows. "The cows, too, Finny."

It hit Fin then for the first time that he was really leaving. It hit him then, and not for the last time, that nothing would ever be the same again.

"Does Lady need defending?"

The existence of Lady was revealed to Fin in pieces, literally. When he was four, someone—a guest? a maid?—mentioned a half-sister and was immediately shushed by Mr. and Mrs. Hadley. Fin was left with the picture of a girl cut off at the waist, of two legs, two feet, two black patent-leather shoes, two white socks. This half-sister was half of the only sister he knew, the sister of the boy down the hall, and so she wore the same gray wool pleated skirt. She was half a sister, the bottom half, no arms, no hands, no face. He was left, too, with a sense that this decapitated sister was secret, and secrets, he already understood, were generally associated with shame.

When he was five, he saw her picture for the first time. It was in a newspaper lying open on the dining-room table. A young woman posed demurely for the camera, a strand of pearls around her neck, like his mother's pearls, but the girl in the picture had skin like the pearls, too. She was beautiful. She wore a white wedding dress, shiny satin. Lace.

"That's my name," he said, pointing to the word "Hadley" in the caption.

"Aren't you clever?" said his mother. "Reading *The New*

York Times." Though she sounded nervous and glanced at her husband. When Hugo Hadley grunted, she said, "That's your half-sister. That's why she has the same last name. And she's getting married."

"Thank God for small miracles. And I pity the poor fool," Fin's father said.

"You'll meet her at the wedding," Fin's mother said.

But he didn't.

The wedding was in a church, and Fin sat in a pew in his gray wool shorts and Peter Pan–collared white shirt. He had new shoes for the wedding. And knee socks. He waited and waited and watched men in black-and-gray-striped pants and long black jackets rush up and down the aisle. He waited and waited and pushed one knee sock down, then the other, pulled one knee sock up, then the other. He waited and waited and watched his father appear from a door in the side of the church, then disappear back through the door, his face changing from its normal color first to red, its color when he got angry, then to purple, a new color. Fin kicked his new shoes against the pew in front of him and waited as his mother whispered nervously to another lady. He waited and waited and waited, in vain.

"Did Lady get married?" Fin asked in the taxi. "Did we miss it? What happened?"

His father was silent. His face had gone back to red.

"There was a change of plans, sweetheart," his mother said. "Lady's not getting married today after all."

Not long after the wedding at which Lady did not get married, Fin saw her picture a second time, a different picture in a different kind of newspaper, smaller, and his sister was on a beach in a bathing suit. She wore sunglasses and held a cigarette in one hand. Fin thought she was even more beautiful than in the last photograph, and said so.

"Beautiful? Yes, she's beautiful," his father said, throwing the paper down. "But she's no lady."

"She is because her name is," Fin said. "So she is."

"What was I thinking?" Hugo said. "Lady. Ridiculous name."

Fin had been named on a whim, too. February 18, 1953, windy and raw outside—"cold as charity," Hugo Hadley liked to tell his friends. His newborn son and his wife both healthy and sleeping, he left the hospital and walked out into the early dark, no thought of where he was going, happy, relieved, just walking and walking, and just when he realized he was bitterly cold, he spotted a revival house. He would slip in to warm up. The film: *Les Enfants du Paradis*. Almost over? Just as well. He couldn't bear to watch the whole thing. The French . . . too theatrical in general. He paid no attention to the movie, arty crap, until it was over. Then the screen went black, and three bright white letters appeared.

FIN.

"I think Lady is a pretty name," said Fin's mother.

Hugo laughed. "Who are you defending, Lydia? My choice of names? Or that little tart? I can never tell with you."

"You don't need defending."

"Does Lady need defending?" Fin asked.

"You have no idea what we're talking about," Hugo said, as if that answered Fin's question.

Which was true, of course, he had no idea what they were talking about, except that they were talking about Lady, and that he knew when something was wrong in the house, and something was definitely wrong.

A few weeks later, a tall, elegant lady visited. She was introduced to Fin as Mrs. Hadley. He looked up at his mother, alarmed. She laughed, her musical girlish laugh, and said, "Don't worry, baby. Mommy's still Mommy. This is another Mrs. Hadley. This is Lady's mother."

Fin shook hands with the other Mrs. Hadley.

His father came out of the living room and said, "Well, well."

Then Fin was told to go and play. Who, he wondered, when they said that, did they think he was going to play with? He went as far as the dining-room door, and from there he watched them settle themselves, the other Mrs. Hadley on a stiff armchair, his mother perched on the edge of the sofa, his father striding back and forth, saying, "I can't just leave everything and go chasing after her."

"I've tried," said the other Mrs. Hadley, who was dabbing at her eyes with a small handkerchief. "I found her in Paris, it wasn't hard, there she was at the Ritz. A runaway at the Ritz! She can be ridiculous. She said she didn't want to get married . . ."

"She certainly made that clear. At the last possible moment."

"But she won't get married, even though . . ." The other Mrs. Hadley paused. Then: "She won't get married, she won't take care of things. Does she think she'll wake up one morning and the problem will have solved itself? You have to do something, Hugo."

"Poor thing," from Fin's mother, a snort from his father, a sigh from the other Mrs. Hadley.

Then: "Damn it." Fin's father.

"Think about how alone she must feel." Fin's mother.

"I doubt that Lady is alone." Fin's father.

"You haven't changed a bit, have you?" The other Mrs. Hadley.

"She's a disgrace. Let her rot abroad."

"You don't mean that, Hugo," Fin's mother said.

"She's nothing but trouble, and I do mean that."

"Nevertheless," said the other Mrs. Hadley, "she is your daughter."

"She needs you," Fin's mother said.

"She needs to be brought home and spanked."

"And so I thought of you," the other Mrs. Hadley said in an acid tone.

"We are going on a trip, Fin," his mother said the next day. "We're going to find your sister, Lady. In Paris. Won't that be fun?"

"Oh, loads," said Hugo.

Fin thought of the newspaper photograph of Lady. "Is Paris on the beach?"

"We are going to find her and bring her home," his father said. "Put the fear of God in her."

Fin didn't want to put the fear of anybody in anybody. Neither, it appeared, did his mother.

"I still don't see the point of taking Fin and me," his mother said. "It's such a long trip. And the whole thing is so awkward . . ."

"Awkward? I'll tell you what's awkward. Having a daughter who behaves like a common . . ." He looked at Fin and stopped himself. "It will grease the skids, okay? She likes you, Lydia. She always has."

He sounded as if he were about to say, God knows why, but he didn't, just shook his head, patted Fin, and said, "Don't mind me." By which he meant, Fin knew from experience, just the opposite. Mind me. Do as I say. Before I say it. As in, go away now, Fin, go away and play.

———

They were off in search of Lady. His mother said it was an adventure. In an airplane. Like Sky King, Fin said, but she did not watch television with him and just nodded vaguely. The airplane lurched off the ground and into the clouds. Fin was too excited to eat his dinner, but he put the packet of sugar printed with the letters TWA in his pocket, a souvenir. It would take an entire night to get to Paris. They were going to rescue Lady. Fin did not understand what they were rescuing her from, and he did not care. He was in a plane and the clouds were below him.

The elevator in the hotel in Paris had no walls, just ornate wrought iron you could see through.

"It's like Babar's elevator," he said.

"I thought Babar was an elephant," his father said, and Fin and his mother exchanged a look of superior knowledge.

The milk in the morning was sour and warm, like no milk he had ever tasted, and he refused to drink it. He ate a croissant, a revelation. He and his mother walked through a park where no one was allowed to step on the grass. They saw a puppet show, which terrified him. The puppets screamed in high-pitched voices and hit each other over the head. The loaves of bread in Paris were as long as baseball bats.

But Lady was not in Paris.

"She skipped town," Hugo said.

And they took a train to Nice. They stayed overnight in a hotel across the street from a rocky beach. In the morning, while his father was looking for Lady, Fin and his mother saw a camel on the beach, and Fin's mother lifted him up so he could have a ride.

But Lady had skipped that town, too.

"At least," Fin's father said, "she hasn't moved on to the casinos."

"She has no sense," he said later.

"She's just a child," Fin's mother said.

"She's certainly behaving like one."

They took another train that night.

"We're going to another country," his mother said. "To Italy."

The train rocked and rattled, and Fin slept on the highest bunk of the triple-decker. Their cabin had a tiny sink. The sink folded up, like the beds. Would they ever find her? He was curious about his half-sister who had skipped two towns and skipped her own wedding. "But when we find her," he said sadly to his mother, "the adventure will end."

His mother hugged him and said, "I hope you're right, my love. But I wouldn't bet on it."

They arrived in Rome early in the morning and searched for Lady there; at least Fin's father did, making phone calls from the hotel, setting off on "wild-goose chases." Fin and his mother took a walk and ran up and down wide steps and threw pennies into fountains guarded by naked marble men. But Lady was gone again, and that afternoon they took a train to Naples and from there a ferry to Capri. Fin sat on a wooden bench, tired, his hands sticky from an ice-cream cone he'd successfully lobbied for in Naples. He watched the shore recede, his eyes half closed. His mother pulled him onto her lap. That's a volcano, she said. Would it erupt while they were in Italy? Oh no, it was extinct.

"The only one who's going to erupt in this place is me," Fin's father said.

The ferry landed, and Fin was so sleepy his father had to carry him off.

"Wait'll I get my hands on her," he heard his father say.

"Hugo," his mother said. "The boy." Then: "Look, Fin.

We're going in a funicular. Up the cliff." And: "Look, Fin. The taxis have no tops, just awnings."

She began humming "The Surrey with the Fringe on Top," until Hugo shifted irritably in his seat. "Never mind," she whispered then, her face against Fin's, her arms around him.

Another hotel, another man carrying suitcases, another narrow cot brought in for Fin to fall asleep on. Blissfully.

When Fin saw his sister for the first time, she was sitting in the piazzetta at a café drinking coffee by herself. She was as beautiful as her pictures. She stubbed out a cigarette, stood up as a young woman walked by, and kissed her on both cheeks, smiling, speaking rapidly in Italian.

Then she saw Hugo Hadley. Her face hardened. The skirt of her white filmy dress danced in a sudden gust of wind. She sat down without saying a word. Then she saw Fin.

He was holding his mother's hand. The sunlight made him squint. Lady was wearing sunglasses. She grinned. Fin, helplessly, grinned back.

"Finino! *Fratello mio, vieni!*"

She does not speak English, he thought in alarm, but when she held her arms out, he let go of his mother's hand and ran to his foreign sister.

"Howdy, pardner," Lady said. Perfect English, to his relief.

Even as an adult, Fin would remember that moment, the harsh sunlight, the circle of crumbly buildings, the cry of the gulls overhead, the smell of coffee, the scent of perfume, and the eyes of his new sister, a young woman in a white dress, those dark eyes. He turned his own eyes away, conscious suddenly of a feeling so overwhelming it made him shy.

"Ah," Lady said, moving on to Mr. and Mrs. Hadley. "Papa!

And *la bella* long-suffering Lydia. What brings you to the enchanted isle?"

Fin had never heard anyone speak to his father in this jaunty, irreverent way. He looked from one to the other. They looked surprisingly alike, their faces long and angry, though Lady was beautiful and young and smiling and angry, while Hugo Hadley was stony and angry. "You know perfectly well why we're here," he said.

Lady said, "Coffee?" and before anyone could answer, she waved to a waiter and said something in Italian.

"Thank you," Fin's mother said softly. She put her hand on her husband's arm and said, "Let's sit down."

"I don't have time for this nonsense," Hugo said.

"We've come halfway around the world to find Lady. I think we can stop for some coffee, Hugo."

"To find me?" said Lady. The waiter came back with three cups of coffee and a large glass of orangeade for Fin. "Well, here I am."

Here she was. They had found Lady, and the adventure was clearly not over, his mother was right. Fin was fascinated by her. She was not a child, though she was his sister. She was not an adult, either, at least not like any of the adults he had ever met. She never stopped moving. She called out a cheerful *"Ciao!"* to a young man passing by. She pulled Fin onto her lap and spooned the foamed milk from her coffee into his mouth. Her hair was long and loose, and she pushed it back from her face. She jumped up, carrying Fin under her arm, and ran to babble in Italian at a girl across the way. She put Fin down and ran back, holding his hand.

"Godamn it, you never could sit still," Hugo said. "Not even for your own wedding. Look, I don't want to be here, Lady, I'm only here because your mother asked me to find you."

"That was very thoughtful of you," Lady said. "You have succeeded. You can go back to New York."

"We're taking you with us," Hugo said. He spoke in an angry hiss. "We're taking you home, do you hear me?"

"I don't have a home."

Fin's father rolled his eyes. "Jesus H. Christ."

Lady said nothing.

"This melodramatic crap has got to stop, Lady."

She waved at someone she knew, smiling, the smile fading as she turned again to her father.

"It's got to stop," Hugo repeated.

"Go to hell," she said. And she got up and walked away, disappearing into a small dark alley behind the café.

"Oh dear," Fin's mother said.

"We did find her, though," Fin said. "Didn't we?"

"Typical," Hugo was saying, pulling out his wallet. "She left me with the bill."

It took Hugo Hadley three days, a frozen bank account, two long discussions with Fin's mother, three or four pleading long-distance phone calls from Lady's mother, the other Mrs. Hadley, and a visit by Hugo to every shop and restaurant in Capri suggesting that the extension of credit to his daughter would be a losing proposition. Three strange, wonderful days for Fin. The town was full of steps and alleys. Enormous lemons hung from vines. The beach was tiny, the harbor full of brightly painted boats. There were dolphins one day. The sun was high and hot. Children kicked a ball in the piazzetta. A bell rang. And he was with Lady.

They were on a flat rock that jutted out to the water, Fin, his mother, and Lady. It had taken forever to get there. A staircase had gone down a mountain to the flat rock. Practically a mountain. Lady lay on her back in the bathing suit she'd worn in the picture in the newspaper. One arm was over her eyes. Fin's mother sat on a red towel looking out at the sky, one foot in the water.

"Everything will work out for you, Lady," she said. "I know it will." She rubbed suntan lotion on Fin's back. Fin made the pebble in one hand jump over the pebble in the other hand.

"I made a mess of things, didn't I?" Lady said. "Do you know my mother has a hope chest for me? Don't you think a hope chest looks like a coffin? But I'm hopeless, I suppose. I should have a hopeless chest."

"You'll find someone you truly love. You'll find a wonderful husband."

"But why?" Lady said, sitting up. "Why do I have to?"

Lydia looked a little shocked, then she laughed. "Lady, you're whining like a child. It's not medicine, for goodness' sake. It's your whole life. It's your future. It's everything! Don't you want to fall in love and get married? To the right man?"

"I want to fall in love. Everyone does. And get married. Of course I do. Someday."

"Then someday you will."

"Oh Lord, give me a husband . . . but not yet!"

They both started laughing. Lady gave Lydia a kiss. Then she dove into the water and swam toward the two gigantic rocks that looked like a bridge and a hat. Fin thought Lady looked like a mermaid. He almost thought she was a mermaid, he told me. Something magical. Everything seemed enchanted. Every moment. At the Blue Grotto, he lay back in a rowboat and watched the arch of rock close around them as he and Lady slipped through a tunnel into the flickering blue cave. A soft shimmering blue light spread beneath them. The water lapped against the sides of the rowboat. "Is it real?" he asked.

He didn't even know what he meant by that. But Lady did.

"Yes," she said softly. "It's real."

Then she sighed and said to no one in particular, "Unfortunately, so is everything else."

The next day they were driven to the harbor in one of the taxis with the striped, fringed canvas tops: Hugo Hadley, Lydia Hadley, Fin Hadley, and Lady Hadley. "The Hadley family," Fin said.

"Active imagination," Hugo muttered.

Fin's mother kissed his head.

Lady said nothing to anyone. Her arms were wrapped tightly around herself, as if she were hanging on for dear life.

The ocean liner was named *Cristoforo Colombo*, and it would take eight days to sail to New York. There were three pools, one on each deck. Their deck was the top deck, the top layer of the cake.

People stood on the pier in Naples and waved white handkerchiefs. Fin waved back, *Goodbye, whoever you are.* The ship's horn brayed like a lumbering animal, but the ship slid effortlessly into the Bay of Naples, past towns clinging to the mountainside, flocks of white stucco houses perched like grazing sheep. Fin kept waving long after the people on the dock disappeared, his chin on the rail, watching the world recede.

In the photos from this trip, Fin is always grinning. In one photograph, which Fin kept framed on his desk as an adult, he sits on his father's shoulders. Standing beside Hugo, Fin's mother holds a sun hat on her head with one hand, the other clasping Fin's skinny leg. The wind is blowing—blowing the sleeves of Fin's shirt, blowing his mother's hair beneath her hat, even finding a bit of Hugo's thinning hair to lift away from his bare head. Behind them, to the right, a young woman lies on a deck chair, her head back as if in sleep, her eyes wide open.

Lydia and Lady spent hours stretched out in deck chairs, their knees covered by plaid wool blankets. Hugo Hadley paced the deck, incongruous in his dark gray suit, his cigar clamped between his teeth. Fin followed him sometimes, other times just watched him pass, once, twice, three times, always serious, always pausing before his wife and daughter as if to assure himself that they were still there.

One afternoon, as Lady flipped through a copy of *Life* magazine they'd gotten in Rome, Hugo paused in his promenade and addressed her: "You have never even said you're sorry."

"I'm sorry you felt you had to come all this way to starve me out of my hole like a rat and stand guard over me on this trip across the wine-dark sea."

"Not at all what I meant."

"I'm sorry you're here, then."

"That does not surprise me."

"Now, now," Lydia piped from the next deck chair. "Now, now."

"Look," Lady said, "I took care of it, okay? I told you. There was absolutely no reason to fly halfway around the world like some Victorian paterfamilias. It's done."

She smiled at him, but there was no joy in the smile.

"Leave the girl alone, Hugo," said Lydia.

"Yes, let us not assassinate this lady further, Senator . . . Have you no decency, sir?" Lady said.

"How dare you!" *McCarthy?* That villain? Hugo, a proudly progressive Democrat, was practically sputtering.

"Oh please."

"You're . . . you're . . ." He was really angry. He had turned his angry purple. "You're not fit," he said at last. He stomped away, his small, uncomprehending son following him, imitating his short, pounding steps.

"We need a drink," Hugo said when he noticed Fin.

Fin drank ginger ale with a maraschino cherry in it. There was a clear plastic swizzle stick, its top in the shape of a ship.

"Look," he said, showing his father. "The boat."

"You're a good guy," his father said. "You know that?"

"Lady is really a very nice person," Fin said, sensing this unusual compliment to himself had something to do with his sister, something uncomplimentary.

"Nice?" Hugo laughed. "'It is very nice to think / The world is full of meat and drink . . .'"

"'With little children saying grace,'" Fin added proudly. It was a Robert Louis Stevenson poem he had memorized for his mother. "'In every Christian kind of place.'"

"If you say so," his father said.

Fin was never bored on those eight days aboard ship. The waves rose up like snow-topped mountains, so close he could almost have touched them, if he'd been a giant. He was reading a Tintin comic book, the only hardcover comic book he had ever seen. At least, not exactly reading it, but looking at it, frame after frame of smooth color and comic adventure. In a rocket ship, a tipsy, weightless Capitano Haddock chases his whiskey. Milu the dog is in a spacesuit. Tintin, too. On the moon! Eleven years later, when men in spacesuits did land on the moon, Fin thought of Tintin climbing down the rungs of the ladder, stepping off the red-and-white-checkered rocket ship, and he thought of Lady. The comic was all in Italian. Lady had given it to him, and sometimes she sat him on her lap and translated. He carried it with him everywhere. When he sat beside the lifeboat where no one could see him, he would open the book, look at the pictures, and listen to passing adults exclaim at the beauty of the sea or the clouds, the prelude to gossip about the other passengers: those two were snobs, that one a lush, this family rather vulgar, that one Israelites without a doubt; now that gentleman, on the other hand, and his lovely wife were charming, they must be quite wealthy, mustn't they, what piercing eyes, so sad about the brother, if it was even true, which was doubtful, although where there was smoke . . .

The engines were loud and exciting. The wind rattled the tarpaulins, the lines, the magazines and books the travelers were reading. And always, trailing the *Cristoforo Colombo* was their own pale, foaming wake.

Fin would rush from one end of the boat to the other, from one deck to another, from the first-class dining room to the swimming pool, always empty of swimmers, its turquoise water sloshing along to its own rhythm, different from the rhythm of the waves in the sea below. Up and down he went, fore and aft, inside and out, sliding his hands along varnished rails and thickly painted white metal studs, along silk wall panels and velvet chair backs. Outside, the air was fresh and cool and whipped by the wind; inside, it was stale and still and sweetened by careful flower arrangements. There were officers in uniform, waiters in uniform, maids in uniform. Sitting on the deck, he watched the legs of passengers promenading by, their shoes, their pant legs, their ankles above sneakers and white wool socks, their painted toenails in delicate sandals. Once, he dreamily dug his hands down between the cushions of a banquette in the lounge and discovered a small but engaging cache of girlie magazines.

"Eight days," his father was saying. "If we'd flown like everyone else, we could have been home in eight hours."

"I think it's lovely taking a ship," said Fin's mother. She patted Lady's hand.

"I didn't ask you to come, Daddy."

Fin's mother sighed. "Your father doesn't really understand fear of flying."

"He doesn't understand anything else about me, so why should he understand that?"

"Your father's just a little old-fashioned . . ."

"That's it, goddamn it," Hugo said. "A conspiracy of fools."
He stood up and stormed away.

Lady snorted.

The magazines had pictures of naked women.

"Woo woo!" Fin said, flipping through them.

"What have you got there, Fin?" his mother asked. Then,
seeing the magazines, she gave a characteristic girlish giggle
and said, "Oh good golly!"

"Dirty magazines?" Lady let out a laugh, too, the wonderful, coveted horsey laugh.

Fin stuffed the magazines back between the cushions. When
he went to retrieve them later, they were gone.

Lady's dresses were crisp and pale during the day, dark and
breathy at night, always cinched in tightly around the middle.

"Look at you, Scarlett O'Hara!" Lydia said, wrapping her
hands around Lady's tiny waist.

"Scarlett O'Hara was a tramp, too," Hugo said.

"You can try it on later, if you like," Lady said to Fin's
mother.

"Over my dead body," said Hugo.

Fin suddenly pictured his father's dead body, cold, waxen,
laid out on a slab of marble like Frankenstein's monster, Lady
standing over it, like Dr. Frankenstein. And beside her? There
was Fin.

He shivered, pressed himself against his father, reached for
his hand.

"Over my dead body," Hugo Hadley repeated, looking very
much alive and rather smug because of it.

"That will be the day," Lady said. And she turned back to
her dinner.

"Hugo, please take it easy on the poor girl. After all . . ."

But Lady, again, laughed.

Lady laughed at Hugo Hadley. Nobody laughed at Hugo Hadley. Not his wife, certainly. Not his law partners. Not Fin. No one laughed at Hugo but Lady.

Fin stared at her, open-mouthed, awed.

"Close your mouth before you catch a fly," Lady said.

When the Hadleys got home, Fin came down with chicken pox, and his memories of the trip were jumbled together with feverish dreams and the long, drowsy hours of daydreams that followed in his darkened bedroom. Lady figured in both. And so he wondered: Did she sing "Whatever Lola Wants" while standing on the piano in the lounge of the *Cristoforo Colombo* or did he dream it? Did she throw a glass of champagne at their father when he called her heartless, a disgrace to womanhood? Did she appear beside Fin's bunk one morning and stroke his hair? Did she cry and hold his hand to her lips and kiss it? Or had he dreamed it all?

"Isn't it terrific?"

Six years later, when their paths crossed again so fatefully, Fin asked Lady: *Was* it all a feverish dream? The singing? The dawn visit? The thrown drink? Even the kiss on the hand?

He asked her in the car on the drive from Pomfret to Manhattan, the drive from his old life to his new life. He stared straight ahead, afraid of this quick, herky-jerky young woman who was all the family he had left: a herky-jerky family, chain-smoking, driving with one hand into the setting sun. Then Lady said, "Finny, remember our voyage?" and Fin blurted out, "Did you really throw a drink at Daddy? Did you sing on the piano? On the ship?"

Lady glanced his way, laughed, looked back at the road, said, "Who the hell knows? I was schnockered, Finny. Across the Atlantic and back again, drunk as a boiled owl."

Fin said, "I had a fever."

But Lady was already on to the next topic. "Now, a trip I would like to take with you would be India. I would like to go to India someday. Find a guru. *Perché no*, eh, Finino?"

"Okay."

"Okay? That's all? *India*, Fin."

The drive was long, and once they pulled onto the thruway, conversation in the convertible was pretty much impossible. Wind blew Fin's hair back sometimes, sometimes blew it in his face. He had fought with his grandparents about his hair. They remembered bowl cuts from the Depression.

"We can afford a barber," they said.

"I don't want a haircut," Fin said. "From anyone."

"He looks like Prince Charles," Fin's mother said fondly, petting his wavy hair as if he were a spaniel.

"Princess Charles is more like it," his grandmother said.

The dog sat on Fin's lap during the first part of the long drive. Fin's legs fell asleep, but he wouldn't disturb Gus.

"Quite a lap dog you've got there, Fin."

Ha ha. Very funny. He held the dog closer, rested his face on top of Gus's silky head, closed his eyes into the wind.

After they pulled into a rest stop to use the bathroom, the dog moved on his own to the backseat. Lady put the radio on, but the noise on the thruway was so loud they couldn't hear anything, and she turned it off. A truck driver pulled up next to them and honked his horn, pointing at Lady's legs. She gave him the finger. She smoked—nonstop. But near Bridgeport, she flicked her cigarette out the window and reached over and took Fin's hand. The day was fading, and to their left a large power plant sparkled with lights.

"Family is family," Lady said. Yelled, actually, above the wind and traffic noise.

"Yup," Fin yelled back. And mine is gone. Except for you. He held her hand tighter.

He must have fallen asleep. The radio was blasting Peter and Gordon. It was dark, though not a true dark, not the kind of dark they had at home. But this was home, he reminded himself. New York was home now, not Pomfret. This was the dimly remembered city dark, the deep black of night washed in daubs of colored light—the streetlamps and banks of windows, the traffic lights, the blinking restaurant signs and glaring storefronts. *A world without love*—the song was being sung directly to him. Yet there was Lady, her face lit by streetlights. Would Lady love him? She was singing along. She swayed to the music.

When she noticed Fin was awake, she smiled, a large warm smile. She put a hand out, took his hand again. But this time, she brought it to her lips and gently kissed it. Just like the dream on the ship. The schnockered dream that was real.

Fin never forgot that moment. It was when he realized he loved Lady, whether Lady loved him or not he loved her, that he would always love her.

Lady turned the car onto a quieter street and then an even quieter one. Fin remembered the elevator in his old building. The wood panels. The brass, shining. Lady pulled her car to the curb and stopped. The buildings were low, skinny—brick houses really, three stories, sometimes only two, steep steps leading up to the front door. No elevators here.

"Greenwich Village," Lady said.

Fin looked up and down the street. Greenwich Village was where Bob Dylan lived.

"That's the house." Lady pointed to one of the high, slender houses. "Our house." The yard in front of their house was the size of a bathmat. A thick, beautiful wisteria grew up from the patch of dirt and clung to the building, purple flowers hanging dramatically over the stairs. Gus went right for the base of the vine and peed luxuriantly.

Inside, Lady switched on a light. The room was long and narrow, two large windows facing the street. A wide doorway led to another room with two large windows at the back, facing what would turn out to be a garden.

"Isn't it terrific?" Lady said. "Isn't it perfect?"

With the exception of a chandelier in each, the rooms were completely empty.

"Home sweet home," Lady said.

Fin looked around him uncertainly. Lady beamed. The place was stuffy and smelled of new paint.

"Home sweet home," he said. Furniture or no furniture, this was apparently where he was going to live. Our house. He liked the sound of that, at least. He walked back to the front door and opened it.

"Wait!" Lady cried. "What are you doing?"

"I'm going to get my suitcase."

"Oh." She looked relieved. "Christ, I thought you were running away. Already." She hustled Fin and the dog back into the car. "Come on, come on, let's split."

"But what about our house?"

Lady seemed not to have heard him. She had turned the radio back on and Louis Armstrong was singing "Hello, Dolly!"

Fin realized how hungry he was. He'd eaten nothing today, nothing at all. He put his head back and stared up at the night sky. No stars in New York City. Just him and Lady. Who cared about being hungry, anyway?

"That house will be our new life," she said after a while. Her eyes were bright beneath the streetlights. She pushed her hair back from her face. She drove quickly through every green light and every red one. "You and me," she said. "Our house."

The lights of the city flashed and blinked. She patted his head with her unfamiliar, lovely hand. You and me, she had said. He gazed at the city. It was all around them. It blocked the sky. It was the sky.

"Our house," he repeated. "You and me."

They parked in front of a tall apartment building, twelve stories—Fin counted. He and Lady lugged his suitcase and cardboard box into an elevator run by a sleepy man dressed like

Captain Kangaroo. Gus stuck close to Fin's side, looking up at his face every few seconds.

"It's all right, boy," Fin said.

"It is, you know," Lady said.

When they entered an apartment, huge and well appointed, it reminded Fin of his parents' old apartment, what he could remember of it. The furniture was ornate. The paintings were large, dim landscapes in curling gold frames. The thick carpet practically bounced beneath his feet. He leaned against the wall, and the cool of the thick plaster, even the faint plaster smell, reminded him of when he was little.

"We'll crash here until our house is ready, okay?"

"Okay."

Fin remembered toddling purposefully from room to room of his old apartment, dragging his small, dirty blanket behind him. He remembered pointing at things and naming them. ("Like God," he would say later. "There is power in names. Things without names don't really exist, do they?") He remembered sitting on the floor while his mother had coffee with her friends, writing his name, FIN, in the carpet with his finger. He remembered a day when she bought daffodils and tulips at the florist, and he held her hand, and the soft pale blue wool of her spring coat brushed his cheek.

"You must never go down to the end of the town without consulting me," he told her.

"Your first literary allusion," she said.

When asked to recite the words to his father, Fin stared up at the figure towering above him. A cigar obscured his father's face, the end a smoldering orange disk. He watched the fiery glow wax and wane, in and out, with the breath of his father. He watched the smoke, a slow, silver cloud.

"Cat got your tongue again?" his father said. He hung up his hat and coat, leaving behind, in the front hall, the familiar wafting smell of tobacco and cold.

"Did I live near here?" Fin asked Lady now. "When I was little?" But it was a huge city with hundreds of buildings just like this one. "No, that's stupid. Forget it."

"Pretty close, though. Anyway, don't worry, we won't be here long." She handed Fin the ice tray. His fingers stuck to it, to the lever, as he pulled and loosened the ice cubes. Lady threw some in a glass, then poured a clear liquid from a bottle. There was a tiger on the label. For a second, Fin thought it said "Fin," but it said "Gin." "My special water," Lady said, grinning. "God, what a long day."

Fin was really hungry now. He had never had to prompt an adult to feed him before. That was what they did, whether you wanted to eat or not. They made you come to the table, they made you stay at the table, they made you eat what was on your plate at the table.

"I should probably feed Gus," he said, hoping she would get the point.

She smiled at the large dog lying at his feet. "Gus." Gus thumped his tail silently on the carpet. "Good grief! Dinner! You probably want dinner, too."

"Don't you?" Fin asked.

"I don't eat," she said, as if she were a vampire or something. "Good grief. I'd be as big as a house."

She opened a can of sardines and a can of tuna fish, which Gus and Fin shared while she recited the nursery rhyme about Jack Sprat and stubbed cigarettes out in the empty cans. There were crackers, too. And an apple.

"Thank you," Fin said. Be polite. His mother would want him to be polite. "We don't want your wife to curse me," she would say in her girlish, bell-like voice, and she would laugh

33

and let him go out to play with dirty fingernails or an unmade bed. Now he felt tears coming, again. He pulled the damp handkerchief out of his pocket. It had been his father's. His mother had given it to him.

"Oh Lord," Lady said. "What have we here? What have we here?"

"I'll stop. I promise. You don't have to yank my arm again," Fin said through his tears.

She put her arm around him. "No, no. Cry away."

Which he did.

"There, there," Lady said awkwardly.

Someone holding him close as his mother had done, someone who was not his mother; he pulled away, then threw his arms around her.

"We're both orphans now, I guess," Lady said softly.

Fin had not thought about being an orphan. He looked up. "You're an orphan?" But he was thinking: I'm an orphan? "I met your mother," he said. "She came to our house when I was little. Before we went to Europe."

Lady laughed. "I'll bet she did, poor old girl. We didn't get along that badly, you know? I mean, compared to Daddy, she was a saint. I miss her."

"I miss my mother."

She pulled him close, but he could tell she wasn't really listening.

"And after all the shit I put her through, she left me everything. I really thought she'd leave it all to the Whitney. She thought they'd never finish it, but there it is, and here we are." She looked at Fin, expectantly.

"Yeah," he said. What was the Whitney? "So now you're rich?"

"You're not supposed to ask people about money. It's considered déclassé."

"Sorry, Lady." What did déclassé mean? It sounded like a dessert.

"I am pretty rich, though. Half of it is in some kind of trust, my mother wasn't an idiot, but we'll make do, you and I."

"You bet," Fin said. He nodded vigorously. He had stopped crying.

Lady took his handkerchief and wiped the tears from his face.

"You got out of school a month early."

"Two months."

"Do you mind?"

"Ha ha."

"I told them I'd enroll you here. But for two months it hardly seems worth it." She kissed his forehead. "Right?"

Fin could only nod. She was the strangest person he'd ever met. Even now, years after he'd met her.

"Well, look at that," she said, tracing the monogram on Fin's handkerchief with a finger. "H.H.H." She laughed.

Fin remembered that laugh—the laugh from the deck of the ship when he was five.

"It's Daddy's," he said.

"Yes, Fin. I see that."

The sarcasm, the set jaw—he remembered that, too, remembered the quick, violent change of mood: a change in the weather, her face clouded over, her voice cold. "I never liked Daddy much. What about you?"

You didn't like or not like your father. It was wrong even to think about it. No one asked a question like that.

"I guess I did."

She handed the handkerchief back. He turned it so he could see the monogram.

Then, just as quickly as this wintry Lady had appeared, she turned calm and sunny again. "Well, it's just us now." She smiled her wide, soft smile. Fin, helplessly, smiled back. "We're a family now," she said. "Lady and Fin."

She lighted another cigarette, and Fin gazed, fascinated, at her face softened by the smoke. She seemed like someone from a sorcerer's land, from a palace or a grove or a fantastical cave.

"Ooof," she said, sniffing a bottle of milk from the fridge and wrinkling her nose. "I'll have Mabel get you some nice proper boy food tomorrow. I should have asked her today. I wonder if I even mentioned that you were coming. Man, will Mabel be surprised."

"Who is Mabel?"

"Who is Mabel? You do have a lot to learn."

He went to bed in a large double bed in a room with heavy rose-colored curtains. He wondered if it was Lady's mother's room. He was afraid to ask.

"Your car is neat," he said. "It's fun with the top down."

"We'll have more fun, too," Lady said. She ran her hand over the top of an ornate dresser. "Don't worry, Fin. We'll be out of this velvet coffin in no time."

Fin had a queasy vision of his own mother's coffin, now buried beneath rich, dark Connecticut soil, and he sat on the edge of the bed. He must have turned green or something because Lady said, "Oh, for crying out loud, Lady, you did it again." She sat down next to him. "Sorry." She put her arms around him. His mother was gone, embraced by no one, embracing no one, her hands crossed on her breast. In a coffin. Was it a velvet coffin? Was it lined in velvet? He was glad he didn't know. He sat stiffly until Lady sighed and said irritably, "I really do lack finesse."

Then she left him alone.

He put on his pajamas but did not brush his teeth, thinking, So there, an act of rebellion against he knew not whom. He lay in the big bed, feeling cold and scrawny, reaching his hand down to touch the dog sleeping peacefully on the floor beside him. The noise of the traffic throbbed on the street below. They were on the tenth floor, higher than the trees. But there were no proper trees, only puny ones growing through the sidewalk. He closed his eyes. He heard a siren. Cars honked their horns. They were so loud he felt as if they were being driven straight through the window, past the curtains, and into this unfamiliar luxurious room, taxis and cars all around him, surrounding him.

But when he opened his eyes, there was no one there, just the white band of street light creeping in beneath the shade as if it were morning.

It wasn't morning.

He closed his eyes and tried to fall back to sleep. He opened them. He remembered another night, when he was six and lived in his old apartment. When he had opened his eyes in the middle of the night and seen his mother in the darkness. When she sat on his bed. When he said, "Mommy," sleepily, then noticed something was wrong. When his mother cried. When her face was white. When she scooped him into her arms and said, "Daddy got very sick." When she pressed her cheek against his. "And now he's gone."

Fin went to the funeral and clutched his mother's hand. *You must never go down to the end of the town without consulting me.*

Was his father sick before he died? Did he surreptitiously sneak small white tablets of nitroglycerin beneath his tongue? Did doctors warn him to stop smoking his cigars, stop gulping his Scotch, stop working so hard, stop scowling and pacing and running his hand through his thinning hair? Yes. He was sick. The doctors did warn him. But no one warned Fin. To Fin, the death of his powerful, imperious father was not only a surprise, it was a mistake. His father, that enormous, growling reality, could not possibly disappear.

Where was the end of the town? he wondered.

"Daddy is in heaven," his mother whispered.

"Yes," he said, though he saw Daddy lowered into the ground.

Fin had searched the crowd for Lady. It was her father's funeral, too. Where was she? Maybe no one had told her. He looked from face to face. They were sad faces. Sometimes they spoke to him, but he could not answer. He turned away from the sad faces and looked for Lady's sad face. He kept looking for her sad face at the graveside. Over my dead body, his father had said. That will be the day, Lady said, laughing. Close your mouth, she'd said, or you'll catch a fly. And he had laughed, too.

At the apartment afterward, people ate and drank as though they were at a party. Fin climbed to the top shelf of the linen closet and lay there in the fresh sleepy scent of ironed sheets. His father was gone. It didn't really matter where. He might have left the house to take a walk. Hugo Hadley liked to take walks.

His mother found him there, later, after everyone had gone home, asleep.

"It's my clubhouse," he murmured as she lifted him down.

She put him in his own bed, then slid in beside him.

They moved to Connecticut within a month. Lydia Hadley had never liked the city, not really, and Hugo's financial affairs were not in the best of shape. He was, Fin told me, one of those strong personalities who does not plan for his own unthinkable absence from the world. There was hardly any money in the bank. No life insurance policy, either.

Fin and his mother retreated to the rolling hills of eastern Connecticut to live with Lydia's parents. The disruption was so complete that the move in some ways helped Fin adjust to his new fatherless state. Everything was different, so why not that, too? It was as if they had left his father in the apartment in New

York so he could make his infamous early-morning phone calls, then storm off to the office, crushing his hat angrily on his large, commanding head. It was, indeed, as if he'd gone out for a walk. Sometimes. Other times, especially at night, Fin twisted in his sleep until the blankets and sheets were coiled around him like ropes.

Now everyone was dead, just like his father. Everyone but Fin and Lady. Fin called Gus onto the bed. He pushed his foot into the soft ruff where he could feel a heartbeat.

Fin met Mabel when he woke up. He followed the smells of breakfast and found himself in a kitchen with a tall, thin, smooth-skinned, middle-aged Negro lady who handed him a plate of fried eggs, toast, bacon, a glass of orange juice, said, "Dogs and children, dirt and devilment," shook her head sorrowfully, and told him to eat up. She had the expression of a policeman giving you a ticket: Don't make it worse.

The large apartment, he learned from Mabel, belonged to Lady's mother. "But she's gone now."

"So Lady lives here?"

"She didn't tell you anything, did she? Well now, Miss Lady has purchased a house down in Greenwich Village, where the beatniks live."

"I saw it last night. It's empty."

"She says she needs to be herself. Why do you need to move from top to bottom to be yourself? I could run a hundred blocks and back and I'd still be myself. I'm myself sitting right here. She needs to be herself? I told her, Miss Lady, I wouldn't wish that on anybody, even you."

"How far is a block?"

"Twenty in a mile."

"They don't have blocks where I live. They have roads. And lanes."

"I've heard of them," she said, laughing. "Well, you live

here now, so enjoy this mess of luxury while you can, because Greenwich Village is no place for a place like this place, I can tell you that."

That was the first day of what Fin would later call the Honeymoon. Lady doted on him as if he were a pet. She ran her hand over his hair the way he patted Gus. "Good boy," she would say softly, out of the blue. "Good boy."

She took him to an ice-cream parlor across the street from Central Park. There were stuffed animals everywhere. She made Fin order hot chocolate in addition to his hot fudge sundae. Then they went to a movie in Swedish in which a little boy shoots his toy gun at a dwarf, who then dresses the boy up as a girl. The boy's mother goes to the opera, but Fin never knew what happened after that, for Lady suddenly said, "Oh Lord," and pulled him out of the theater. Lady laughed as they stood on the sidewalk outside the theater, shaking her head and looking wild and horsey, and Fin laughed, too, though he had no idea at what. Lady took him to the zoo in Central Park after that, and he fed peanuts to the elephant and ate a hot dog from a cart on the street. Then they got in a cab and went to see *Hello, Dolly!* He sat in his plush seat, stunned at the vibrant spectacle, the immediacy, waiting for Louis Armstrong to appear.

"Sextillions of infidels"

When he looked back on it years later, Fin could not recall exactly how many of these Honeymoon days he had with Lady. There was a toy store bigger than his old town hall, a red wooden sailboat as a present, a walk to a pond in the park to watch it cut through the water, then drift and stall with the breeze. More ice cream, at Schrafft's this time—an ice-cream soda, coffee with vanilla ice cream. Another musical, *Fiddler on the Roof.* Pizza. Chinese food. And Lady.

It was Lady even more than the sweets or the horse-and-carriage or the toys or the egg roll or the theater late at night. She held his hand when they crossed the street, as if he were a toddler, but he was proud to hold Lady's hand. Her long legs flashed beneath her short skirt. Her hair moved with her stride, her smooth horsey gait. People noticed Lady. Fin saw that. She talked to everyone, as if she knew them, as if they were her friends. She talked to them everywhere—on the steps of the public library, in the elevator, at Bonwit Teller.

Fin took in everything about her—sandals, scent of perfume and cigarettes, white teeth, palms damp with perspiration in the heat. This was his new life, and it was so colorful and powerful, so fast, that it was hard to relate it to his old one. Lady walked so quickly. Everyone on the sidewalk did. When Lady poked him in the back to hurry him along, he said, "Are we late?"

"No, Farm Boy. We're alive."

And he picked up his pace to match hers.

"Damn it," she said suddenly. "I did it again. No finesse."

But we are alive, he thought, a little guiltily. It's not Lady's fault we're alive. Or mine. He was alive, even if his parents and grandparents were not. They had abandoned him to this noisy, busy city, to this sister who raced everywhere she went. He was no longer a little boy on a farm. He moved his legs faster. "You do, too, have finesse," he said.

At night, Lady read to him:

"Afoot and light-hearted, I take to the open road,
Healthy, free, the world before me . . ."

Only in the morning, when he first woke up, did he have time to think. Then he would lie in bed and listen to the screeching of brakes, the slamming of delivery-truck doors, the petulant car horns, the whistles of the doormen, and he would recall morning at home, at the home he had left behind. There was the rooster, though he was not a reliable rooster and often crowed at night as well as in the morning. The cows made their soft, sweet lowing complaints. And there were birds, more and more voices joining together as the sky grew lighter. Crows and robins and blue jays and sparrows and mockingbirds and catbirds and red-winged blackbirds—his grandfather had always been trying to get him to hear the difference. But all he heard was song. At these times, in the struggling light of a New York City morning in spring, Fin hugged the dog to him and felt almost faint, whispering his mother's name, "Mommy," into the dog's white ruff.

One day Lady took him down dirty cement steps at Eighty-sixth Street and Lexington Avenue. "The subway!" she said. With a puff of hot, filthy air, the train roared into the station. They boarded and Fin held the pole happily until the subway stopped at Ninety-sixth Street and Lady grabbed his hand and pulled him off.

"There!" she said. "One of the wonders of modern transportation. What's left on our list?" And they took a cab to the Empire State Building.

"Aren't we going in?" Fin asked, staring up.

"Ye gods, no," said Lady.

Instead they went to count the stars in Grand Central Station and admire the Kodak Colorama taking up one wall, a huge photograph of four girls in white gowns, America's Junior Miss Pageant. Or was that a different day? Was that the day they went to Chinatown and saw the dead ducks hanging upside down? Or maybe the day they had tea at the Palm Court and listened to the musicians playing waltzes? Or contemplated the swords and armor and mounted knights at the Metropolitan? The days glided so carelessly, one into the next, each so surprising and new and yet, exactly because they were so surprising and new, so similar. He couldn't recall exactly which was which or even how long the Honeymoon lasted. What he did remember, piercingly, was the fullness of those days and the heady fatigue.

What he remembered, too, and just as piercingly, was the day the Honeymoon ended.

It was a warm evening, and outside, the light was soft and indolent in the golden sky. He came in from a walk with Gus and plunked himself down on the little foldout seat in the elevator. He liked watching Mike the elevator man. Mike had a quiet, melodious Irish accent. Fin found his company soothing after a day with Lady. The Honeymoon days were always hectic and bounteous, and to walk the dog, alone among the men returning home from work, among the nannies skippering baby carriages along the sidewalk, that was Fin's time, not so much to contemplate his new life as to stop thinking about it altogether, to breathe.

Today Lady had been even more accelerated than usual, walking faster, talking faster. She'd taken him to the Museum of Natural History, his favorite, then rushed him through the exhibits so quickly he had no time to feel the threat and size of the grizzly bear above him or sneak past the yellow-eyed wolves in the dark or find the horizon of the painted savannah backdrops or pity the dead rabbit clotted with dusty maroon blood. They walked home through the park, practically ran.

"I have to get away," she kept saying.

"From where?"

"Here. There. Everywhere."

Sometimes Lady said she was free as a bird. Sometimes she said she was in a gilded cage. Today had been a gilded-cage day.

In the elevator, Fin balanced on the flipped-down wooden seat. Gus sat beside him, ears pricked forward. Mike the elevator man sported a mustache, but wore white gloves, which detracted from the dignity of his uniform considerably. They looked so much like Mickey Mouse hands.

"Aren't you hot in those gloves? It's almost summer, I guess."

Mike grunted. "From the mouths of babes."

Gus flopped onto the floor with an abrupt dog sigh. Mike let Fin pull the brass lever himself, steering the elevator, as Fin thought of it, to the top floor and down again with a series of sickening, thrilling lurches. After a while, Fin said he guessed he ought to go back to the apartment for cocktails, a new ritual Lady had introduced him to.

"What a world," Mike said.

But just as Mike was about to close the elevator door, a

young man entered the building door. He tipped his hat to the doorman, greeted Mike with a wink, and, on seeing Fin and Gus, backed up with exaggerated surprise.

"Lassie!" he said. "You came home."

Fin had never liked winkers, and now the man had taken off his hat and was spinning it on one finger.

"It's been a while, hasn't it, Michael?" said the man.

"Yes, sir, Mr. Morrison," Mike said, giving Fin a sidelong glance.

The elevator stopped at Lady's floor and the man got out. He turned to Fin and Gus with an expression of mock dismay.

"Are you two following me?"

Fin was about to speak when Mabel opened the door. "Look who's here," she said.

"With bells on," said the cheerful Mr. Morrison, handing her his hat.

In the living room, Lady was slouched in a chair smoking furiously, as if smoking were something you worked at, practiced, like playing the piano.

Mr. Morrison said, "You look wonderful, Lady."

"Merry as a cricket," said Lady, but she did not look merry. She looked ready to bolt, trailing her reins behind her.

"It's been a long time."

"Has it?"

"Too long."

The conversation was stilted, as if it couldn't breathe.

"I'm home," Fin said loudly. "Lady, I'm home."

"Yes, I seem to have acquired an entourage." Mr. Morrison glanced at Fin and Gus. "Do you know them?"

Mr. Morrison was nattily dressed and, Fin noticed, had beautifully manicured hands. Fin put out his own rather grubby hand and watched with pleasure Mr. Morrison's brief hesitation before taking it.

Lady poured whiskey into a glass and handed it to Mr. Morrison.

"You remembered," he said.

"It's a drink, Tyler."

Mr. Morrison said, "Skoal?"

Lady turned to Fin. "Mr. Morrison is . . . an old friend."

"I hope I am," said Mr. Morrison. "I want to be friends with you, too, son."

"My father's dead."

But then, to Fin's chagrin, Lady asked him to leave her and Mr. Morrison alone to discuss business.

In the dining room, Fin helped Mabel set the table. "What *business*?" he asked.

"He's a lawyer."

"Why does Lady need a lawyer? Did she get in trouble?" He tried to sound concerned, but he was relieved. A lawyer, not a friend, not a boyfriend.

"White people have lawyers before they get in trouble. Especially when they've got boys around. Eleven-year-old boys."

He grinned at her. She gave a small twitch, which he took to be a smile in return. Mabel wore a wig. She adjusted it slightly.

"Is that hot?" he asked. "Like a hat?"

"You ask too many questions."

"But is it?"

"Hot as all get-out."

"So it's good in winter. And winter's longer than summer."

This time, Mabel really did smile.

A little while later, Lady called Fin into the living room. There were a few things they had to discuss, she said. A few things about Fin's situation. "You see, Mr. Morrison is your fiscal guardian—"

"*You're* my guardian," said Fin.

"Oh, absolutely, Finino. Tyler is another kind of guardian. He guards your money. Like Fafner."

"Who's Fafner?"

"A dragon."

"Thanks so very much," said Mr. Morrison.

"I don't need anyone to guard my money. Guard it from who?"

"Whom," said Fafner.

"From me, I suppose," Lady said with a laugh.

"Don't worry about it, son. It's called a trust."

"But it means you don't trust," Lady said.

"I don't have any money," Fin said.

"Sure you do. A whole farm's worth. I'm here to help you and Lady handle the sale."

"Oh no," Fin said, shaking his head. "Not for sale."

Lady sat on the floor and pulled Fin down, facing her, as if they were going to play patty-cake. "That's what we were just talking about, Finny." She took a drag of her cigarette and blew a smoke ring. "Your mother's will is still the same one our father drew up for her." Fin watched the smoke ring rise and stretch and droop and disappear. "Naturally, being the enlightened man he was, he didn't think Lydia could take care of any money herself." Fin started at the sound of his mother's name. Lydia. He thought it was a beautiful name. "As it turned out, she didn't have to take care of any money," Lady was saying, "because the bugger didn't leave her any."

"Okay, okay," Fin said. He hated it when Lady talked about their father.

"And that's where I come in," said Mr. Morrison.

Fin looked up from the floor at Mr. Morrison, whose hands were in his pockets, legs spread slightly, a sincere expression clamped onto his face.

"I've never even seen you before," Fin said.

"Finny, your mother inherited the farm from your grand-parents, but she never changed her will, the one Daddy drew up for her."

"Now, you can follow that, can't you, buddy?"

"For this one act alone I could kill Daddy," Lady said. "I really could."

"Lucky for him he's already dead," Fin said.

Mr. Morrison laughed. "You're a cocky one. Must run in the family. You know, you're a lucky little boy to own a whole farm."

"Jesus, Tyler, his mother just died. I don't think 'lucky' is the word."

"Just trying to get this settled. Just a servant of the law."

She shrugged.

"Let's look at it like this," Mr. Morrison said to Fin. "I'm here to help look after you, not the way Lady does, but to make sure you're protected financially, you know, having enough money, a big, big piggy bank full of money for when you grow up. Get it?"

"Don't sell the farm," Fin said. Get it?

"Oh, for crying out loud, it sounds like a cowboy song." Lady started singing in a twangy voice, "*Don't sell the fa-arm. Don't sell that fa-a-arm.*"

"Cowboys don't have farms," Fin said. "They have ranches."

Mr. Morrison pulled a gold cigarette case from his jacket pocket, then a lighter. Just the way he flipped open the case, the arrogance of it, infuriated Fin. Mr. Morrison drew deeply on his cigarette and blew out a large puff of smoke.

Fafner, Fin thought.

"Well, you see, young man, that decision is up to me, to liquidate your property or not to. As I see fit."

"Yakety-yak. You sound like my father. Were you always so

pompous? *Liquidate your property*," she said, mimicking his voice. "They're *cows*, Tyler."

Fin turned to her in alarm. He hadn't even thought of the cows.

Mr. Morrison said, "Ah, Lady, fairest Lady. You really haven't changed, have you?"

Maybe it was the way he said it, but Fin suddenly felt embarrassed, and Lady, he noted, turned red. He looked away and wrote his name in the carpet, the way he had as a little boy. Mr. Morrison tossed his cigarette lighter up and down in his hand.

"Maybe not," Lady said at last. "Maybe I haven't."

"And why should you?" Mr. Morrison said, the words loud, hearty, and false. "I've changed, though. I really have."

"Tyler . . ." Lady's voice softened a little. "There's no point. I mean, good if you've changed and good if you haven't, but it wasn't your fault and . . ."

"What wasn't his fault?" Fin said. What were they talking about?

The slap, slap of Mr. Morrison's lighter landing in the palm of his hand filled the room. Lady stared at the carpet. Fin had written his name twice. Finfin. Like Tintin.

"It's history, I know," Mr. Morrison said. "Ancient history."

Cows, Fin wrote, dragging his finger heavily through the carpet. He began chanting, "Cows, cows, cows, cows . . ."

"Lavender Jesus," Lady said. Then, suddenly, her arm on Tyler's, she said, very gently, "Do it for now. Do it for me."

Tyler laughed an odd laugh that Fin would come to know so well, a laugh that was carefree and forced at the same time. Then he smiled at Lady and said, "As always," holding up his hands in a cloud of exhaled smoke, "I surrender."

Fin knew something had happened in that moment, *do it for now, do it for me*, something he did not understand, something he did not want to understand. Still, he had won. Tyler Morrison had surrendered. Victory! He ran around the living room, shouting it out: "Victory!" Gus followed him, barking.

"At least this devastating bovine defeat has brought me one victory of my own," Tyler said to Lady. "I got to see you again, if only for a moment." He looked around the living room. "Brought me back to the Hadley residence. Brought me back, that's for sure."

Lady looked around the room, too. "Oh, I won't be here long," she said lightly. "No, no. I have to get out of here, have to get away from this gilded cage."

"Ah yes," said Tyler. "So you've always said."

Lady came into Fin's room at bedtime that night and read more poetry by Walt Whitman.

" '*And the cow crunching with depress'd head surpasses any statue,*' " she read softly, smiling at him in the dim room. " '*And a mouse is miracle enough to stagger sextillions of infidels.*' " And it sounded like a prayer.

Sextillions of infidels. That's what Fin decided to call Tyler, after he looked the words up in the dictionary. If he ever saw him again.

Which he did.

Why? Why did Sextillions of Infidels keep showing up when there was no more business to discuss?

"Why are you here?" Fin asked him the first time he appeared.

"Pyrrhic victory," said Sextillions of Infidels. "Look it up."

Lady insisted Fin call Sextillions of Infidels Uncle Ty.

"But he's not my uncle. If he was my uncle, he'd be your uncle, too, you know."

She thought that one over, then said, "I'll call him Uncle Ty, too!"

"Here I am again," Uncle Ty said to Fin at the door.

Fin stood in the doorway, not moving.

"You're in my way, young fella."

"Did you sell my farm?"

Uncle Ty picked Fin up, pinning his arms to his sides, and moved him out of the way. "No," he said. "Not yet, anyway."

"Then why are you here?" Fin said to him.

"Go polish your overalls or something, kid. I'm here to see Lady."

Fin watched him leave with Lady, his arm around her shoulders.

"Why does he keep coming here?" Fin asked Lady the next morning.

"Why do any of them?"

"Any of who?"

"Ty is an old friend. I told you."

"Uncle Ty."

"Him, too." She laughed and ruffled Fin's hair. "When in Rome," she said. Then she looked sad. "Or Denmark." Then she said, "The past is never where you thought you left it, Fin." Then: "I forget where I read that." Then she kissed Fin and said, "Fear not," and they made ham-and-cheese sandwiches and had a picnic in the park on a white damask tablecloth.

But Uncle Ty kept returning. He brought Lady flowers, he rushed to light her innumerable cigarettes with a click of his gold lighter, he took her to the theater. Victory? This was more like an occupation. He wore cuff links and a tie clip that matched the lighter. Fin loathed him in feverish, fervid silence, and he watched Lady and Uncle Ty when they were together. There were places you could watch without being seen, sometimes just curled on the sofa in the same room, but reading a comic book, being quiet. They would forget he was around. Uncle Ty would give his odd little laugh, say, "Shit," shake his head, and say, "Everyone has to settle down sometime, Lady." Lady would move away from him and say, "Oh, absolutely."

Once, when Uncle Ty had downed several glasses of Scotch, he grabbed Lady's wrists and yelled at her. He said she needed him. "You need me," he said again, and then again. Fin had looked up from Superman as Lady gently pulled her arms away. Fin waited for Lady to yell back. Lady didn't need Tyler Morrison, the thought was ludicrous, how could Uncle Ty not know that? Fin waited for Lady to storm out of the room. How dare you? she would say. But she did not storm anywhere. She sat quite still and looked thoughtful. Then: "I can't think what for." It was Tyler who stormed out of the room.

He turned up again, soon enough, as if nothing had happened, nothing at all. Like a bad penny, he said, chucking Fin beneath the chin and popping his hat on Fin's head.

"I come before you as a suppliant," he said to Lady.

"Don't be an ass," Lady said. She smiled and shook her head like a filly, flicking her hair back from her face, but she did not really look like a filly, like a horse frolicking in a pasture. She had that desperate, wild look, like a horse straining at the end of a rope, rearing in the air. Maybe Tyler didn't notice, but Fin did.

"Let's get out of here," she said, and she grabbed her pocketbook and rushed out the door, Tyler behind her, scrambling to keep up.

Lady went out on other dates, it wasn't just Tyler Morrison, but Tyler was the one who turned up the most, and he was the one Fin knew he had to watch out for. He could feel it every time Tyler walked in the door.

"Tough growing up with just that beautiful girl to raise you, isn't it?" Tyler once said.

"No."

"Sometimes a guy needs another guy around to talk to."

"I don't."

"They've done studies, you know. Better to have a mother

and a father. Even, say, foster parents. It's healthier. Emotionally."

"I'm very healthy," Fin said.

Then Lady came in the room, and Uncle Ty changed the
subject and did a magic trick, pulling a quarter out of his ear.
Fin had to pretend to laugh. He didn't want Lady thinking he
was emotionally unhealthy.

"Uncle Ty went to boarding school," Lady said once. "He
really liked it. He said he felt independent. He said boys like
boarding school. They play lots of sports and they play tricks on
each other."

"Yeah, but look how he turned out."

"Mmm."

Fin was on the couch reading the obituary section of *The
New York Times*. Lady sat beside him. "Here's a lady named
Faustina," he said. "That's a funny name."

"I hope I'm doing the right thing with you."

"And a lady named Kat."

"After all, I went to boarding school." Silence. Then: "Of
course I hated it. But maybe boys are different."

"Faustina and Kat went to school together."

"Boarding school?" Lady asked absently.

"They hated it. They ran away to sea disguised as pirates.
They were shipwrecked on an island and had to marry canni-
bals, but they escaped in a rocket ship . . ." He went on until
Lady noticed and kicked him and laughed and said, "Okay,
okay, no boarding school."

"Why does Lady like Tyler Morrison?" Fin asked Mabel one
morning. They sat at the kitchen table while Fin picked at his
breakfast and Mabel had a cup of coffee. "He acts like he lives
here."

"Well, he almost did, didn't he?"

Fin slapped his hands on his face like one of the Three Stooges to portray frustration. "What?"

"She jilted him. Left him standing at the altar."

Fin stared at her. "You mean like a wedding?"

"That's what I mean."

"I went to a wedding that was Lady's wedding, but Lady never came."

"That's the wedding, then. Even Miss Lady didn't skip out on two of her own weddings. Went off to Europe on an ocean liner. She's never taken an airplane in her life, and I don't blame her."

Lady and Uncle Ty? Impossible. Of course she had jilted him. He was so obviously inferior to her with his trim, insolent manner. Lady, unconstrained and rash, *afoot and lighthearted*— Lady could never have capitulated to Tyler Morrison and his little spinning hat.

"Our Miss Lady is foolish, but she's no fool," Mabel said.

Our Miss Lady. Fin smiled. It sounded like a church. Or a television show.

"Yeah," he said. "Our Miss Lady is no fool."

"Foolish, though."

"Yeah. Foolish."

"But no fool."

"She wouldn't get married to him again, would she?" he asked Mabel.

"That," Mabel said, "is the question."

Lady appeared, bleary-eyed. "What is the question?" she said. She poured herself coffee. "My head is pounding."

"Will you marry Uncle Ty," Fin said, "this time?"

Lady frowned at Mabel.

"The truth will set you free, Miss Lady," Mabel said.

"Well, I *didn't* marry him, did I?" Lady said. "Good grief.

What is this, the Spanish Inquisition? I was eighteen years old, for crying out loud."

"It was one of those arranged child marriages," Mabel said to Fin. "Like the Hindus."

"Close enough," Lady said.

"You're not eighteen now," Fin said.

"Neither are you. And I'm your guardian until you are, and I have a headache. So dry up."

Lady drank her coffee.

"Hangover?" Fin asked.

"No." She glared at Fin. Then: "*Yes*. So sue me."

"So will you? Marry him this time?"

"You don't own me, Fin," she said. "Or you," she said to Mabel. Then she started singing the Leslie Gore song.

She sang it all the way through. It was one of her favorites.

The Promised Land

Lady was unpredictable, that was the one thing you could predict. That's what Mabel told Fin. So every morning he woke up in the rose-colored bedroom that had belonged to Lady's mother and looked out the window to try to predict the weather instead. But the city sky would be just the same—smooth, metallic—and he knew it would be hot, the same as yesterday, and he waited for the day that would not be the same, dreading it, sure of it, curious and impatient.

It arrived in July.

"You're up," Fin said to a bustling, showered, beaming Lady. "It's so early."

"When you're up, you're up," Lady said. *"And when you're down, you're down / And when you're only half-way up / You're neither up nor down."*

"Okay." What else could he say? What do you say to a nursery rhyme? She spread jam on a piece of toast. Even that, even the way her hand held the knife—it was not the way other people spread strawberry jam. Swipe, swipe—giant motions, graceful, but really giant. As if she were wielding a sword.

Mabel was there earlier than usual, too. "Pack your bag and

grab your hat," she said grimly. "We're setting sail for the promised land."

A sail? The *Cristoforo Colombo* . . . "Capri?"

"Capri?" Lady said. "What are you, the beautiful people? No, no, we're going to Greenwich Village!"

"With the ugly people. You got your bongo drums?" Mabel asked Fin. "That's what they do down there. They drum and they sing nasty old field songs. They wear sandals on their dirty feet. They cohabitate. And they dress raggedy. That's where your guardian, who is charged by the United States of America to take care of you, that's where she's taking you." She poured him a glass of orange juice. "And me."

"Why didn't you tell me?" Fin said. "Is the house ready?"

"No. Nearly done. But I have to get out of here," Lady said, almost frantically. "Why does nobody understand that? I have to get away from here."

A gilded cage day again. They had become quite frequent, paralleling the frequent visits of Tyler Morrison.

"You could go to boarding school. With Uncle Ty."

"Uncle Ty," Lady muttered, her tone satisfyingly sarcastic.

"Then you're not going to marry him?"

Why did everyone assume she needed someone to tell her what to do? Lady said. Why did everyone think they needed to be like a father to her, like her father? One Hugo Hadley in a lifetime was enough. This was 1964. She wanted to live her own life, a big life. She needed a big life, a real life. Bigger than the lives of the girls at Rosemary Hall, bigger than the lives of the other girls at Wellesley, bigger than her mother's life, her father's life, and certainly bigger than Tyler Morrison's life.

"He asked you again and you said no!"

"I'm not ready to settle down," Lady said, ignoring him. "Is that a crime?"

"No!" Fin gave Lady a thumbs-up.

"Life is big and bountiful. I want to go to Africa to live with chimpanzees."

"And that's why we're going to Greenwich Village," said Mabel.

"Freedom in our own backyard, Mabel. Freedom from this big bourgeois ball and chain, freedom from charity balls, from suitable suitors, from lawyers and stockbrokers and bankers. Freedom from Hadley hell!"

"Freedom from Uncle Ty!" Fin said.

"Freedom from all of them!" Lady cried, taking Fin's hands and dancing him around in a circle. "Come on, Mabel! Freedom!"

But Mabel just watched them, silent, her expression unreadable.

Lady and Mabel climbed into the front seats, Fin and Gus into the back of the convertible. They drove down Fifth Avenue and Fin watched the cars driving uptown. Were those cars leaving Greenwich Village? Why? That was where everything was happening. He smiled a superior smile. Goodbye, Uncle Ty, and good riddance. Goodbye, as well, to the cool, cushioned ease of Lady's mother's sprawling apartment, goodbye to the doormen, who smiled at him and accepted the enthusiasm of Gus's greeting with patient equanimity, goodbye to Mike and the other elevator men. He would miss them. But Fin already missed so much, he told me, that he was getting used to the feeling.

The buildings hung over them, blocking out the sun but not the heat. Lady wore sunglasses and a blue chiffon scarf on her head. She sang along with the radio, the Beach Boys, "I Get Around." The sound of her voice, just off-key, came back to him on the hot car breeze.

As Lady had said, the house was not finished. There was no

front door, for example, just a makeshift plywood barrier. There was no electricity. There was no staircase from the main floor to the kitchen downstairs, partially below street level: you had to walk past the plywood barrier and down the front steps, then down two more steps around the side, and then, finally, into the kitchen. But the house was no longer empty, either. There was furniture, all right: weird furniture, low and angular. The paintings were enormous and bizarre, some geometrically bizarre, some shapelessly bizarre, but all bizarre all the same to Fin. There was a haphazard feeling to the whole enterprise, as if someone had thrown his clothes on the floor. If his clothes were furniture. Nothing was where it should be. Huge pillows, not on the couch but on the floor. The rug? Not on the floor but on the couch. A mirror stood on the floor, leaning against the wall. The curtains on the window were Indian cotton bedspreads, a different pattern for each window.

A small man had pulled back the plywood for them, beaming, his face almost perfectly round. His eyes were round, too, and black, like someone in a comic strip. He was smaller than Fin, but he had a mustache as thin as a pencil line.

" 'Groovy' is the word you are searching for." He had a heavy accent. He held out his arms toward the jarring arrangement of jarring items. "For the groovy debutante."

"Oh, I left the debutante uptown, where she belongs . . ."

"Uptown with all the real furniture," Mabel added.

"Mabel does not approve," Lady said, laughing. "Mabel does not approve of anything I do, do you?"

"No," Mabel said. "I do not."

The small man was named Pierre. He was the interior decorator. He had made the house look like this on purpose. Was he an adult? Yes, of course, obviously: his hair was thinning, he had a mustache, and he was dressed like a man in a suit and tie. A little man. In a little suit and tie.

"The child's eyeballs are popping out of his head," Pierre said, staring back at Fin.

"Put them back, Fin."

"How do you do," Fin said. He held out his hand.

The little man's little hand took his and shook it vigorously. "The door will be here tomorrow. Electricity tomorrow. The stairs . . . this will take another week or so. You're impulsive, my friend Lady. And impatient. It is what we love about you, yes?"

"You're a genius. It looks like we've lived here for years."

Fin caught Mabel's eye. She opened her mouth a little, as if to speak, then shook her head, and closed it.

"And now we will live here for years to come."

On the second floor, there were two rooms. One was Lady's bedroom, the other her study.

"What are you studying?" Fin asked.

"Life!" Lady said.

Fin's room was on the third floor. Next to it was a room with a television.

"Color television," Lady said. "Just for you."

"Color!" He laughed out loud. "Can I watch it whenever I want to?" His grandparents had favored wrestling and *Walt Disney's Wonderful World of Color* in black-and-white on Sunday nights.

"When do you want to?" Lady asked.

Fin looked at her blankly. Did she not understand the simplest thing? He knew Lady was the wisest person he had ever met. She was certainly the most sophisticated. But there were times, like this, when she seemed almost asleep, with her eyes open, her voice clear and loud, standing upright on her lovely legs. Like a horse. A beautiful, powerful horse. Fast asleep.

"Oh well, if you don't know, I certainly don't," she said when he did not answer.

Fin's bedroom had a fireplace in it. The walls were decorated with rugs of colorful geometric design, but there were no rugs on the floor. Nor were there curtains on the windows. He could see the back garden—some flagstones, a tree in the middle, a curved wooden seat encircling the trunk. Beyond it, another garden and the windows of another house staring back at him. When he got into his pajamas that night, he did it in the bathroom, a flashlight balanced on the radiator, trying to hold the door closed with his foot as Gus nudged it with his long nose. He woke up in the middle of the night, confused. Where was he? Not home. Not which home?

Out his window he saw yellow squares of light, the windows of the brownstones backing onto the garden. He was in Greenwich Village, in Lady's house, the terrific, perfect, groovy house.

He lay there in the unfamiliar semidarkness, the sheet pulled close in spite of the summer heat, and he wondered what more he could do to make Lady like him. She liked him, but did she like him enough to keep him with her? Forever? He often felt that Lady was just ahead of him, just out of reach, rounding the corner, leaving just a glimpse of her hem as she disappeared, a tiny flag.

"Stop blowing smoke in that boy's face!" Mabel said the next day, lugging the vacuum cleaner into the new living room. "What is wrong with you, Miss Lady?"

"Please don't call me Miss Lady, Mabel. This is a new age for the Negro."

"When *you* work for *me*, that'll be the new age. And when you get married, then I'll stop calling you Miss Lady." Mabel glowered at her. "I'll call you Mrs. Lady."

"You'll have a new name, anyway, when you get married," said Fin. "Then we won't be the same."

"Our dear departed father wouldn't let my poor old mother

give me a middle name so that I'd be able to use Hadley as my middle name. So we'll still be the same in a way."

"My middle name is Hugo."

"There, you see? We just can't escape, can we?"

"While you two sort yourselves out, I have to vacuum," Mabel said, and pushed the button of the new silver vacuum with her foot. Fin jumped on to ride like a jockey, knees to his chin, then got off and stared out the window. A Checker cab went by. A man scraped something off his shoe on the curb. Fin wondered where the beatniks were.

"Where are the beatniks?" he said when the vacuum was dragged up the stairs and out of earshot. Now all they could hear was the banging of the workmen on what should have been the stairs to the kitchen.

"Oh, Fin, what am I going to do with you in Greenwich Village?"

Fin did not answer. It was not a question one answered, he understood that. And, too, what *would* she do with him? He had no idea.

"Let's see," Lady said. She tapped her lip with her finger. "You could come with me to the beauty parlor! And the dentist!"

Fin made a face.

"No?"

Fin shook his head.

"What would you like to do? What did you used to do?"

"Ride my bike. Play baseball."

Lady considered this. "I don't know how to ride a bike."

"I could teach you."

The next day, they bought bicycles. English bicycles with leather pouches full of little tools attached to the backs of the seats. Fin's was dark green, Lady's was dark blue, and they had three speeds, not at all like his fat-tired bike at home.

Fin held the back of Lady's bike and told her to pedal as fast as she could. He ran behind her, holding the bike steady. Then he let go.

"You did it!" he cried as she pedaled down the sidewalk.

"I did it!" she said when she had turned around and come back.

It did not occur to Fin for years, many years, that she had known how to ride a bicycle all along. "But she did," he told me. "Of course she did! I see that now."

They rode their bikes around the Village that afternoon, but they never took them out of the storeroom behind the kitchen after that. It wasn't much fun to ride a bike in New York after the initial excitement of teaching Lady how to do it. There were too many cars. Too many people. Too many potholes. Too many stop signs and traffic lights. Too many buses. Fin put his shiny green English three-speed bicycle into the storeroom and spent the rest of the day unpacking while Lady was off doing errands. He read an old comic. He studiously picked at a scab on his elbow for a few minutes. When it began to bleed, he panicked and pressed a piece of toilet paper against it, praying it would not leave a stain on his clothes. He did not want to hear Mabel's opinion of boys who picked at scabs on their elbows.

When he got hungry, he went outside, through the new heavy door, down the front steps, and in through the kitchen entrance.

"Boys," Mabel said accusingly, then handed him a tuna-fish sandwich and a glass of milk.

"You should be playing baseball with your friends. Correct?" Lady asked him when she got back.

"I don't know anyone here," he said. "I don't have any friends."

"Then I'll just have to do for the time being." And she taught him how to blow smoke rings.

She was going out that evening. "Do you want to come? It's a nightclub. The man I'm going with is a bit of a bore. Are you interested in synthetic fabric? He's very interested in synthetic fabric."

"Are kids allowed in nightclubs?"

"I don't see why not."

"You don't?"

"In Europe they let dogs into restaurants."

"You could take Gus."

Lady laughed. The big laugh. Fin was happy to get the big laugh. The big laugh made everything seem adventurous and full of joy through the drawn-out summer day. He complacently worked on a model airplane that afternoon. A World War II Flying Tiger. While it dried, he stared curiously out the window at the neighbors' backyards. He could see a lady washing dishes at her kitchen sink. A little black-and-white dog ran out into a yard, barked at the sky, and ran back inside. He could hear someone playing scales on a saxophone. Someone had put bras on a line to dry. Greenwich Village was everything he had hoped it would be.

"Just like the Bible"

A week or two after they'd moved downtown, Lady came sweeping into Fin's room. She was wearing a short dress with tiny straps she called spaghetti straps. Fin thought for years that she had made that up to amuse him: spaghetti straps. She was going out to dinner and a movie with some friends. She sat on the floor in her dress. She was made up, but had no shoes on. She said, "Finny, I've got it!"

Fin had been arranging toy soldiers on his pillow.

"Oh, Finny, none of that," Lady said, eyeing the soldiers. "We're pacifists, babe. Didn't I mention that? Well, now you know. Now listen, I've thought it over carefully, and I have the answer to what we can do with you while you're here."

"*While* I'm here?" He was going someplace else? So soon? When did he have to leave? Was Lady coming, too? "Where am I going?"

"You're not going anywhere, for the love of Mike. But we have to have something for you to do, *n'est pas?*"

"*N'est pas!*" Fin agreed, relieved.

She was shimmering in the late-evening sun, her shoulders

so thin, bony compared with his mother's. Except when she was sick. But Lady wasn't sick. She was healthy and alive, she smelled like wild roses, intoxicating. She had painted her toenails a bright white. He thought she was magnificent.

Then she said, "You will help me get married!"

Fin sat silent and shocked.

A husband? What had happened to Fin and Lady, the orphan family? Would the husband be an orphan, too? But the husband would obviously be Tyler Morrison, and Fin would have to help Lady marry him. How could Lady have changed her mind so fast? It was Fin's fault, that's how. Fin hanging around Greenwich Village, where everyone was groovy and free except him, an eleven-year-old with nothing to do. It was Fin. He was holding Lady back in her quest for a big life.

"You don't have to marry Uncle Ty," he cried out. "I'll be good. I'll play by myself. I'll help Mabel. I'll make friends, too . . ."

"Uncle Ty? Good God, no. We're downtown now, Fin."

A new husband he had not even met? What if the new husband did not want an eleven-year-old brother-in-law?

"Who?" he asked. "When? When are you getting married?"

"Well, let's see . . . I'm twenty-four. The deadline is twenty-five. After that you really do become pathetic. So we have a year. A little less than a year."

Fin tried not to let his relief show.

"Just like the Bible," Lady said. "Except that was seven years. And I won't have to share my husband with my sister."

"Because you don't have a sister."

"Well, that's one reason. So, what do you think, Fin? Can you help me find someone to fall in love with in a year?"

"Don't worry. Everyone falls in love with you, Lady."

"That's not what I said."

Fin thought about that for a moment.

"Twenty-five," Lady was saying. "Then it's all over. How's your Shakespeare, Fin?"

"I watched the Beatles in *A Midsummer Night's Dream* on television."

"How about *Taming of the Shrew*?"

"Uh-uh," Fin said, but Lady was already reciting, standing, one hand on her heart, her other arm flung out.

"I will be master of what is mine own:
She is my goods, my chattels; she is my house,
My household stuff, my field, my barn,
My horse, my ox, my ass, my any thing."

She poked Fin's chest. "I don't want a master. And I don't want to be an ass."

"Me, either." But Fin was thinking more of the barn and the ox, which was almost a cow.

"And that's where you come in, Finino."

Fin thought, Me? I can't marry Lady; then, for one fleeting second: Can I?

"You really have to help me. One year to find one, a good one, one I'm in love with. Is that too much to ask?"

"No!"

They shook hands.

"One year, Fin. One year, twelve months, three hundred and sixty-five days. Or thereabouts.

"No lemons," she added. "There are a lot of lemons out there," and she left the room trailing smoke and scent and confusion.

Fin was able to begin his search for Lady's future husband the next day. He wasn't sure how Lady had managed to make so many friends so quickly, but almost every night there was a party at her house, some planned, some spontaneous. People dropped in, Fin noticed, as if they were in Connecticut bringing round a pie, but these people came late, after midnight sometimes, and brought not pie but a bottle of bourbon or wine. Fin sat at the top of the stairs in his pajamas and watched the young men and women drinking and laughing. And talking. He had never seen people talk so much.

Sometimes he came downstairs, ostensibly to get a glass of milk from the kitchen, but really to see them talk as well as to hear them. *Stagnating in the swampland of collectivism. Extremism in the defense of liberty is no vice, moderation in the pursuit of justice is no virtue.* Then they said something about being a crazy cat. At first Fin thought they were talking about Krazy Kat and asked if they knew if Krazy Kat was a girl or a boy. The cartoons had always unnerved him. But they said, No, they wished Goldwater was a cartoon, he should be a cartoon, he was all too real.

He watched them dance, waving their arms and jiggling crazily. He watched them argue. Young men, standing so close they nearly touched, would shout at each other, forefingers poking the other's chest. There were factions, so many factions, musical factions, political factions.

"What's a Trotskyite?" he would ask the next morning. "Who's A. J. Muste? Why shouldn't honkies play trumpet? What's a honky? Where's Port Huron? What pill?"

Gus roamed among the partygoers, his nose occasionally sniffing crotches regardless of faction, his tail knocking over cocktail glasses, his loud, shrill bark punctuating the music.

The New York City Fin encountered with Lady was utterly different from his earlier years of safe and comfortable routine. Lady did not believe in routine, or safety, or, frequently, in comfort, either. Lady's downtown world was one of urgent, restless urbanity. Everything about his new home was full of color and noise and movement. To Fin it was as good as a circus.

Spumoni

What you don't know about Lady, because I haven't told you, is that she was a great reader, and reading was something she was determined to share with Fin. It was she, as I've mentioned, who gave Fin the Tintin album on the ship and translated it aloud as they gazed at the bright, clear drawings. It was she who sent him a copy of *Just So Stories* on his sixth birthday, which his mother read to him. It was she who gave him *The Phantom Tollbooth*, *Huckleberry Finn*, and *Alice's Adventures in Wonderland*. Later, when she saw that his interest in toy soldiers was abiding, she presented him with a copy of H. G. Wells's *Little Wars* (the man was a pacifist, after all), and a copy of *Tristram Shandy*, so he could read of Uncle Toby's bulwarks. He never read past Uncle Toby, but he never forgot him, either.

On the day Fin met Biffi Deutsch, he was reading *The Spy Who Loved Me*, which was not at all like *Chitty Chitty Bang Bang* and sometimes confusing, but he could not be seen on the steps reading a book written for a child. Biffi was a Hungarian Jew who as a small child had survived the war in Budapest, survived the invading Germans and then survived the invading Soviets. Fin knew nothing of this when he met Biffi, only learning of it much later, from an obituary of Biffi's mother. Odd, to know so little of a man who had meant so much to you, Fin told me once.

After the war, Biffi and his mother came to the United States to join Biffi's father, an art dealer who had been safely stranded in New York since 1939. On a picnic with his wife and son, Mr. Deutsch was struck by lightning. And killed. How could you not mention that your father was struck by lightning? But Biffi never did. He walked with a buoyant, unhurried step, as if the evils of the world had never chased him from country to country and never could. He often said the world was cruel, but he never seemed to mean it. After all, he had been named after a café in Milan that made exceptional cake, the Caffè Biffi, or so he said. It was not easy to know when he was joking. He was handsome, funny, and fierce, a diabolical black goatee surrounding a wide, beautiful mouth, angelic brown eyes shimmering above. His accent was musical, his name a confection. He might as easily have hailed from Freedonia as from Hungary. Fin was crazy about him.

"You're crazy about him," Lady once said.

"Yeah, but you're just crazy." Fin could say that to Lady. He could say almost anything to Lady. That was because most of the time she wasn't really listening. Most adults never listened to children, and she didn't listen most of the time, either. But then, when you least expected it, there she was, intent, curious, open, her eyes locked on yours, her whole being locked on yours.

No wonder Biffi Deutsch fell in love with her.

"Good lad," Biffi said when he introduced himself that first day. Lad? No one had ever addressed Fin as "lad." "Good lad." When he shook hands, he left a dollar bill resting on Fin's palm.

Fin tried to hand it back.

"No, no, it's for you."

Like a tip. Who ever heard of tipping a kid? Maybe in this man's country they tipped kids. Or at least lads.

Fin led him into the living room, where Lady lay on the couch, her head covered by a pillow. Fin made his way closer, close enough to lift a corner of the pillow and whisper, "Someone's here. A man. From not the United States."

Lady emerged, ravishing, her skin as clear as porcelain, her eyes bright. "*Ciao*, Biffi! I wasn't expecting you!"

"Not? You have invited me, you see."

He settled down on one of the low curvy chairs and crossed his legs. As he did so, his pant leg rode up, exposing bright purple socks, a dazzlingly pale leg, and a dark garter.

Fin made them martinis.

"Who taught you this sophisticated skill?" asked Biffi.

"Lady did."

"Did she?" said Biffi. "Did you?" he said to Lady, raising an eyebrow.

"He doesn't drink them," Lady said. "Do you, Fin?"

"No. They're disgusting."

Biffi laughed. "Well then."

When Biffi and Lady got up to go to dinner, Biffi said, "Come on, you, too," and Fin said, "Really?" and Lady said, "*Perché no?*" and Mabel said, "Wash your hands."

They went to a small Italian restaurant with red-and-white-checked tablecloths and candles stuck in wine bottles that were wrapped with woven straw. There was sawdust on the floor, and Fin felt as if he were in a horse stall. He had spaghetti and meatballs. "Where are you from? Is Hungary near Italy? I've been to Italy. And Paris. Have you been to the World's Fair? Do they have a Hungarian pavilion at the World's Fair?"

"He's usually as quiet as a mouse," Lady said.

"I am?"

"Are you?" Biffi asked.

Fin thought for a moment. He heard his father's voice: *Cat got your tongue again?* "Maybe."

"I was a quiet boy," said Biffi.

"Quiet children hear things," said Lady.

"All children hear things," Biffi said.

Fin watched as a beautiful striped slab of ice cream was placed before him.

"Spumoni!" he said. Just the word was festive.

"A traditional Hungarian dessert," said Biffi.

"Ha ha," said Fin.

"Oh yes!" said Biffi. "It is true. And Spumoni is my middle name."

"Biffi Spumoni Deutsch," said Lady. "It just rolls off the tongue."

They all started to laugh. They repeated the ice-cream middle name, laughing and laughing. He had never laughed like that with adults. He had not laughed like that with anyone in a long time.

Biffi took them to a Mets game. "A baseball match," he said. "A matinee." And Fin could not tell, as usual, if he was joking.

They sat on the first-base line. His first Major League Baseball game. The field was so green. Lady got him a Mets cap. People screamed and ate. The players swung and missed.

"They seem to miss hitting the ball an awful lot," Lady said.

"Nor catching it," said Biffi.

"If you strike out twice and then get a hit, that's like a three hundred batting average, which is really good," Fin said. "Everyone misses a lot."

"So that's why they call them the Lovable Losers?"

"Sort of."

Biffi furrowed his brow and said, "Next time we go to the races, eh?"

"What about the World's Fair?"

"I have lived through the World's Fair, boy. The horses are more dependable."

But they did go to the World's Fair. They went on the simulated helicopter ride, on the flume ride, the monorail, the outrigger canoe ride at the Hawaii pavilion. They waited in a long line to see the *Pietà*.

"Don't you want a Belgian waffle?" Fin asked Lady.

"No," Lady said. "And if I did, I would go to Belgium. Not to Flushing."

Biffi came to the house for dinner, he took Lady out to dinner, he took Lady and Fin out to dinner. Fin and Gus came to recognize the sound of his car and would both rush out to meet him.

"I choose Biffi," Fin announced. The house was hot and damp that afternoon, and he and Lady had migrated outside. She was in a bathing suit, stretched out on her stomach on a towel, the transistor radio beside her tuned to Cousin Brucie.

"For what?"

"Husband."

She peered at him over her sunglasses. "I do like Biffi."

"Me, too."

"But you have a full-year contract. Don't fink out on me, Fin."

"No. Okay. But what if he's the really, really good one?"

"I can't give up so fast."

Fin could also not help but notice that Lady was a little wary of Biffi.

"You're too serious," she said to him once.

They were sitting in the garden having drinks. Fin had climbed up the tree, and after a while they seemed to forget he was there. He looked down at them through the fat green maple leaves. The air was heavy and still in the treetop, but cooler than below. The leaves themselves were cool to the touch.

"Certainly not I am serious," Biffi said. "I am a joker. Everyone says I am a joker."

"Everyone is wrong. You're a superficial joker."

"I am a deep joker. That is my charm."

"No, but you're deep. And you scare me."

"I am deep. And I am a joker. This is on my positive, surely."

"And I don't buy that pidgin-English bit, Biffi."

"Perhaps it is a joke."

"Perhaps," Lady said, and that seemed to cheer her up.

They often argued. Screaming kinds of arguments. Then they made up. Then retreated to the bedroom. Then, a few days later, argued again, until Biffi started to seem almost as jumpy and changeable as Lady.

The parties continued, if anything getting bigger and more frequent after Lady met Biffi, as if she needed chaperones, dozens of drunken chaperones. There were other suitors, too. An earnest young civil rights worker, a cynical musician, a journalist with a magnificent beard and a pen that leaked on the sofa. Fin did his reconnaissance, but his heart was not in it. His heart was with Biffi. That one in the suit and tie? Boring. Turtleneck? Smug. Boots? Too loud. Loafers? Too quiet. Sandals? Obnoxious. Leather Pants? No, a simple no, Leather Pants was out, it was summer. What about Nehru Jacket? He approached Nehru Jacket while shaking the icy martini shaker.

"Mittens," said Nehru Jacket, nodding with approval at Fin's protective hand wear. The martini shaker was so cold. "Smart."

"What are your interests?" Fin asked politely. It was his standard opening salvo.

"Aeronautics," Nehru Jacket said, "and sex."

Well, he's out, Fin thought. Lady knew nothing about aeronautics. Ha ha.

There was one guy Fin thought Lady might like. He came one night with Pierre, the dwarfish interior decorator. He was taller than Pierre, but who wasn't? There was something appealing and boyish about him, he had very blond hair, and he was Danish, but none of that mattered much. What mattered was that he was an artist.

"Lady likes artists," Fin said when Pierre introduced Jan as one. "What are your interests?"

"Toy soldiers," said Jan.

"No, really, what are your interests?"

"He paints toy soldiers at a factory in New Jersey," Pierre said. "It's his day job."

"It is, *au contraire*, my passion," Jan said.

Fin could hardly believe his luck. Here was a man who threw in French phrases, just like Lady, and loved toy soldiers, just like Fin.

"Lady," he said, tracking her down at the door as she greeted a man with a large beard and a large stomach.

"He's a famous poet," she whispered when the man had gone into the living room.

"Okay, but what about Jan the painter artist who's over there with Pierre? He could be the one. As a backup to Biffi. He's not a lemon at all."

Lady glanced over. "Oh, but, Fin, he likes boys."

Fin almost blurted out, *Yeah, I know, and toy soldiers, too.* Then he realized. Jan liked boys *that way.*

"That's so unfair," he said.

"Life is unfair," she said. "President—"

"—Kennedy said that, I know."

"How do you know?"

"You told me."

"Oh. Good for me!"

And Lady went back to float among her would-be suitors.

Biffi was not there that night, banished temporarily from the house after a particularly loud and violent fight. Lady had thrown a coffee cup at him, and he had said something in Hungarian and slammed the door behind him. You couldn't rely on either of them, not to know what was best for Lady. The only one who knew, who truly knew Lady, Fin thought, was Fin. Lady had not really told Fin that President Kennedy said life was unfair; at least the first time she told him was not the first time he heard it. His mother had sometimes said it in a soft, wistful voice, *Life is not fair*, when she was sick. *President Kennedy said that*, she would add, as if that made it more true or less sad or both. Lady said it, too, of course, but usually when someone wanted something from her she was unwilling to give.

Fin watched her now as she made her way to the window and stood looking out. She turned off the lights for parties and lit candles everywhere. She was so glamorous, so romantic, her hair gleaming in the flickering light. So unguarded, just for a moment, that moment, like a kid, a girl in a world in which life was not fair.

I'll take care of you. The words sounded so silly, even in Fin's head, even as a thought, a silent thought. He was eleven. Lady was Lady. She hated to be taken care of. No one took care of Lady. But I will, he thought. I'll take care of you.

He retreated to the top of the staircase and sat there sleepily petting Gus, listening to the party below. Flirtatious laughter. Blustering arguments. The noise got louder and louder as more people arrived. Smoke wafted up with the noise. Cigarette smoke. Marijuana smoke.

And then Lady wafted up, too.

"What are you doing here, Finny?"

"I don't know."

"Couldn't sleep? Come on, night owl." She tenderly took his hand. She led him into his room. Tucked him in, the covers up to his chin, his arms uncomfortably pinned to his sides. He didn't mind. She was smiling at him, stroking his head.

"Everything will be okay," he said.

Lady looked surprised.

"It will, Lady. I promise."

"Thank you," she said. "Thank you, Fin." And she kissed his forehead as softly as his mother used to do.

Friends

Every Tuesday night, Lady and Fin would drive to Fifty-seventh Street and eat Chicken Kiev at the Russian Tea Room. Butter bubbled out of the chicken, and Fin said it looked like the oil bubbling out of the sand at the beginning of *The Beverly Hillbillies*. He had red soup with dill in it, the first time he had tasted dill. Then they would go to drawing class at the Art Students League, and Fin would try not to stare at the nude model.

"Don't be silly," Lady said on their first visit. "Haven't you ever changed your clothes at a country club?"

"No."

"Oh." Lady pondered this. "Well, if you did, and you were a woman, this is what you'd see." She smiled triumphantly.

Two of her friends from college were also in the class. Mirna was one. She was dark, wiry, always on edge, "the edge of *what* we thankfully don't know," Lady said. Mirna's face was permanently puckered with worry. When she talked, and she talked a lot, she seemed to be squeezing her words up from somewhere, somewhere you probably wouldn't want to go. Ever. She had seriously muddy brown eyes. You could get stuck in them, leave a boot behind.

"Hi!" he said as they entered the studio, and he grinned. He always grinned when he saw Mirna, but it never did any good.

Mirna came closer. "Are you *all right?*"

Am I all right? Fin thought wildly. I thought I was. But I must be wrong.

"How are *you?*" he said, tilting his head brightly, like a terrier.

"You don't have to be afraid of me, Fin," Mirna said, nodding when really she ought to have been shaking her head. It was like someone patting her head with one hand, rubbing their belly with the other. She often nodded like this. Who was she agreeing with?

"Nope," he said. He tried to nod as he said it. "Not afraid."

"Someday," Mirna said. She squeezed his hand in hers. Then went off to take dark charcoal stabs at the large sheet of paper propped on her easel. Lady once told Fin Mirna was a bit upsy-downsy, mostly downsy.

Lady's other friend, Joan, was beautiful, not beautiful like Lady, more like a cake, Fin told me. She was sweet, substantial, blond, her long hair a shining yellow, cut in bangs across her forehead, her skin white, her cheeks pink as a birthday frosting flower. Maybe it was the candy coloring, maybe her high-pitched voice, but there was something childlike about her. Fin attached himself to her, the way a dog attaches itself to the only person in the room who hates dogs. She clearly found him annoying. He sensed this, but could not resist her. When she began to give him treats to make him go away, it just made it worse.

"Here," she said, handing Fin a Life Saver. "Go see what your sister is drawing."

"She's drawing the same thing you are. The naked lady."

"Well, go see if hers is any good."

"It's not."

Fin tried to imagine the three of them, Lady, Mirna, and

Joan, in the same dormitory. Joan, after curfew and a few too many, had climbed in the window of the wrong room, then climbed into Lady's bed; that's how they met. They met Mirna the next year when Mirna did the same thing. They were the Gleesome Threesome, the Bra Trois—Fin had heard them reminisce. But he still could not picture them in the same room, even when they were in the same room.

"That's why we like each other," Lady said, trying to explain. "We're friends in spite of ourselves. See?"

"I guess."

"And then, soon enough, you have so much history together. I've known them a long time."

"Did they know Uncle Ty?"

Uncle Ty had appeared only once at the house on Charles Street. Business, supposedly.

"Maybe," she said.

On one of these evenings of art class, the three friends arrived early enough to set up their three easels in a row.

Fin waited patiently beside Joan until she noticed him and dug out her roll of Life Savers. "Here. Take the whole roll. Don't you feed him?" she asked Lady.

Fin took the striped pack and sat on the floor, pulling the Life Savers out, separating the orange ones.

Mirna was talking to Lady in a loud whisper. "Do you ever"—she paused. She was a great one for pauses—"*regret* it?"

"Regret what?"

"You know. The *operation*."

"Jesus, Mirna, shut up."

"Well, you know . . ." Pause. "With this"—pause—"*situation* . . ."

At the word "situation," Joan looked at Fin, then, abruptly, back at her easel.

Lady said rather loudly, "I can never do hands. They look

like paws." She glanced at Fin and smiled. "Don't they?" she said.

"Yup." Fin pretended to read the book he'd brought with him, *The Cricket in Times Square*. Lady had given it to him. "You're like the cricket," she'd said. He stared down at the page, at a drawing of enormous men and women hurrying past a tiny cricket. He stared down and pretended he was reading. He knew when they didn't want him to hear. Why do they say things, he wondered, if they don't want you to hear?

"This situation, as you put it," Lady said softly, very softly, to Mirna, "is sitting right here."

"You were so *young*," Mirna went on, implacable, in a tone that suggested being young was on its way to being an incurable disease.

"I'm still young," Lady snapped.

"You know, Mirna," Joan said in her pouty voice, "you're only a year younger than we are. I don't know why you make such a big deal about it."

"But you were practically a teenager . . ." Mirna said.

"I *was* a teenager."

"And you dropped out of college."

"I attended the school of hard knocks."

"And you got knocked up!" Joan said.

They all started laughing.

"Ladies," said the teacher.

Lady's friends also came to the house every other Sunday morning. Mirna brought bagels and lox, and Joan brought coffee cake. It was their girls' ritual, they said. But Fin noticed they talked mostly about men. When he left the room, they talked about sex, but in voices too soft for him to make out the words, even when he sat on the new stairs between the kitchen and the floor above. Quiet, whispery words, peals of laughter, the pop of the percolator. It got boring there in the hot stairwell. Fin would take himself outside and sit on the front steps, snapping his ball into his mitt, waiting for something to happen.

And then, one Sunday in August, something did happen. A girl, about his own age, ran down the steps of a brownstone across the street.

"Hello," she said.

"Hello."

"I just got home from camp. I live here. Why are you just sitting there?"

"I can't think of anything else to do, I guess."

She was taller than Fin and very tan. She wore dark green shorts and a short-sleeved white shirt.

"This is my uniform," she said, seeing his glance.

"Okay."

"You look really hot."

Fin looked down at his heavy jeans, his old sneakers. He had on a brown plaid short-sleeved shirt that was too small.

"Where did you go?" the girl in uniform asked. "Treetops or something?"

"What's Treetops?"

"A camp where they have farming, stupid."

Fin felt himself coloring. "I don't need a camp," he said. "I have my own farm." And he raced up the steps and slammed the door.

"Do you know the people who live across the street?" he asked Lady that night.

She was applying pale polish to her fingernails. He watched the brush, watched it dip into the glass bottle, watched the pink polish cling to it, watched it spread, smooth and shining, across the nail.

"Which people?"

"I don't know. The ones with a kid."

"The shrinks?"

"Do Mr. and Mrs. Shrink have a daughter? Like my age?"

"They're both shrinks, I think. Poor kid. Diamond? Is that their name? Ruby? Raising a kid according to its bowel movements—I wouldn't know where to start."

"You're disgusting."

"I didn't write the book, Fin. In fact, I didn't even read it. So don't blame me."

The next morning Fin sat on the stoop untangling a knot in the dog's ruff, hoping the girl would reappear. And, yes, the door of the brownstone across the street opened and there she was, the girl whose parents raised her according to a book about bowel movements.

"'Ello again," she said. She didn't have her camp uniform on. But why was she speaking with an odd, stilted Liverpudlian accent? "I'm practicing my Beatles accent," she said, sitting beside him. "What do you think, mate?"

"I really do have a farm, you know. A dairy farm. I'm renting it out until I get old enough to go back and take over."

"Groovy," she said.

She petted Gus. "Is this your dog, mate? What's 'is name, then? You live 'ere now?"

The girl's name was Phoebe and she was in the grade above his. "But that's all right," she said, obviously referring to Fin's lesser status. "I don't mind." She was allowed to charge any books she wanted at the bookstore on Eighth Street, any records at the record store. "No clothes, though," she said. Her accent had returned to normal. "No posters, either. Just books and records. My parents think they're educational."

They browsed through bins of records, leaving with an album of Dave Van Ronk and one of Herman's Hermits. They bought a copy of the *Tao Te Ching*. Gus waited patiently outside, then followed them back to Phoebe's house, a brownstone furnished rather more formally than Lady's.

"My parents are really old," Phoebe said. "Like, really old. I was a mistake. I'm not supposed to know."

"I just moved here. I live with my sister," Fin said, trying to do his part. "I'm an orphan."

He felt slightly sick, as if he were bragging about his parents' deaths.

Phoebe was looking at him thoughtfully.

"I used to want to be an orphan," she said. "And a nun."

They were quiet for a moment.

"Now I wish I was a spy."

"Ian Fleming just died."

"Yeah, so?" Phoebe said, and Fin could tell she didn't know who Ian Fleming was.

"He wrote James Bond," he said. "The books."

"Oh."

"I'm sort of a spy."

"Sure you are. And a farmer."

Then Fin told her about his mission to find Lady a good husband. "I really like Biffi. I wish they would stop fighting. Then she could marry him. Because what if Tyler comes back? He'll send me away. She makes me call him Uncle Ty."

"She can't marry her brother, Fin."

"He's not her brother. I'm her brother. Her only brother."

"Why should she get married to anyone? She's rich. She doesn't need any husband at all. Not like that finky Jane."

"Who?"

"Jane Eyre. She's a character in a book. Who is so stupid. Why doesn't she just live with Mr. Rochester? But no, she has to wait until he's ruined and blind. And, listen, you can't be too good at finding someone, because then she won't need you to find someone. Mate," she added in her English accent. Her bed had photographs of the Beatles, torn from magazines, taped to

the canopy. She disappeared behind the curtain of the Fab
Four, then reappeared with a copy of *16 Magazine*.

"She doesn't want to be a spinster," Fin said.

"How old is she?"

"Twenty-three-and-a-half," he lied.

"Well, I don't know . . ."

"No, okay, she's twenty-four."

"Oh. Well, yeah, then."

"Anyway, I *like* Biffi," Fin said.

"So *you* marry him."

"No, *you* marry him."

"I'm never getting married," Phoebe said. She looked up
from her magazine. "I want to be a bachelorette."

That week was cool and crisp. The silver haze gave way to a
blue sky, to white clouds riding a soft breeze. Lady flirted at her
parties. With a musician. With a Spaniard. But she flirted everywhere, with everyone, Fin told me. The Good Humor man. The
waitress at the coffee shop. The bus driver. It was how she steered
her little boat through the rocks and cliffs and sandbars. Fin said
he had never realized how many people there were on a street
until he walked down a street with Lady. "Flirting was like so-
nar for her," he said. "She was like a bat, flitting around in the
dark."

So Fin didn't make too much of the appearance of Jack Jordan at the house on Charles Street.

Jack appeared on a Saturday morning. Fin was in back of the
house, throwing a ball methodically against the brick garden
wall. Gus sat beside him, not even looking. Fin was Jim Bunning, the Phillies' pitcher; it was Father's Day, he was throwing
a perfect game, pitch after pitch—*stee-rike*. The guys swinging

so helplessly were the Mets, which was sad, but it was a *perfect game*. He couldn't help himself. He hurled the famous sliders, his knuckles nearly scraping the ground. Jim Bunning would fall apart with the rest of the Phillies at the end of September. He would later become Senator Bunning from Kentucky, a right-hander who turned into a right-winger. *But how was I to know that?* Fin would ask years later. And even if he had, he'd say, why would he have cared in 1964? The guy pitched a perfect game.

In the radiant light of a late-summer morning, he lifted his leg and moved into his motion. The pink rubber ball snapped smartly from his fingers. It made its precise, unpredictable arc. Just over the plate. Just catching the inside corner. Then, thwack, it hit the redbrick garden wall and flew obediently back to his glove.

Lady had never mentioned it, but he knew he had to start school soon. A New York City school. A Greenwich Village school. The other kids would holler or they would squeal when they caught sight of one another, they would talk about what they had done over the summer, it would be just like going back to school in Connecticut—except every detail would be off. The slang would be different. The shoes would be different. The book bags, the notebooks, the names. They would think he went to farm camp. Friends would drift into small groups, laughing and talking, but they would not be his friends. He would greet no one, and no one would greet him.

Fin worried about school and threw Jim Bunning's strikes. The rubber ball bounced obediently back. And then, suddenly, the ball smacked not against the wall but against a man's cheek, and the man was chasing Fin, and Fin was running, into the house, up the stairs, screaming, "Help! Help!"

Jack Jordan had rung the doorbell, but he'd been too impatient to wait for Mabel or Lady to open it. Or, just as likely,

Lady had told Mabel not to answer the bell. Whatever the reason, Jack Jordan, athlete, former college football player, vaulted
over the gate at the side of the house. He landed in the garden,
where, with what seemed at the time to be the force of one of
the real Jim Bunning's deceptive fastballs, a Spaldeen smacked
him in the face.

He spluttered, as if he'd been splashed by an ocean wave.
The veins stood out on his forehead. The stain left by the ball
on his cheek was bright red. Then he caught sight of Fin.

"Hey! You!" He held his arms out as if to catch a football.
But it was no football he was after.

Fin took off. "Help! Police!" he yelled, as if he were in a
cartoon, up the stairs, the crazy man behind him; in front of
him, Mabel. He smashed into her. The crazy man smashed into
Fin, a tackle that brought all three of them down. Mabel
screamed. Fin, on the bottom, struggled to get free, Gus standing over them barking as if they were renegade sheep.

When a sudden calm descended.

They all simultaneously caught sight of a pair of shapely legs
and pretty bare feet, one of which moved forward in a gentle
nudging kick.

"Who's hiding in this pile of wrinkly laundry?" Lady said
pleasantly. Her toe inserted itself between Fin's elbow and Mabel's face. "*Mabel?*"

"I warned you," Mabel said. She stood, smoothed her blue
cotton uniform dress, straightened her wig, and stalked off.

"What bullies men are," Lady said.

"I'm not a man," Fin muttered. "I'm just a boy."

"Get up, Finino *mio*. Jack, I'd like you to meet my brother,
Fin. Fin, this is my dear, dear friend Jack . . . Jordan, right? Jack
Jordan. He's come to take us golfing."

Fin and Jack stood up and sullenly shook hands.

"You can call him Uncle Jack."

"Another uncle?"

"Shut up, Fin," Lady said, laughing.

Jack did not seem very happy about being an uncle, or about taking Fin along. "Oh come on, Lady. Golf is no fun for kids."

"He's brilliant at miniature golf."

Uncle Jack was strong, strapping. His hair was silky and stylishly long. But it looked pasted to his big square rugged face, as if he were a paper doll.

"What are your interests?" Fin asked.

"My *what?*"

When he was older, Fin tried to picture that day from Jack's point of view. Jack, twenty-two years old, football star at Yale, soon-to-be vice president of something at his father's business selling something, still living in the enormous, gracious seaside house in Sands Point, Long Island, with his doting parents. Jack hops in his car to make the trip into town to Charles Street in Greenwich Village, invited there by a mystifyingly beautiful girl he's met at a party, Twilly Chandler's party—"Quite a donkey roast, isn't it?" the beautiful girl had said. "Who are you, anyway? I feel absolutely crapulous. Will you take me inside like the well-brought-up young man you undoubtedly want me to think you are?" And she had collapsed decorously into his arms, smiling, murmuring, *"Bravo ragazzo . . ."*

And so, a few days later, enchanted by her eccentricity, her pale skin and wide dazzling smile, by the sense that she would do absolutely anything and probably already had, he sets off with visions of exotic positions and wild gasps of uncontrolled, uncontrollable pleasure, and he arrives at her street, such a promising street, so small and unlikely and bohemian, and he leaps out of his car, rushes up the steps, rings the bell, rings it again and then again, and then, full of his memory of that slender body relaxing into his own at Twilly Chandler's donkey roast, of the lemony scent and the odd, arousing pale lipstick on those delicious lips murmuring their anachronistic and incomprehensible slang, he runs down the steps, two, three at a time, sees the gate, leaps over in a great gazelle-like motion—if only Lady could see him—and finds . . . Fin. Finds a younger brother, a skinny, weedy kid who whacks him in the face with a pink rubber ball, who runs away and leads him into a pile up with the old Negro maid, who makes him look like a jerk.

Golf was fun. Even tearing up the grass when you missed was fun. Fin got to steer the golf cart.

The next day Jack sent Lady flowers, a long box of roses wrapped in tissue, like something out of a movie. Even then, Fin didn't worry. Corny flowers? Lady had gotten flowers before. You didn't make your way into Lady's heart with flowers. Fin didn't worry the first time Jack took Lady out to dinner, either. Jack was a dumb jock. Not Lady's type at all. The guy could barely speak. Jack wasn't even as old as Lady. He was just out of college. He was no match for Biffi, worldly, cosmopolitan, bearded, funny Biffi. No match at all.

Jack did emanate a strong, athletic energy. That was true. But so what?

Fin opened the front door and said, "Hello. Lady will be down in a minute." Fin was the gatekeeper. He was the sentry. Enter. Your audience with Lady has been arranged. She will receive you . . . and then toss you out on your ear. "Please sit down and wait."

He followed Jack into the living room. He wondered if Jack used hair tonic to keep his light brown hair in place. Or spray. His boots were polished to a mirrorlike sheen.

"In Victorian England, men used to polish their boots so they could see up ladies' dresses. In the reflection," Fin said. It was one of the scattered odds and ends of information Lady occasionally came out with.

"Yeah, well, this isn't Victorian England, is it?"

But when Lady came downstairs looking ravishingly beautiful in her very short skirt and coltish legs, Fin was gratified to notice that Jack glanced down self-consciously at his shiny boots, frowned, and blushed.

It was only a few days later that Fin began to worry about Jack. It was only when Biffi phoned and Lady told Fin to say she was out.

"She said to say she's out, but she's not," Fin said.

"Ach."

"Yeah, ach. There's this guy, and he's a jerk."

"We will get hamburgers," Biffi said. "You and I." He liked to get hamburgers. He believed they were the secret of America's health and prosperity. "Not the hot dogs," he would say. "That is nonsense."

"So that's the story. Pretty bad, huh?" Fin said as they sat in the coffee shop.

"Love," said Biffi, "is bondage."

"Lady likes freedom."

Biffi put his chin in his hands.

Fin did the same. "Do you want to go to the World's Fair again? Or something?"

"The world," Biffi said, "is not a fair."

"No, the World's Fair is a fair."

"You are very young, Fin."

"God, you're as bad as her."

"No one can compete with Lady," Biffi said.

After the hamburgers, they walked back to the house and sat on the stoop.

"If your sister finds me here on her doorstep, I am a dead duck."

He sighed. He took out his pipe, rubbed the bowl on his nose, then pulled out a yellowing tobacco pouch. "Here," he said, handing both to Fin. Fin filled the pipe, used Biffi's little tool to tamp it down the way Biffi had taught him, then watched the flame of the lighter sucked down into the bowl as Biffi puffed. The smell of the smoke was sweet and dark. Biffi's hands were large. How long had it been since Fin had held his father's hand?

"Sometimes I miss my father," he said. "Although I guess he wasn't such a nice man."

"I miss my father every day, and he was a terrible and selfish man."

Biffi puffed on the pipe. Fin closed his eyes.

"You'll tell me what goes on with this unworthy uncle?"

Fin opened his eyes. "Like a spy," he said.

"Like a friend," said Biffi.

Spies

He asked Phoebe if she would help, and she immediately pro-
duced a pair of binoculars from a closet. She positioned herself
at her window, which faced Lady's window across the street.

"I don't want to look in Lady's window," Fin said. "What if
she's getting dressed or something?"

"You're such a pervert."

"No, I said I *don't* want to . . ."

"Only a pervert would even think of that."

Fin said, "Just aim them downstairs, okay?"

And they looked through the living-room windows and
watched Mabel emptying ashtrays.

"This guy has got to be removed from the picture. We have
less than a year. Our mission is clear."

"We will not fail," Phoebe said.

That night, they met in the space beneath Phoebe's stairway
where the door to the kitchen was.

"They just left," Fin said. "They went to the Café Au Go
Go. Can we get in there?"

"What did you *do* all summer, Fin?" It was a coffeehouse, of
course they could get in, Phoebe went all the time. Sometimes

she just listened from outside, sometimes she had ice cream inside.

They stood outside this time. Stan Getz and Astrud Gilberto were performing. "The Girl from Ipanema," soft and seductive, floated out to them. At about ten o'clock, when Fin and Phoebe sat sleepily on the sidewalk, backs against the wall of the building, Lady and Jack walked out. Jack had his hand on the small of Lady's back. As if he owned her. Phoebe put her finger to her lips. Fin watched Lady put her head on Jack's shoulder.

"Criminy Dutch," he whispered to Phoebe when Jack and Lady had turned the corner.

"That was close."

"Come on," he said. "We have to follow them."

They kept at least a block behind Lady and Jack. They followed them home, home to the house on Charles Street. Watched them stop abruptly. Heard Lady's voice: "What the hell are you doing here?" Heard a male voice: "Thought I'd stop by." It was a drunk male voice.

"That's *him*," Fin said.

"Who?"

"Uncle Ty."

"I thought it was Uncle Jack."

"No, the other one."

"You broke my heart," Uncle Ty was saying. Loudly. "Do you know that?"

"Yes, of course I know."

"It's still broken. I bet you didn't know that."

"Of course I know that, Ty. Am I blind? Now, come on, let's get you home."

"I hope someone breaks your heart, Lady," Uncle Ty said.

"I don't have a heart."

"True, true . . ."

"Jack!" Lady said, as Tyler collapsed against her. "Help me, for God's sake."

"Who is he?" Jack said.

"Just someone."

Jack put Ty's arm around his neck and hauled him away from Lady.

"Who are *you*?" Tyler asked Jack.

"He's no one," Lady said.

"Hey!" said Jack.

"Are you going to help me or not?"

Uncle Jack pulled Uncle Ty toward Seventh Avenue.

"Taxi," Lady called, and a cab stopped at her feet. She unloaded Uncle Ty into the backseat and slammed the door.

"Taxi!" she called again, and another cab pulled up, like magic. She opened the door and motioned Jack to get in.

"Where're we going?" he said.

Lady closed the door on him, too.

"*You're* going. Home."

"Hey!"

"You said that already. Off you go."

Fin and Phoebe ran home to get there ahead of Lady, Phoebe peeling off to go up her steps, Fin bolting up his.

"Lavender Jesus, what a night. What are you doing up, Fin?" Lady said when she came in.

"Nothing."

She mixed herself a martini, and Fin got up to go to bed. His heart was still pounding from running.

"Stick around," Lady said. "Keep me company."

They sat beside each other on the couch.

"Sometimes it gets to me," she said.

"What?"

"It."

"Yeah," Fin said. "Me, too."

"What if I really don't have a heart?"

"Like the Tin Man. But he really did."

She put an arm around him and drew him close.

"I do love *you*, that's for sure," she said.

"I guess you have a heart, then."

But how could you have a heart when everyone wanted to tear off pieces? And everyone did, until there was nothing left, that's what she meant. Everyone tearing like wolves. Except him.

"I'm still only twenty-four," she said. "You know? So how am I going to do everything I want to do in one year? How?"

Fin sleepily closed his eyes. He already had Lady's heart. In his own heart.

"We have half the same DNA," he said.

"Poor you," she said.

It had gotten hot again, so hot that it seemed as though summer wouldn't be able to end even if it tried. Fin was at Phoebe's house, sitting as usual between her open window and a large, noisy fan. The binoculars rested on the windowsill. He and Phoebe took turns looking through them.

"Maybe we should be out seeking clues. Instead of just sitting here," she said.

"We could go observe the uncles," Fin said. "In their native habitats."

"Yeah, not your sister, who sleeps all day."

"Tyler came over again."

"Crap. She has a complex, I guess."

"She's still seeing that dumbbell Jack, too, but she won't even speak to Biffi."

Phoebe said, "Did you ever think that maybe Lady was just sowing her wild oats?"

"That's what guys do. Not girls." Fin lay on the floor and stared at the ceiling, which Phoebe had painted with yellow stars. Jewish stars.

"Those stars are sort of depressing, Phoebe. Like concentration-camp depressing."

"No kidding."

Fin went home and flipped through his sister's address book, which she kept in the kitchen on the counter below the wall phone. Beneath the ballpoint doodles and pencil squiggles, he found Tyler Morrison; Morrison, Frost and Morrison, attorneys-at-law.

"Do you know which bus to take?" he asked Phoebe.

"I shall not dignify your inquiry with an answer. Of course I do."

They sat side by side on the bus, the window open, the air streaming in hot and heavy, almost solid. The night before, Tyler had come over and told Fin if you wanted to get ahead you needed to go to prep school. "You want to get ahead, right?" he said.

"Ahead of what?"

"Ahead of this," Tyler said, raising a fist, laughing.

Then Lady came downstairs and Tyler handed Fin a wrapped box. It was a G.I. Joe doll. "You like toy soldiers, right?" he said.

"He doesn't know the difference between a toy soldier and a doll," Fin said to Phoebe.

When he'd asked Lady what Uncle Ty was doing skulking around again, she said it had just happened, the way things do. "I don't know, Fin. Tyler is a part of my past. Sometimes history makes you feel more . . ."

"Historical?"

She laughed. "Wretched child. *Young.* It makes you feel young. No, that's not it, either. Secure? No. What am I trying to say? I guess it's that I remember him. Which is okay, until he reminds me of Hugo Hadley, Esquire. History can only take you so far, I suppose."

"To the present," Fin said to Phoebe. "Which Tyler Morrison occupies too much of."

"This has something to do with an Electra complex," Phoebe said. "But don't worry too much. Lady is a drifter."

Would Lady just drift and drift, he wondered, down the stream, merrily, merrily, merrily, bumping one shore, then the opposite shore, with another little leaf following in her wake, floating past her on its way to boarding school? Fin used to place the curled leaves of a tulip tree in the stream near his grandparents' house and watch them navigate. Until they sank. He remembered the dappled shade for a moment, the sound of the stream. It was a treat, sometimes, to look back, to savor the loss, as if it were something sweet to eat. The sadness. His mother's voice. The smack of a cow's tail against its side, swatting away flies. Even the flies. Flies were different in the country. Lazy. Slow. Maybe that's what Lady meant about history.

"Tyler didn't really do anything yet, did he?" Phoebe's voice interrupted his thoughts. "He didn't sell your livestock."

"They're not livestock. They're cows."

"They're alive. And they're stock."

"They're cows."

And no, Tyler hadn't sold them. Yet. Fin called Mr. Cornelius, the music teacher renting the property, every two weeks to make sure, no matter what Lady said trying to reassure him. Mr. Cornelius said the cows were all doing beautifully, though they missed Fin.

"How can you tell?" Fin asked.

"A mournful moo," said Mr. Cornelius, who was considered artistic and therefore, pardonably, eccentric.

"Let's wait till Tyler comes down for lunch," Phoebe said. "They go to lunch and drink martinis."

"Who?"

"Lawyers. My father told me. Then they're too tired to do any work in the afternoon. So they go see my father. Because they can lie down. Because he's a shrink."

"Sure."

"Well, the martini part is true."

"Sure."

Tyler appeared and left the building with two other men. Five blocks later, the three men went into a restaurant. Fin and Phoebe stood uncertainly outside, watching through the plate glass as the trio sat down.

"See?" Phoebe said when martinis arrived.

"Are you children lost?" a woman asked them. Several lavender shopping bags hung from her arms. She carried a large pocketbook, too. She stopped and placed her packages on the sidewalk, obviously glad for a break.

"Oh no," Phoebe said. She pulled a compass out of her pocket. "See?"

"We're waiting for our mother," Fin said. Why had he said that?

"She's in the ladies' room," said Phoebe.

"Would you like me to wait with you until she comes out?"

You will have a long, long wait, Fin thought.

"I'll go tell her to hurry up." Phoebe disappeared into the restaurant.

Fin looked down at the sidewalk. Splotches of ancient chewing gum, cigarette butts, spit, heat. I'm sorry, he thought to his mother, to have used you in a lie.

"You're very nice to wait," he said to the woman. "But you really don't have to. I see my mother coming." He pointed to a woman walking through the restaurant. "But thank you very much." He lifted the woman's bags and handed them to her. A funeral phrase drifted through his mind. "For your concern," he said.

"You have very nice manners, young man. Tell your mother that."

Fin nodded and watched the woman walk on, lavender shopping bags banging against wide thighs.

The sun beat down, and the woman who was not his mother exited the restaurant and walked north, leaving behind a quick air-conditioned breeze before the restaurant door swung closed. He stood on one leg for a while. Then the other leg.

Phoebe came out a few minutes later trailing the same air-conditioner chill wind.

Fin said, "What took you so long, anyway?"

"Ladies' room," she said. "They're talking about baseball, by the way, if you're interested, since that was the whole reason we came here." She looked disgusted.

"So?"

"Yankee fans."

They walked over to the bank where Jack Jordan worked. Two blocks. The suitors were conveniently concentrated in a small area. Even Biffi's gallery was close by. If someone wanted to surround them, to lay siege, someone could. The suitors would slowly starve. Eat their own children. If they had children. Which the suitors did not. So they would kill each other, feed on their own freshly slaughtered flesh, and disappear.

"We'll wait here." Phoebe stood behind a tall potted plant. She gestured for Fin to join her.

When Uncle Jack returned from his lunch, his seersucker suit coat was slung over his shoulder. His tie was loose. He said, "Richard! Poker tonight," to a man who had come in just after him. "Jim's place."

"Bring your wallet," said Richard.

"Yeah." Jack laughed. "But tonight I'll win back every cent. My wallet will be bulging."

And they both were whisked upstairs by the elevator.

"Uncle Ty is a Yankee fan," Fin told Lady.

"I'm sorry, Fin."

"And Uncle Jack is a gambler."

"What is it you want me to do, Finny? Send them to bed without any supper?"

Yes, Fin thought. Why not? *Perché no*? You said I should help you find the lemons."

"But I didn't say you should spoil all my fun."

Fun was important to Lady. It was one of the seven virtues. She never mentioned what the other six were.

One night Fin followed Lady and Uncle Ty to a Spanish restaurant. Phoebe didn't want to come. She had decided that spying was dull. "And babyish." And it was too hot. "I'm going to write some 'Embarrassing Moments' and 'Bright Sayings' and send them to the *Daily News* and get five dollars instead."

Fin didn't blame her. Even the dog had elected to stay home, lying on the marble slab in front of the living-room fireplace.

When Lady and Ty came out of the restaurant, they did not look happy. Fun? Lady wasn't having any fun that night.

"You're making a huge mistake," Uncle Ty said. "Huge."

"Maybe I am. But I get to make it. It's mine."

"You belong to me, Lady."

"This is 1964. I don't belong to anyone."

"Yeah, yeah, yeah. What're you going to do, Lady? Be a lawyer?"

"Maybe."

"You never even finished college, for Christ's sake."

"Thanks to you."

Uncle Ty said something Fin couldn't hear. Lady said, "Fuck you, Ty." They were home by now, and she marched up the steps and in the door without looking back.

Ty turned and walked away, in Fin's direction.

"Jesus!" He jumped when he saw Fin. "What are you doing here? Shouldn't you be in bed?"

"Indubitably."

"You're an even bigger pain in the ass than your sister, you know that?"

"I'll tell her you said so."

"I wouldn't if I were you." Ty gave Fin a long look, then said, "Moo, mooo." Then: "You know why Lady likes you so much?"

"Because I'm her brother. I'm her only brother. She loves me."

"Yeah, you're her brother. But you know what else? You're the kid she never has to have. You know what I mean?"

"No."

"Sure you do," said Ty, and he gave Fin a mock sock to the gut and continued on his way.

"All because the *Times* has no funnies"

There was a lot more going on in the world than Lady's love
life, even at the house on Charles Street. Fin read the newspaper every day. The *New York Times* obituary section had been
his grandfather's favorite. Fin's, too. He would sit on his grandfather's lap pointing to names, *Hatfield*, *Jerome*, *O'Connor*, and
sounding them out.

"Two *Warner*s today," he said one Sunday morning, bent
over the obit page he'd spread out on the kitchen floor. "Natalie
and William S. Jr."

"Isn't it a little morbid?" Mirna said. "Reading the obits?"
She said it hopefully, as if she'd given him a piece of pie—*Isn't it
delicious?*

"*You're* reading the wedding announcements," Fin said.

"Well, that's to see what's going on, what my friends are
up to."

"Well, same here," Fin said. He grinned.

"Anyway, our friends got married a long time ago," Joan
said. "There are no holdouts but us."

"Holdouts," Lady said. She gave a sarcastic grunt.

Fin made a series of little pig grunts.

"*Basta*, Finino," Lady said. "Tell us how the Mets are doing. *They're* alive."

Fin snorted again. "Barely."

He watched them sipping from their coffee cups. Sip, sip, sip. The cups clattered back into their saucers. They each put a chin on a fist and stared at nothing. Fin gulped some orange juice and listened to the sound, loud but somehow private, internal. What did they hear when he gulped? What did they hear when he sipped? The same thing he heard when they sipped? He sipped. It sounded almost as loud as the gulping. But it did sound like the word "sip." He sipped again.

"What on earth are you doing?" Lady asked.

"Sipping."

She turned back to the wedding announcement page. "Oh, look! Misty Cardiff got married."

"That anti-Semitic bitch."

There was silence as they all seemed to remember some incident.

Lady said, "Well, somehow I'm getting married by the time I'm twenty-five. Period." She tapped the wedding announcement page.

"You already had a wedding announcement," said Fin. "Are you allowed to have another?"

Mirna, momentarily silenced by the first bite of a bagel, looked at Fin over the pile of pink salmon and red onion and white cream cheese with her troubled, knowing look.

"I saw it," Fin said, suddenly very uncomfortable. "I saw the picture in the newspaper. When I was little. That's all."

"Did you?" Lady asked, smiling at him. "I didn't know that."

You were so beautiful, he wanted to say. You looked like a pearl. And a horse. He licked cream cheese off his fingers.

"Just for the record," Mirna said, "*I* am not technically a holdout. *I* am technically unlucky. And *I* will clearly never find anybody to marry."

"Me either," said Joan.

"Me either," said Lady. "Who am I kidding?"

"Come off it, Lady. You have guys proposing right and left."

"Why can't I just fall in love, then? Just the thought of living with any of them for the rest of my life . . ." She shuddered. "What's wrong with me?"

"Well, I do have a career, at least," said Joan.

"I have one of those, too," said Mirna, "and you know what? Your career doesn't give a shit about you, Joan. Does it take you out to a nice dinner? It never even takes you out to lunch. It certainly doesn't take you to bed . . ."

"Enough," said Lady.

Mirna glanced at Fin, then pointed to the plate of smoked salmon. "You have to actually watch them slice it. Or they give you the tail."

"Well, I happen to love my work," said Joan.

"Except for the children," Mirna said.

"Oh, them." Lady started laughing.

"I *love* the children." Joan was a kindergarten teacher.

"*Miss Cooper, look at my picture; Miss Cooper, she pushed me; Miss Cooper, Miss Cooper* . . . You can't stand the brats," Mirna said. "You're always complaining about them."

"And you sure won't meet a guy at that girls' school, Miss Cooper," Lady said.

Lady met people everywhere, of course. She stopped to chat with strangers on the street. She jumped into taxis with strangers and asked if they could drop her. She admired a stranger's handbag on the bus or pointed out a sunset shimmering between the buildings to a stranger passing by.

"She'll meet lots of little girls," said Fin.

Mirna gave him a look. "Read about your dead playmates,

Fin . . . Now," she said, addressing Joan, "Helen Gurley Brown is married. Even Hannah Arendt got married. So why not us?"

"Yeah," said Fin. "Even Jane Eyre."

Joan had been piling a bagel half with lox. She frowned at Fin, pushing the plate over to him. "Here. Shut up, okay?" Then: "Yeah, I really am sick of kids."

"Hey, here's a man who fought in the Spanish-American War," Fin said, going back to the obituaries.

"Too old for us," Lady said.

"*William H. Hands*," said Fin. "And his son is named H. William Hands!"

"Good grief," said Lady. "And all because the *Times* has no funnies."

That summer, Fin read the *Post* and the *Daily News* as well as the *Times*. He checked the sports section of the *Daily News* in the morning at the newsstand, then bought the *Post* in the afternoon and brought it home to examine the box scores, study the standings, read the sports features, then skim through the rest of the paper, through the stories about students from New York going to Mississippi to register voters, stories about the two students who never came back. The riots in Harlem that summer were in the newspaper, too, and Fin read about them, but Harlem was so far away from Charles Street it might as well have been Mississippi. It wasn't the Long Hot Summer for him. It was long and it was hot, but when you're eleven, you're eleven, and that's just the way it was, though even an eleven-year-old knew something was happening. You could feel it in the air, even in the air of Lady's house in Greenwich Village.

On the day Flannery O'Connor died, which he always remembered because she lived on a dairy farm like him and because someone enthusiastically referred to her in the obit as a "white witch," a "literary white witch," but still, Lady was having a dinner party for which she seriously considered using her mother's finger bowls.

"Don't they know how to use napkins?" Fin asked.

Lady sighed. No finger bowls. "But they used to look so pretty. A lemon slice floating on top . . ."

Mabel cooked all day in preparation. Pounds of shrimp, an entire salmon.

"We'll serve it cold," Lady said. "No one could eat a hot dish. Not in this heat."

"No one eats dishes, even cold ones," Fin said. "Ha ha."

"Ha ha."

"Food's got to cook," Mabel said. "It's got to get hot before it cools off."

"What a terrific slogan, Mabel. Like something the Freedom Riders would say," said Lady.

"Not a slogan," said Mabel. "A fact."

In the kitchen, Fin helped Mabel. He dumped slippery gray shrimp into the sink and shelled them, the stink of the ocean overwhelming the sweltering kitchen. Steam rolled from the pot on the stove, almost indistinguishable from the hot moist air. "I used to think they started out pink," Fin said, watching the shrimp when Mabel dropped them in the pot.

"Color, color, color," Mabel muttered, wiping sweat from her face with a dishcloth, "that's all I hear these days. Now look at all those shrimps. Why'd Miss Lady go to all this expense, anyhow? Same old riffraff with their sandal feet . . ."

"Nope, she's having rich people tonight."

"Don't call Miss Lady 'she.'"

"Even Mirna and Joan aren't invited. It's to raise money."

"First I heard." Mabel dumped the shrimp into a colander in the sink.

"She thought you'd get mad," Fin said. "It's to raise money for Negroes."

"Oh Lord," said Mabel, scowling just before a fog of fishy steam obscured her face. "Lord save us from Miss Lady and her whims."

When Fin came downstairs later in his navy wool funeral suit, Lady took one look at him and said, "Good God, Fin, what have you done?"

Fin stood at the bottom of the stairs, his wrists poking three inches from his jacket cuffs, his pants high above his shoes. He had grown, that's what he'd done.

Lady tapped her lips thoughtfully, a gesture Fin remembered from his father.

"Daddy used to do that," he said, tapping his own lips.

"Nonsense."

"I could wear Levi's."

"Nonsense again. Here's ten dollars. Go buy yourself some decent pants, for God's sake." She handed him a few more bills. "And a couple of shirts. Good grief."

Fin went to a children's clothing store he'd spotted on one of his walks, and though the proprietor of the establishment looked surprised when no one but a big collie dog followed the eleven-year-old in, he was nevertheless able to produce a pair of chinos and several long-sleeved button-down shirts.

"Your mother will be proud," the man said when Fin came out of the dressing room. Fin rolled the cuffs back and admired himself in the mirror.

"My mother's dead," Fin said. He watched the man's face in the mirror. They all did the same thing, exactly the same thing. They glanced away, quickly, as if they'd seen the rotting corpse, then they looked back at Fin with a kind, determined smile.

"Dear, dear," the man said softly.

Fin relented. "My guardian will be very pleased," he said.

The relieved proprietor gave him a lollipop, a red one, which Fin stuck in the corner of his mouth. He wore his new pants and a new blue oxford shirt out of the store.

At dinner, he was seated beside a very old lady with powdery white skin and frail birdlike hands that trembled as she reached for her glass of wine. On his other side sat a woman of about forty. Her dress was pale green silk. There were dark half-moons beneath each pale green silk arm. She insisted Fin call her Cee Cee. The old lady was named Mrs. Holbright.

"And what's your name, young man?" Cee Cee asked.

"Fin. It means 'the end' in French. My father wanted me to be the last of his children."

"Sounds like Hugo," said old Mrs. Holbright. Her mouth made a clicking sound when she spoke, as if she were a mechanical toy. "He's Hugo's boy," she said to Cee Cee. "Same eyes. Is Lady good to you? I'm sure she is. Excellent fellow, your father, up to a point. Do you have a temper, Fin?" Her mouth clicked shut, and she stared expectantly at Fin.

"I guess," Fin said. He smiled politely.

"Ha!" Mrs. Holbright said. "I don't believe it for a minute. You're as sweet-tempered as a lamb, just like your poor mother. And as polite. Aren't you? Don't dare contradict me, young man. I enjoy being right. Most people do, you know. But you will find that I am particularly inclined in that direction."

Cee Cee, who had been effectively silenced by the older woman, gave a tiny, demure cough in apparent agreement. She patted her décolletage with her napkin, as surreptitiously as possible, sopping up a thick film of perspiration.

Fin thought of his mother, her girlish laugh. He tried to remember his father's eyes. He envisioned only the end of a cigar burning high above him.

"Now," Mrs. Holbright was saying, "what do *you* make of the colored question, I wonder."

Fin realized she was addressing him. "The Negro question," he said automatically.

Cee Cee looked embarrassed, as if he had said a word like, say, "penis." "What a warm night," she said.

"Good heavens. Colored, Negro . . . Mabel, which is it?" Mrs. Holbright's voice was piercing. All conversation in the room stopped. All eyes turned to Mabel.

Mabel stood holding a silver pitcher of ice water.

More silence. General, awkward silence. Cee Cee looked as though she wanted to throw her damp napkin over her head and hide. A few guests looked down. Someone coughed. Lady, who had just lifted a large shrimp to her lips, held it there like a Milk-Bone in front of a dog and smiled broadly, clearly enjoying herself. Drops of water beaded the pitcher.

Mabel looked thoughtful, considering the question.

"Well," she said at last, "call me anything, just don't call me late for dinner."

Lady swallowed her shrimp like a sea lion. "Ditto."

Fin, horrified by the entire exchange, tried to catch Mabel's eye to somehow apologize for the guests, for his sister, for the entire Caucasian race, but Mabel deposited the pitcher on a silver dish and disappeared without a glance at him.

"Segregation is wrong," Fin said to Mrs. Holbright, a little too loudly.

"Yes, yes, I suppose it is. So shall I give Lady and her Negro friends a donation?"

"Of course you should," Fin said.

"Or shall I march?" the old lady was saying, not having waited for the answer.

March? Fin looked at the old lady. They would have to carry her on a litter.

"Although I should not like to go to jail, I'm sure," she added.

Carry her to jail on a litter.

"Anyone can march," he said. "Not everyone can give money."

"Clever, clever. A little diplomat. You've got Hugo's tongue in you. Charming man, your father. Charmed everyone. Except his own daughter, of course."

"Don't gossip," Cee Cee said.

"Oh pooh. I'm old and I can behave as badly as I want to. Isn't that right, Fin?"

Before Fin could answer, Cee Cee reached across and pinched the loose flesh of the old lady's arm. "Mother!"

Mrs. Holbright was Cee Cee's mother? Fin looked at them both curiously. He tried to imagine pinching his mother. Would his mother ever have gotten as white and slack as Mrs. Holbright, if she had lived? His young, tender mother?

"My mother's dead," he said to Cee Cee.

She pulled her arm back, as if Fin had been about to sink his teeth into it.

"Oh dear," she said. "Let's concentrate on the Negroes, shall we?"

Jack Jordan had not been invited. He was currently out of the picture, which at first had been a relief to Fin, except that Uncle Tyler now seemed to be back in the picture in a prominent way. He sat at what he considered the head of the table, which Fin, as of that moment, considered the foot. Pierre, who decorated all the rich people's houses and apartments, was there, too. Fin didn't know anyone else. He wished Biffi were there. He often wished Biffi were there.

"In Europe, the Negro is far better off," said Pierre.

"That's because they don't have any," said Uncle Ty.

"What is that supposed to mean?" Lady said.

110

Fin leaned on his elbows and happily listened to Uncle Ty and Lady disagree about civil rights. All the guests became louder as more wine was served. Even Mrs. Holbright seemed tipsy.

"Young man!" she shrieked at Fin. "A shoulder to lean on!"

He helped her to the bathroom. She had a gigantic pocketbook swinging from her arm.

"Keep an eye on your sister," Mrs. Holbright said as he helped her back to the table. "I'm very fond of her."

"Me, too."

"You do look like your father, you know. Handsome man when he was young. And don't mind Lady about him. She was fond of him."

"Ha ha."

Mrs. Holbright stopped to get her breath. "Divorce, temperament—they took a toll, I'm not saying they didn't, but remember, Lady is one of those people who likes a good enemy, needs one. The drama, I suppose." And they resumed their slow waddle, Mrs. Holbright's hand heavy on his shoulder. "Yes, she really does like to bat them around a bit." Mrs. Holbright gestured toward a smiling Lady and an exhausted, defeated Tyler Morrison. "I had a cat like Lady," Mrs. Holbright continued. "Cee Cee! Cee Cee!" She reached across and poked her daughter.

"Mother! For goodness sake . . ."

"What was the name of that cat? The one who played with the mice? While they were alive?"

Cee Cee grimaced. "Latimer," she said.

"Yes! Latimer." Mrs. Holbright sighed. "We had to put him down."

"Never tell a child what he can learn for himself"

Lady seemed to move from one suitor to another without warning, without rhyme, without reason. This time, though, Fin knew he had civil rights to thank. Finally, as August drew to a close, Tyler was out and, after a week or so of frenzied parties, Biffi was back. Fin followed him wherever he went in the house. Gus followed Fin.

"A parade," said Lady.

Lady was a force of nature, Biffi said. A hurricane, a tornado, a sunrise, a shower of gentle rain. "Never be angry at the weather," he told Fin. "There is no gain in it."

Fin was not angry. He was relieved, relieved to have Biffi back, relieved not to be in boarding school, but mostly relieved to have discovered, even in the short time he'd been living with Lady, if not rhyme or reason, then at least a rhythm, a pattern, some order to things. The path Fin had been on since the death of his mother had seemed such a vague one, fading off into the mist, unmarked and going nowhere. But now he began to see his days as parts of weeks, his weeks as parts of months, all of them marked by short, specific seasons. There was cold, gray Tyler season and bland, humid Jack season, and there was Biffi season, bright cloudless skies that darkened dramatically into violent storms, then lifted to reveal the sudden blue sky again. It was Biffi season now.

"Tell the boy about his education," Biffi said one day.

"Good grief, what's your hurry?" she said.

"Where am I going to school? When?"

"Who said you were going to school at all?"

"I want to go to Phoebe's school."

"Okay, okay." Lady solemnly put her hands on Fin's shoulders. "You start school next week. And, yes, Phoebe's school. I didn't want to tell you until I had to. The prison-house walls and all that."

Fin gave her a hug.

"Thanks, Lady."

"It's against my principles."

"I know."

"It is the American law, I believe," said Biffi.

"Unless you get kicked out. Like Holden Caulfield," Fin said.

"It's not prep school, Fin!" Lady said. "For criminy Dutch sake."

"I know. You would never do that." Not now. Not with Biffi here.

"They sent me to boarding school because they didn't like me around the house. But I like you around, Fin."

"Did you go to boarding school?" he asked Biffi.

Biffi shook his head. No, no boarding school.

He took Fin for a celebratory hamburger.

"I'm glad Lady let me know I'm going to school before school actually started." Then Fin told Biffi everything he could about the uncles. "She doesn't even like Uncle Ty at all," he said. "But there's this hold he has over her."

"History," Biffi said.

"I guess. And Uncle Jack, forget it, she doesn't like him, either. Not really."

"But here is a question, my friend: Does she like Biffi?"

Fin wanted to say yes. He wanted to say, Of course she does, she's in love with you. Instead, he ate his French fries, four at a time, covered in ketchup, until he could stuff no more in, a way to say nothing at all.

"And," Biffi continued, "really, does she like anybody? Really like them? Sometimes I don't know." He handed Fin an extra paper napkin. "But we know she loves you."

"Ty said I was the son she would never have to have," Fin said through the French fries. But Biffi must not have heard, because all he said back was "You eat like a peasant."

The first day of school, Fin arrived half an hour early and nervously entered what was supposed to be his classroom. There were no desks. There were no chairs. Just a man who seemed to be kneading dough on a long table by the windows. Fin said, "Sorry," and turned to leave.

"Are you Fin Hadley?" the young man asked him. "Your mother said you'd be here early."

"My mother is dead."

Fin watched with delight as the young man flushed and cleared his throat. "I'm so sorry. I thought . . ."

"You mean my sister, I guess."

"Oh. I see. Yes, she did seem rather young. Well! Here we are!"

"Is this Mr. Shelby's classroom? Sixth grade?" Fin asked. But it couldn't be. What kind of classroom had no desks?

Mr. Shelby explained that he was Mr. Shelby, but he was not, for all intents and purposes, Mr. Shelby at all: no one was called Mr. or Mrs. or Miss at the New Flower School.

"We're all one here," Mr. Shelby explained. "No distinctions."

"Okay."

He said his name was Rufus, but he liked to be called Red. Then he laughed. "For all sorts of reasons; the only one you need to know is that Rufus means red in Latin."

"Do we study Latin?" Fin asked, excited. He was reading a book about the Battle of Actium.

"This is a progressive school," the teacher said, obviously taken aback.

Mr. Rufus Red Shelby. What a jerk.

When the other kids arrived, ten in all, they sat on the floor in a circle. There were six girls and four boys. Even sitting, the girls towered over the boys.

Red's pedagogical method became clear that first morning. When a little girl raised her hand, he ignored her. When she began violently swinging it in front of his face, he tilted his head away and did not otherwise respond.

"Red! Red!" she cried out at last.

"Finally!" he said. "You have learned your first lesson. We do not submit to establishment imperatives like 'raising hands.' If you want to ask a question, just ask your question! You have as much right to speak as I do."

By now the little girl was squirming pretty desperately.

"Can I please have permission to go to the girls' room?" she said.

Red considered this for a moment, then said, "Permission? This is not a matter of permission, Betsy. I like to put most of our endeavors to a vote." He eyed the wriggling child. "But under the circumstances, yes, you can."

Looking relieved, the girl asked, "Where is the girls' room, Red?"

"Ah," said the teacher brightly. "Never tell a child what he can learn for himself."

New Flower was so different from Fin's old school that he hardly thought of it as school at all. They began each day with Community Meeting, usually a song by Woody Guthrie or Pete Seeger, once with Pete Seeger actually there to lead them. Sometimes, when they went back to class, Red would ask them to be a tree, which took about fifteen minutes. They would stand or sway, whatever their tree was feeling like that morning. In Science, they raised fruit flies and made posters of different generations of fruit flies, coloring in their fruit-fly eyes with red or yellow, depending. They built a longhouse for Social Studies and ate beef jerky in it, then made posters of it. Some of the kids were bored with the longhouse because they had made a longhouse the year before, but Red said that wasn't a longhouse at all, that was a wigwam. In Language Arts, they read and discussed the liner notes of Bob Dylan albums and made more posters. For Math, they had a different teacher, an older woman with lint on her sweater, who gave them colored blocks to arrange. No posters.

"Fin attends the New Flower Poster-Making Academy," Lady said to Joan. "I like his 'Vote for Goldwater, Vote for Death' best myself."

When the day was nice, the students would all troop out to Washington Square to Observe. There might be a toddler on a tricycle looking up at a mounted policeman on a huge horse, the horse towering above, its hooves clacking on the cobblestones, the reins pulled tight as the giant animal pranced and snorted. The uniformed officer might wear polished boots. A dark blue station wagon might cruise past. A fat girl on roller skates might clump behind . . .

Sometimes they painted their Impressions of their Observations. Sometimes they discussed them in the Sharing Circle.

"I wish I had roller skates," a girl would say.

"Do you really?" Red would ask. "I mean, *really*?"

"Well, yeah, kind of. Yeah, I do."

"But is it you wishing or is it the message you're getting? To want roller skates? To want *things*?"

"Oh, like a message from a ghost? Or from God or something?"

"No," Red would say wearily. "Not from a ghost. Not from God."

Fin learned very quickly that the correct answer to most questions of this nature was "Advertising" or, even better, "Society."

"Right. Exactly. Society. You don't really *need* roller skates, do you, Missy?"

"Well, to skate I do."

"Someone implants the idea of need, and that someone is . . ."

"Society," Fin would say again.

"What did you do at your hotty-totty school today?" Lady asked when he got home.

"The fruit flies got out, so we don't know what color this generation's eyes are."

"No wonder the school costs a fortune." Lady handed him a package. "Here." It was a book. *Kim*, by Rudyard Kipling. "Don't let your teacher see it."

"Is it dirty?"

"Nope. Imperialist."

The Mets went 53 and 109 in 1964, finishing tenth in the National League. The Cardinals beat the Yankees in the World Series, a series in which Mickey Mantle hit three home runs. But even with the World Series as a reminder, autumn snuck up on Fin. Without the flocks of goldfinches, the flutter of dull-colored warblers in their fall plumage, the moon shining big and orange in his window, the humps of baled hay in the fields, the smell of the leaves sinking deeper and deeper into the wet earth, without the fading of the cicadas' song, he was unprepared. One day he smelled wood smoke and realized autumn was all around him. He looked up to see geese flying south in formation over the Hudson River. The wind blew flurries of small gold leaves down the street.

"We're segregated," Phoebe said that afternoon as they turned onto Charles Street. "By grade." She was in seventh grade, one higher than Fin. They never spoke at school. You couldn't. You really couldn't.

"Grade ghettos," Fin said to Lady when he got home.

"Oh please, what puerile bunkum. Go talk to Mabel about that one, Finny."

"What does puerile mean?"

"Boyish."

"Is that bad? That's not bad."

"Okay. Childish. It means childish. Don't they teach Latin in that school?"

"No. Latin isn't relevant. Did you know that Cole Porter wrote a whole song in the subjunctive? He died last week."

"Do you even know what the subjunctive is? Do you even know who Cole Porter is?"

"I read his obituary. And I *am* a child. So childish isn't bad, either. Is bunkum Latin?"

"I've never heard of a private school without Latin. Do you want me to take you out? Put you in a real school?"

"No! I just made two friends."

"In your ghetto?" Lady said, grabbing him by the neck and kissing his head.

"But they *are* grade ghettos," Phoebe said the next afternoon. "They separate us. Based on our grade."

"But we get to get out of the ghettos. So they're not real ghettos."

"But a sixth-grader can't come into a seventh-grade class-room."

"Unless they skip a grade."

Phoebe thought this over. Then they argued over which was the real attitude of the Beatles: "I don't care too much for money, money can't buy me love" or "Give me money, that's what I want."

Phoebe's grandmother had gotten her a guitar. Phoebe had immediately charged a book of chords to her parents at the bookstore, and she and Fin took turns trying to teach themselves the chords for "On Top of Old Smokey." She had an album cover of Dave Van Ronk taped to her wall, and she tried to imitate the roughness of his voice, with mixed success.

"You know what 'House of the Rising Sun' is about, right?" she asked Fin when they decided to move on to that.

Fin pretended to be concentrating on getting his pinkie in the proper position for an F chord.

"Prostitutes," Phoebe said. "It's a whorehouse."

"I know," Fin said.

"You did not."

Fin looked up from the guitar, and in spite of the contemptuous expression on her face, he grinned at her.

"I knew you didn't know. You probably don't even know what a prostitute is."

"I do, too. They follow armies around. Did you know that?"

Phoebe did not, and furthermore, she declared, she did not care.

Thanksgiving dinner was spent with Biffi and his mother, a sharp-eyed woman in a well-cut camel-hair suit and laced suede shoes who had spent two days cooking a traditional Thanksgiving dinner. There was a huge turkey on a platter surrounded by plates and bowls of mashed potatoes, peas and onions, creamed corn, and extra stuffing, all of it, somehow, tasting vaguely of cabbage. The table was covered by a thick white linen cloth, and the silver was heavy and bright. Fin could barely lift his elaborately decorated crystal glass of water.

"What lovely dishes," Lady said.

"Queen of England," said the unsmiling Mrs. Deutsch. "Same."

Lady had brought a bottle of champagne, a glass of which seemed to cheer Mrs. Deutsch considerably. She toasted the New World and insisted Fin have some bubbly, which she pronounced "boobly." It was the first champagne Fin had ever tasted. "Like Gigi!" said the now quite jolly Mrs. Deutsch.

The next day, Lady gave Fin a paperback of Colette's novella.

"What's a courtesan?" he asked, reading the back cover.

"Look it up."

The book had an old-fashioned drawing of a girl on it.

"Don't mind that," Lady said.

"Is it dirty?"

"Is love dirty?"

Fin raced upstairs and read the little book straight through.

Wasn't it a little . . . inappropriate? I once asked him.

"Is love inappropriate?" he said. "Or beauty? Or literature, for that matter?"

Well, sometimes it is, I said.

But Fin would always be a bit of a romantic, at least when it came to books. That was one of the things, one of the many things, bequeathed to him by Lady.

Money was another. It's true that Lady went through quite a bit of it at first. People said she was careless with money, but Fin always said they were wrong, that she was not careless at all, but carefree. He understood Lady's relationship to money. She loved it, he said. Not the way a miser loved it, or a gambler. She wasn't consumed by desire for money. For Lady, money was a pal, a generous pal, generous to her, to Fin, to her friends when they needed generosity.

"Money," she said, "is freedom."

Freedom, that highest good, along with Fun.

"You will have both, Fin. Freedom and Fun. *Perché no?*"

She meant: Not like me. She meant: I won't be like our father. She never said so in so many words, but it's what she meant.

It was harder and harder for Fin to remember his father. Sometimes he would hear something, a door slamming, or smell a cigar, or see a man in an overcoat and hat, and his father would come back to him, his deep voice, his sudden corrosive presence.

He would remember being curled on his mother's lap. She stroked his hair in her sweetly absent way. The room was silent, just the rhythmic sound inside his head of her small hand gliding across his scalp. Then she sang to him, songs he would not remember, but the musical sound of her voice, clear and intimate, he would recall always. And into the scene of one of these cherished memories of his mother, into the room where he lay, a little boy on his mother's lap, a great noise, a banging of doors, and cigar smoke, all would announce the arrival of his father. The reverie was over, the oasis gone like a desert hallucination.

"Damn fool," his father might say. His mother would ask, Who?, or not. His father would answer, or not.

Fin would look up at his father. That's most of what he remembered: looking up.

"Did you study your spelling?" Hugo would ask. Fin remembered that, too.

And Fin continued looking up, silent.

" 'Dog'?" said Hugo.

Silence.

"Go ahead," Fin's mother whispered.

"D.O.G."

"Okay, then," Hugo said. " 'Rabbit.' "

Rabbit? How many *b*'s? How many *t*'s? How many *a*'s? Fin felt hot. Felt his heart beating. He had practiced with his mother. "R.A.B.B.I.T.T.?"

"What do you do all day with him?" his father said, angry, turning on Fin's mother. Fin clutched her hand.

"He's only a child," she said gently, then she stood, let go of Fin's hand, and took his father's. She gave her husband a kiss as Fin got up and backed out of the room.

"R.A.B.B.I.T.?" he said suddenly, from the doorway.

"Well, why didn't you say so in the first place?" his father said, suddenly jovial, and held his arms open to let Fin jump inside his heavy embrace.

His father had been like that. Encompassing, like air. Unpredictable, like Lady. "Demanding, like life," Fin told me, with a shrug.

But Lady didn't think her father was a bit like life. He was everything that kept her from life. He was strict. Severe. Cruel, Lady said.

"The prison house," she called her home. "A prison you couldn't escape, a prison you were born into."

"But that, surely, is called existence, no?" Biffi said when she told him this.

"You can't possibly understand how awful it was because you experienced so many things so much worse," Lady said.

Fin checked her expression. Yes, she was serious.

"So don't even try," she added.

———

Fin's best friends at school were a boy named James, who could play the guitar, and another named Henry. Lady referred to them as Henry James, thinking it hilarious. It's true they were a pair. They looked like brothers, both with black shiny hair and enormous, round blue eyes. Fin, they discovered, was a good pitcher, and they spent their recess time playing wiffle ball on the closed-off street or, in bad weather, in the small gym. Sometimes, instead of playing ball, they flipped baseball cards.

Phoebe had an impressive stack of baseball cards that her grandmother, who lived in Omaha, Nebraska, had gotten for her on a recent visit. Instead of buying a few packs of cards with the powdery slab of pink gum inside, Phoebe's kindly and ancient grandmother had been convinced that one was supposed to buy the entire display box, which held twenty packs. At ten cards each, that was two hundred altogether. An instant collection.

"You're so lucky," Fin said.

"You think? It's kind of destroyed my will to succeed."

Parent-teacher conferences were held twice a year at New Flower. There were, of course, no grades given out, so these meetings were supposed to be taken very seriously. Lady swept off to the first one on a blowy December evening, late before she even stepped out the door. Fin put on an album. Buffy St. Marie.

What would his teacher make of his glamorous sister?

He opened a box of cookies and poured himself a glass of milk. He lay on the couch and stared out the windows. The wind blew through the slender trees, scattering their last few leaves. From his position, lying on the low couch, he could see Phoebe's window on the second floor across the street, but no light was on. Her parents ate dinner every night at eight o'clock, and Phoebe was expected to join them. She claimed it was the only time she saw them. He imagined them seated around the oval dining table, politely passing dishes. He envied them, the little family of three. "Pass the butter to your father," he imagined the mother shrink saying, smiling sweetly at the shrink father. "It's *margarine*," said Phoebe's imagined voice, and Fin's imagined family dinner was over.

Lady came back from that first parent-teacher conference with a smile Fin was beginning to understand—the Smile of Conquest. He would talk about that special smile years later, with his own special smile, the one that crept across his face whenever he thought of those early days with Lady.

"Lordy Lou, your teacher sure can talk!" She gave the smile again.

"N.O.," Fin said. "No. Really, Lady. Not him. I forbid it."

His words brought back a memory—his mother, her pale blue coat, her slender fingers around his. *You must never go down to the end of the town . . .*

"My little captain," Lady said, ruffling his hair. "Your poster-making is above average, apparently. And can I help it if your teacher finds me fascinating?"

"Yes," said Fin. "You can."

Then came Christmas, Fin's first without his mother. He pretended it was a different holiday, not the one he'd celebrated in Connecticut with his mother and his grandparents, not the one with snow and trees, not the one with the silver early-morning sky as he shook his mother and begged her to get out of bed. He pretended it was another holiday, but still a holiday with a tree, a Christmas tree. He wanted a Christmas tree, he just did. He begged for a tree, following Lady from room to room until she said, "Okay, okay. A tree. Two trees. A forest. Just stop whining." They selected the biggest tree in the lot, then began to drag it along the sidewalk, laughing and gummy with sap, stopping every few feet to rest.

By the time they got home, two young men were carrying the Christmas tree on their shoulders. Lady invited both of them to her Christmas Eve party. Fin and Phoebe decorated the tree with ornaments from a huge box that Lady seemed surprised to find in a closet. "Well, look what we have here," she said.

"You knew they were there," Fin said.

"Did not."

"You wanted to get a tree all along."

"Not."

The ornaments were glass balls mostly, a few wooden reindeer and teddy bears and sleds, a tin giraffe, a car driven by Santa, some stars. The lights were red, yellow, green, and blue. Mabel appeared with popcorn balls wrapped in colored cellophane.

"My parents won't let me get a tree," Phoebe said. "Because we're Jewish."

"You're Jewish?" Fin asked. "Like Biffi?"

"I guess so. Does he eat bacon?"

"Yes."

"Then, yes. Jewish like Biffi."

The Christmas Eve party went on so long it seemed to Fin that it must be New Year's Eve when everyone finally left. In the morning, it was Christmas, though, not New Year's, and the flat winter sun poured through the windows onto the tree and the packages beneath. Fin's stocking was filled with oranges and walnuts. Biffi's gifts to him, left under the tree the night before, were a jackknife and a copy of *The Wind in the Willows*. Mabel had left a harmonica. Lady gave him new pajamas, slippers made of deerskin, the new Beatles album, *Beatles '65*, a hat like John Lennon's, and a subscription to *The New York Review of Books*, along with the most recent copy.

"A grown-up paper," he said, rather awed.

"Don't be silly. Look—Gore Vidal writing about E. Nesbit.

A book by Eric von Schmidt, you like him. And it won't kill you to read a little Lowell, you know."

He threw his arms around her. Then it was time to give Lady her present. He'd thought long and hard about what to give her, Biffi, and Mabel. Phoebe was easy—a Coke bottle with an elongated neck and a huge paper flower, both of which he'd seen on Eighth Street. He finally decided on a paisley scarf for Mabel. A package of multicolored pipe cleaners for Biffi, which Fin really wanted for himself. And for Lady, a wooden box he'd made at school. "To keep your love letters in," he said.

Little Wars

And then, briefly, sadly, it was Jack season again. There wasn't much snow that Jack season, but the sky was gray and gloomy and Fin spent most of his time inside, listening to records or reading. He started *Native Son*, but he could read it only during the day. It was too disturbing at night. At night, he read Lady's old copy of E. Nesbit's *Five Children and It*. Gore Vidal highly recommended it.

He wasn't sure what exactly had ushered Biffi out of their lives this time—an enormous argument, as usual, but he didn't know what it was about or even if it was about anything. Lady now simply declared that Jack was a breath of fresh air. And there was something fresh about Jack, in a hygienic and scrubbed way. He was extremely physical, a big strapping guy, a jock. A jock after a shower.

"You can't marry a jock, Lady."

"Says who? And who said I wanted to marry Jack? Who said I wanted to marry anyone?"

"You did."

"Do you hear any wedding bells?" She put a hand up to her ear. "I don't."

"You don't have to get married ever, you know."

She gave an odd, horsey snort and said, "I can't not get married forever, either."

"Why not?"

"Do you want me to be an old maid?"

Now it was Fin's turn to snort. An old maid. Lady. "That would never happen."

"Damn right."

And so Fin lay on the floor on the flokati rug reading *Native Son* and waiting to let Jack in while Lady finished getting dressed. Uncle Jack arrived right on time, as always. He nodded at Fin, said, "Hi," then began pacing.

Fin followed him, bent over, pretending to be Groucho Marx.

"Cut it out." Jack took out a cigarette.

"I can blow smoke rings," Fin said. "Lady taught me."

"She would." Jack sat, then got up and began circling the room again. Gus came into the room and began to follow him.

"Cut it out," Jack said to the dog.

"Something wrong?" Fin asked.

"Tell me something," Jack said. Fin stopped. The dog stopped. "Does your sister confide in you? You know, about things?"

Fin said, "What kind of things?"

"Well, if I knew that, would I be asking?"

"You mean like adulterous things?"

"You mean adult."

"No, I don't."

At this, Lady came into the room looking lovely and innocent, with big false eyelashes like Twiggy.

"We're talking about adulterous things," Fin said. With great pleasure, he watched Jack color.

"*Adult*," Jack said.

"Let's go, Jack. Be a good boy, Fin," Lady said. "Don't corrupt anyone else tonight, okay?" She took Jack's arm, but Jack turned back to Fin.

"Adult. Not adulterous," he said. He smirked at Fin. "Because I'm not married."

"I never said you were."

Jack looked mildly pacified.

"*She* is," Fin said. He smiled innocently at Lady. "Or was supposed to be."

"You *are*?"

"No, of course not. It was a long time ago, anyway." She led Jack through the door. "Good night, my little duenna," she hissed at Fin.

"Married in the eyes of God," Fin yelled at the two figures as they descended the stairs to the street. Gus began to bark his shrill bark.

"The eyes of God?" Mabel said, coming up behind Fin. She slammed the front door shut. "Get to bed or I'll give you the eyes of God but good."

On Fin's twelfth birthday in February Mabel baked a coconut cake and Lady took Fin and Henry James to a Knicks game.

"Gorgeous," she said.

"Willis Reed," Fin told me. "He was a rookie then and he was the one Lady had her eye on. She had a good eye."

When she came up to bed late that night, she saw Fin's light on. "Why are you still awake, birthday boy? It's two in the morning. I told you you're too young to read *Native Son*. It would give anyone nightmares. It is a nightmare. This whole country is a nightmare if you're Negro."

"I didn't have a nightmare. I finished *Native Son* a long time ago."

He held up the book he was reading. *The Mysterious Island.* "Biffi gave it to me. For my birthday."

"Biffi," she said, obviously annoyed. "You never give up."

"I didn't say anything."

"Four and a half months left before I become an old maid: that's what you're thinking."

"I'm not thinking anything. Honest."

Lady pushed him over and lay down beside him. "Would you read to me a little?"

Fin picked up the book. He was on page 284, when the castaway, who has become almost subhuman in his isolation, is found.

"'It is a great misfortune to be alone, my friends . . .'" he read.

"Man," said Lady, "even Jules Verne has an opinion."

This was the winter of Martin Luther King's march to Selma, Alabama. It was the year the United States first sent troops to Vietnam. Lady took courses at the New School. Fin read Alan Watts.

One evening, Tyler showed up with his briefcase, the first time in months. He and Lady had to discuss taxes, apparently, Fin's taxes. He didn't stay too long, but afterward Lady said, in the dull, resigned voice she often was left with after a visit by Tyler, "Maybe Tyler's right. Maybe you would benefit from someone more mature and responsible to look after you. No one has ever accused me of being mature, or responsible."

"You're taking child-rearing advice from *Tyler*? I don't get it. I thought he controlled my money, not my destiny."

"No one controls your destiny, Fin. Not even you."

"*That's* profound," he said. From the kitchen table he picked up a soldier he'd been painting, and pretended to examine it.

But he barely saw it, barely saw the blue tunic of the French cuirassier, the glistening black boots, the bowed legs meant to slip over the black horse he'd left lying awkwardly on its side, its hooves still lifted in their never-ending gallop. "So Jack is out and Tyler's back? Is that it?"

"No one is out and no one is back. I'm allowed to go out with my friends, aren't I?"

"Ask Tyler."

"Wow, you really dislike him, don't you?"

"News flash."

"He said you assume a nauseated expression when he enters the room."

"Observant."

"He wants to take you skating."

"At my boarding school or my foster parents'? He's such a hypocrite. And a brownnoser."

"That's a truly vulgar expression."

Fin, who had never before considered the literal meaning of the word "brownnose," reddened. "Gross, Lady."

"He wants to take you skating at Rockefeller Center, okay? Right here in New York City. Anyway," Lady continued, "they're all brownnosers, let's face it."

"Gross, gross. Uncle Ty has ulterior motives, okay?" said Fin. "*And* he's not worthy of you. At all."

"I know," Lady said, suddenly serious. "Don't think I don't. But sometimes, well . . ."

"Ulterior motives. Unworthy. *And* ubiquitous."

"Spelling test at school?"

R.A.B.B.I.T.T.

"I can't spell them. Only say them."

"Tyler has your best interests at heart, Finny. He didn't mean . . ."

"Yes, he did."

"Christ, it's just skating."

"Tyler wants to get rid of me. You just said so."

Lady sighed, a soft, light sound that could mean anything from distress to confusion to coffee ice cream, her favorite. Then she put her arms around Fin, quickly, gently—so quickly and so gently he hardly noticed, until there she was, holding him tight against her. Awkward, angry, hands still in his pocket, Fin did not move.

"I won't let anyone send you away," she whispered. "Ever."

You better not. You better not, Lady.

"I'm sorry, Fin. I'm no replacement for a mother, am I? I know you miss her. You probably miss your father, too. Poor Finino *mio*."

"He's your father, too," Fin mumbled. "I keep telling you."

"I know it's not the same." She kissed his head. "Not the same as a real family."

Fin pulled away. "Of course it's not the same!" Everything blurred, he was so angry. His own voice sounded harsh and high and far away. "It can't be the same. I don't want it to be the same. I want it to be the way it is. Why don't you ever listen? No one listens. Tell Tyler to go break up someone else's family. Tell Tyler to go to hell!"

Fin ran up the stairs, two at a time, trembling. He slammed the door to his room. He opened the window and leaned his head out, breathing in the evening urban hush, the cold air.

There was a knock on his door, and Lady came in carrying a shoebox.

"Why do you flirt with everyone and go out with everyone and, and, you know . . . if you don't even really like them?" Fin didn't look at her. He closed the window and leaned his head against the pane. "Why?"

"I don't know, Fin. How should I know? I'm trying, that's all. Maybe I think that the next one will turn out to be The

One, like in a song. I *do* think that sometimes. I *hope* that. Why shouldn't I hope that?" She sat down on the floor and put her face in her hands. "Even if it's not true."

"Maybe it's true," Fin said, sorry now. Lady looked pitiful, sitting there, her elbows on her thighs, her cheeks smashed up in her hands. "It's true. It's definitely true. But . . ."

"But what?"

"But it hurts people, it hurts their feelings."

Lady twisted a hank of hair around her finger. Like a Shirley Temple curl. "Love is cruel," she said. "Right? But it really is. It just is."

Sure. Love was cruel. In books. In movies. Even on television, love was cruel. Even in comic books love was cruel. Poor Superman. Poor Lois Lane. But this was not a book or a movie. It was not about a superhero. It was Fin's sister, Lady, kind and tender and inattentive. And Fin sometimes could not help wondering if it wasn't love at all that was cruel, if it was Lady.

"Anyway," she said, "I have feelings, too, believe it or not."

The room was dark and Lady was outlined by the light in the hallway. Like a Buddha. A thin, elegant Buddha with long, long hair and a Shirley Temple curl.

"Are you in *love* with Tyler?" Fin asked.

"Fin, come on."

"No, really."

Lady stood up and switched on the light and the Buddha vanished. It was just Lady. "What are you, the House Un-American Activities Committee?"

"And what about Uncle Jack? You can't be in love with all of them."

Lady looked tired. "Who said I was? Some people make you feel easy and good when you're with them, that's all."

"Like Biffi," Fin said. He, anyway, felt easy and good whenever Biffi was there puffing on his pipe.

"No, not like Biffi. Biffi is *triste*, which means sad. He skips around and grins and jokes, but Biffi carries the world around with him. And the world is *triste*."

"Well, Ty *should* be *triste*. And Jack is stupid."

"Jack is a little stupid, granted. You have to be a little stupid to be happy."

"But you're happy."

"Q.E.D."

Now Fin had to laugh.

She picked up a kneeling English soldier from his bookcase and turned it over in her hand, admiring his paint job. He had glued tiny puffs of cotton to the end of the rifle. "Like smoke," she said dreamily.

"This is Waterloo." He pointed to the squares of British soldiers he had set up, to the rows of French cavalry waiting to charge. "The front row would shoot, then kneel down so the next row could shoot. It was an innovation. That's how we beat Napoleon."

"We?"

Fin laughed again. He found it so difficult to stay angry at Lady. Maybe that's what the suitors experienced. First you got angry, justifiably angry, a burning anger. Then she caught you off guard, she made you laugh, and the laughter swept the anger away like a strong wind sweeping a cloud over the horizon.

"What's in the box?" he asked.

"I got these for you."

"That box has been in the hall forever."

"Mmm. I got them for you, for your birthday, and then I forgot to give them to you."

She had already gotten him a present, a perfect, wonderful present. A record player, actually a stereo with separate speakers, a KLH.

"You're impossible," he said, unconsciously mimicking her. Inside the box, he found a pair of desert boots.

"Do you like them?" Lady asked. She was leaning eagerly over his shoulder. He could smell her perfume and her body beneath it. He blushed. "These are the ones, right?" she said. "The ones you wanted?"

He took them out of the box and set them on the floor.

"These are exactly the ones," he said.

"I meant to give them to you; then, I don't know, something or other, you know me . . ."

As Lady rambled on, Fin slid his feet into the shoes.

"Lady?"

"Yes?"

"These are about five sizes too big."

"But I told them twelve."

"That's my age."

Lady contemplated the big clown shoes on Fin's feet.

"Crap." She looked distraught.

"That's okay," he said, patting her hand consolingly. "We can exchange them tomorrow."

She grabbed him in a tight hug. "How could you think I'd ever let anyone take you away? Especially in those shoes. Lavender Jesus, who would take you? P. T. Barnum?"

It was a few days later that she handed him the book about toy soldiers by H. G. Wells. *Little Wars*. She had inscribed the first page: "To Fin, My Little General, once more unto the breach, dear friend, once more!" Her signature was large, full of flourishes. Fin has sworn to me that she splashed her favorite perfume on it. I've seen him hold that book up to his face and breathe in its scent. And say, "Once more."

"Boys don't have babies"

In spring, the little trees flowered. The vine in front of the house on Charles Street flowered, too, with purple fragrant wisteria. The wind shook the branches of cherry blossoms, their petals blew down the street like confetti, and there was sun at last, bright and generous. From his window, Fin could see daffodils in someone else's garden.

Clouds were brisk and white. Apple tree blossoms were white, trembling on their dark branches, as white as the clouds, as white as the men's shirt sleeves against dark suit jackets thrown over one arm. Little girls played hopscotch, the path of boxes drawn on the sidewalk with white chalk.

On April 12, 1965, opening day, the Mets would lose to the Dodgers, Don Drysdale would hit a home run, Drysdale, the pitcher, a humiliation that would sting for years. But that afternoon, after school on a beautiful spring day, before the game had even started, everything was still possible.

"It's spring!" Fin yelled, running into the house after school, slamming the door behind him.

"I hate spring," Lady said savagely. Her allergies. She had a wet washcloth pressed against her eyes, a cup of coffee on the kitchen table in front of her, a pack of cigarettes. She held the washcloth out to Fin. He wondered why water from the kitchen tap was never as cold as from the bathroom tap. Lady draped the thing over her entire face this time. Fin laughed.

"It's like a mask," he said. "Like plaster of Paris and they make a mask."

"That's called a 'death mask,'" Lady said dryly. The finches sang joyously outside. "Stop that racket." She reached out, blindly slamming the window shut. "Light me a cigarette, angel," she said.

Fin grabbed her pack of cigarettes from the table and put one in his mouth, catching a glimpse of himself in the window's reflection, posing for a moment. He lit a match, puffing carefully until the cigarette caught, then lifted one corner of Lady's terry-cloth death mask and placed the filter end between her lips. Lady was convinced that clouds of cigarette smoke protected her from pollen.

"That's my boy," she said, inhaling deeply, exhaling, the smoke spiraling above her. She waved the cigarette around like a stick of incense.

Fin pictured the two swollen eyes beneath the washcloth, pink like rabbit eyes, and her nose swollen and red. She sneezed, making the edge of the heavy wet washcloth jump. "I'm so miserable."

Fin went into the living room and put on a record. Lady's record collection had grown since they moved to the Village. There had been pop and rock uptown, which in a chronologically backward migration had journeyed into jazz and then blues and folk when they first moved into the house on Charles Street. Down all those uneven coffeehouse steps she went to hear old black men and young white men rasping out songs accompanied by their big, booming guitars. Lady had gotten a guitar herself, but had yet to play it. Sometimes Fin would stretch his hand around the shiny wood neck, the frets and metal strings tearing into his fingers.

He put *Bringing It All Back Home* on the spindle, stacked on an Ian and Sylvia. Mississippi John Hurt, the Rolling Stones. He turned the volume down low.

"Lie down on the couch," he said. "Just pretend it's a hangover."

Fin sat in the low lounge chair, his legs out, his head back. It was so peaceful, just him and the sniffling Lady and "Subterranean Homesick Blues." He could see the sky above the brownstones. He could see the soft, quick clouds. No Tyler, no Jack, no Biffi, no uncles or suitors of any kind.

"We want the old Bob Dylan," Lady chanted halfheartedly from behind her washcloth. The song changed. "She Belongs to Me." Gentle. Liquid. "And the new Bob Dylan," she said.

You will start out standing proud to steal her anything she sees . . .

Yes, Fin thought. He looked at Lady, her terry-cloth death mask turned to the ceiling.

She never stumbles / She got no place to fall . . .

Lady pulled the washcloth from her face and stared at Fin. Her face was sullen, swollen, blotched. "Nothing," she said, as if he'd asked her what was wrong. She put the damp washcloth back on her face. Her hand patted the coffee table, a search, here, over there.

"They're in the kitchen," Fin said.

As he went to fetch Lady's cigarettes, Fin walked past the small guest bathroom. He remembered Mrs. Holbright, remembered walking her to the powder room the summer before, waiting outside the closed door trying not to hear the tinkling sounds on the other side, walking her back to the table, to her daughter, Cee Cee. *You do look like your father,* she'd said. *Hand-*

some man, she'd said. *And don't mind Lady about that, you know. She was fond of him.*

"Why do you hate Daddy so much?" he asked Lady when he came back into the living room.

"Who said I hate him?"

Fin shrugged. "Anyway, you never talk about him."

"I don't hate him," Lady said. "I don't hate 'Daddy.'"

Fin was sorry now that he had brought up the subject. The way she said "Daddy." The way she sat up, holding the washcloth on her face like a bandage, a World War I bandage.

"I didn't hate him," she said. "He hated me."

"He did not." But Fin thought of his father on the ship, thought of how he glared at Lady, how he spoke to her. Was that hate? You can't hate your daughter, though. It's unnatural. "He didn't hate you. He was concerned about you."

Lady laughed. "After a while I figured out how to protect myself from his 'concern.'"

"How?"

"Stop hearing him. Stop seeing him. Stop caring about him. Like those three monkeys."

"Yeah, exactly like the monkeys. Except the speak-no-evil part."

Lady turned the washcloth over. "Oh, Finny."

"Anyway, why? Why would he hate you?"

"Because I grew up."

"Would he have hated me when I grow up?"

"No."

"Why not?"

"Because you're a boy."

"So what?"

"Maybe you're right. Boys grow up, too. Boys come in late from parties. Boys wear clothes their fathers don't like. Boys go on dates . . ." She trailed off and was silent for a moment. "Just one difference," she said then. "Boys don't have babies."

Boys don't have babies. But Lady had never had a baby, either. "But neither did you," he said.

"No," Lady said.

There was an uncomfortable silence.

"Lady?"

She did not answer.

"Lady?"

These dreamy states would come upon her sometimes. Fin hated them. She was too far away. "Lady, Lady, Lady," he chanted. She absentmindedly stroked his hand, as if it were a kitten. "Finny," she murmured, but nothing else.

He thought of the Pounds' baby in Connecticut, round and sticky and eager.

"I hate babies," he said.

He was the baby Lady would never have to have. That was what Tyler said. Fin stood up, startling the dog, who had been asleep on the floor at his feet. "Tyler said I was the child you'd never have to have."

Silence. Then: "That fucker."

"That fucker," Fin agreed, seizing at the opportunity to say the word "fucker."

Lady usually drew the line right about there. But she said nothing.

"But why did that fucker say that?" Fin said.

"Never mind, Fin. And stop saying 'fucker.' "

"Okay. Well, I guess I'll go do my homework," he said.

The washcloth said nothing.

"Will you help me with my homework? It's a science project," he said after a while.

"Another fucking fruit-fly poster?" asked the washcloth, and suddenly, like a seething, roaring cyclone, Lady flew to her feet, ripped the cloth from her face, her blotchy, crimson, carmine face, and began to yell at Fin. "Homework?" she yelled, as if homework were Hitler. Or Fin were Hitler. Or she were Hitler. "*Homework?* At that pitiful excuse for a school, that overblown kindergarten?" Her eyes were slits in her swollen face. Lady had never yelled at him before. She looked like a monster. She sounded like a witch.

"So what'd you even send me there for?" he yelled back. She had startled him, scared him. And the dog. "Why'd you send me to that kindergarten?" She'd insulted him, too. "Huh? Why?" he yelled over Gus's high hysterical yelps.

"So you would never, ever have to do science homework on a beautiful spring afternoon." Her voice and the dog's voice rang together like ugly, jangling bells. "So you could do the things that are really important . . . So you could be fucking *free.*"

Fin knelt to hold the dog, to calm him down. To calm himself down. To make Lady stop yelling.

"Sorry," said Lady. Quietly. "Sorry, Fin."

"You're nuts," he said.

"I know," she said. "But he really is a fucker." And she went upstairs to her room.

Fin sat on the floor with his arms around Gus. Babies. Hateful, babbling babies. They wore dirty diapers and smelled and could not say what they wanted. They made Lady angry. And she didn't even have one. "I will never have a baby," he said softly to Gus. Boys don't. Boys are free. And he thought of the stray dog he and Gus had seen on one of their walks by the river. He had tried to pet it, to catch it and take it home to feed it. When he told Lady about the dog, she said, "At least he's free."

———

The Saturday after Lady yelled, she suggested she and Fin go to a museum together. "Just the two of us."

"What about your allergies?"

"Pills and sunglasses. The answer to many of life's challenges."

Fin usually played baseball with Henry James on the weekends, going uptown to their apartments, one or the other's. They lived a few blocks from each other on Park Avenue. They would meet, then march off to the baseball field in Central Park and play, a three-man team matched against itself. But that Saturday he and Lady took the bus up to the Museum of Modern Art, to the Op Art exhibit.

Lady kept her sunglasses on in the museum. "And I thank my lucky stars I've got them. Good Lord. It's an assault."

Fin spun around in a circle. He loved it. It was tricky art. Glossy. Impersonal. Fast. Black-and-white. Clean and glaring.

"Showy," Lady said. "By show-offs. Let's go get doughnuts."

They went to Chock full o'Nuts, where a man who would have been handsome if he hadn't had that odd roll of flesh on the back of his neck between his shirt collar and his hairline flipped open his lighter and held the flame up to Lady's cigarette.

Fin stared at his neck roll uncontrollably.

"I saw you at the museum," the man said to Lady. "I'm a painter, you see."

Oh, we see, thought Fin. He tried to catch Lady's eye. But the sunglasses, the huge sunglasses, kept her distant.

"You probably know Biffi," Fin said. "Biffi Deutsch. He's a dealer."

"I have no use for dealers," said the artist.

A fraud, a complete phony, as suspected. Though his shoes were freckled with paint. Maybe he was a housepainter.

"Biffi specializes in illuminated manuscripts," Fin said.

"The past," said the "artist." Did he sneer?

Lady hadn't said a word. She sipped her coffee.

"What are your interests?" Fin asked the housepainter.

"The present," said the man.

He ignored Fin then. Sat on Lady's other side, asked what she thought of the exhibit. She stubbed out her cigarette, slowly.

Just get it over with, Fin thought. He'll ask you for your number and you'll look surprised. In fact, you'll be surprised. Why? I'm never surprised. But you are. Genuinely. Every time.

Lady spoke at last. She found the exhibit simplistic but entertaining.

The housepainter said, on the contrary, the show was revolutionary.

And Lady sighed wearily and said, "Oh, that again."

Fin ate his doughnut placidly now. No need to participate further. No phone numbers would be exchanged. Not after "revolutionary."

The housepainter eventually came to the same conclusion and went on his way, never having ordered so much as a cup of coffee, to the annoyance of the girl behind the counter, who said, "What a drip."

Lady laughed, said, "Ain't it the truth," and gave the girl an extra half dollar.

" 'What am I to do?' " she sang gaily in her Marlene Dietrich voice. " 'I can't help it.' "

But she could help it. Fin knew it. He wondered why Lady didn't know it, too. Men clustered to her like moths around a flame. And the flame wanted them there, needed them there. They were a kind of fuel. They singed their poor, battered white wings. And Lady glowed and shone.

"Ha ha," he said.

He took Lady's hand in his and squeezed it. He looked at her and smiled. He was as tall as she was now. When had that happened?

He said, "I'm as tall as you are."

He loved her so much, loved even her cruelty, which was not cruelty at all, really. Just fear and confusion. He could see it in her eyes sometimes. No one knew but him. And Mabel, maybe. What was she afraid of? Getting old? Getting married? Not getting married? Losing her glowing looks or her fiery freedom? Which? Maybe all of them.

"When I grow up . . ." he said.

But Lady interrupted him. "No, God, don't ever do that, Fin. Not ever."

What, like Peter Pan? Played by a woman hauled around the stage on wires? He had watched it every year on TV with his mother.

"When I grow up . . ." he said again.

"I forbid it!" said Lady. She was laughing, holding his hand, swinging her arm so that he had to swing his, too. She began to run. The sidewalk on Fifty-first Street was crowded. People stared at them. People always stared at them.

"Where are we running?" Fin said, running beside her. He was laughing, too.

"Away," said Lady. "Where else?"

They ended up running home, or at least walking there. Whenever Fin complained that he was tired, Lady would grab his hand and start running again.

He lay in bed that night replaying the day, the flashy art, the man with the neck roll, the waitress, the doughnut, the journey downtown. Lady was never the same. How did it feel to be never the same? Yet a day with her was as predictable as a calendar. How could that be? He thought, Because I know how people react to her, but I never know how she will react, to anything.

"If you don't push it, what's the point?"

It had been one year since Fin's mother died, one year since coming to New York City to live with Lady. He'd been an orphan for one year. It felt like ten.

They went back home to Connecticut on the anniversary of Lydia Hadley's death, a lovely, gentle Saturday in May. Fin sat in the same seat, in the same little Karmann Ghia convertible, the same Lady beside him at the wheel, darting from lane to lane, honking back at the truck drivers who honked at her, the same Gus in the backseat, his head poking out, his ears pushed back by the wind.

Just a different direction. Everything turned around. A turned-around Fin.

Lady was always happy when she was driving. "It makes me feel as though I actually have someplace to go," she once said. She pulled across two lanes and whipped off the thruway at exit 18. "Ice cream for lunch," Lady said. "Carvel!"

They had cones dipped in chocolate, Brown Bonnets.

"Who would wear a brown bonnet, though?" Lady said when they were back on the road. "What a sad bonnet that would be."

Fin didn't have much to say. He was looking at the sumac

that grew along the thruway. It was so familiar. He didn't sit in his room on Charles Street or walk along Eighth Street or stare out the window in school and think, I miss the stalks of sumac that grow alongside the New England Thruway. But he had missed the sumac, anyway. Just hadn't realized it.

They pulled into his driveway. What else had he missed that he didn't know he missed? The apple blossoms were out and perfumed the air. And there was that other smell of spring, the wet, green smell. And the sound of the peepers. And a red-winged blackbird. He was almost dizzy with the sounds around him, with the scent of hay, with the dry, hot dirt in the drive-way and the warm animal presence of the cows. Moo, moo, that's what Tyler had taunted him with, a drunk Tyler. Moo, moo. He laughed suddenly. Moo, moo. The cows were mooing. Tyler could stagger down the street and taunt him all he wanted, but cows still said moo, moo, and no one could ever change that.

"Moo!" he said, turning to Lady.

Gus jumped out of the car and Fin followed. The dog rolled in the grass, his legs sticking up, kicking. Fin wished he could roll in the grass and kick his legs. But here came Mr. Cornelius, the music teacher.

"Welcome home, my liege," said Mr. Cornelius, who always was a little weird. He bowed.

Fin bowed back. Then—he didn't mean to, he just did it—Fin hugged Mr. Cornelius. Then, and again he didn't mean to, he burst into tears.

Mr. Cornelius, who might have been odd but was used to children, said, "You're as tall as I am." Which wasn't saying much, as he couldn't have been more than five foot six, but was saying it at exactly the right time and in exactly the right tone of voice.

Lady took Fin to the cemetery. He had picked wild roses,

three bunches, one for his grandfather, one for his grandmother, and one for his mother. The blossoms were small, fragrant and white, except for one rose that had a faint pink blush. He put that, last and alone, on his mother's headstone. He cried and didn't care if Lady saw.

They had dinner that evening in his grandparents' dining room, which Mr. Cornelius had not changed in any way. Fin half expected his mother to come in from the kitchen with dessert. He half expected her at every turn he took, expecting his grandparents with the other half. And knowing, with the whole of himself, that they were gone, absent, missing, that the house full of their possessions and memories was empty.

The cows were just the same: cows. Their nostrils were wet. They chewed rhythmically, like machines with hot, grassy breath. You could lean your head against their flanks and hear their breathing and internal rumbling. Their tails flicked at the flies. Their eyes rolled as they followed your movements. He sat in the barn and marveled at their shifting feet, their calm.

Lady found him there, sitting on a bale of straw. "Do you miss them?" she said. She pushed him a little, made room, and sat next to him. "Do you miss all this a lot?"

"Every day," Fin said. "Well, every day I remember to. But sometimes I forget, which is worse."

"Do you want us to move back? To live here?"

Fin thought, Yes! Yes, I want to go back. But then he realized he couldn't, not really. There was no back to go to. The only ones left were Darlington, Daisy, Burgo, and Fleur, the cows. Not his mother or grandmother or grandfather. Just a house, a barn, and four cows chewing their endless cud. Anyway, what would Lady do here? He tried to imagine her on the little farm in the little town. She would run around and around until she turned into butter, like the tigers in "Little Black Sambo," which was prejudiced, anyway.

"No," he said. "Then I would miss New York."

"Thank God," Lady said. "This town is for the birds."

He slept in his old bed in his old room. There was nothing of his in it anymore. It was just a small bare room at the back of the house. But he could close his eyes and hear the mockingbird and picture the raccoon staring at the garbage can, trying to outwit it, and there was the creak of a floorboard, the flush of the toilet, and the soft panting of the big dog asleep on the floor beside his bed. Fin was home in a home that was immediate and real, in a home that did not really exist.

The next day he went around on his old bicycle, the one he had long since outgrown, and looked for his friends. He found some on the school baseball field. When he told them about New York, about his house there, about his bizarre school, about his friends Henry and James and Phoebe, they laughed and exclaimed at the right parts, and they told him about the boy who cut off his finger in shop and the teenager who died diving into the pond. It was as if he had just slipped back into his old life. Like getting on his old bike.

By the time he got back to the house, Mr. Cornelius had fallen in love with Lady, and Lady was bored and ready to return to the city.

"Thank you for taking care of everything, Mr. Cornelius," Fin said.

"You don't have to worry about this place, Fin. I love it like it was my own." He must have noticed Fin's expression. "Which of course it is not. I see myself as the caretaker, you might say."

Fin nodded. "Yes." The caretaker. He liked that. The caretaker who would take care. "Thank you."

"The guardian of the place, you could call it."

"Guardian angel," Lady said.

"Come back soon!" said the guardian angel.

Fin thought about the house and the pastures and cows for

weeks, for months, afterward, but he never worried about the place. Mr. Cornelius had confided that, sometimes, he brought his guitar out to the barn and sang to the cows.

"It really has been quite a year," Lady said on the drive back.

"It feels long and also short."

"It does."

The traffic came to a halt, and two ambulances passed them in the emergency lane.

"I have an announcement to make," Lady said. "You know, since it's been a year."

In the car in front of them, a little girl stuck her tongue out, then pushed her face against the back window until she looked like a small pig. An announcement. Fin did not want to hear an announcement. He tried to breathe normally, but he was sure no air was really getting in. Or out. An announcement.

"You know how I said I have to get married before I turn twenty-five?"

Fin nodded. Yes, he knew, but her birthday had come and gone last month with no mention of the deadline and he had thought he was home free. The little girl in the car ahead pulled her ears to the sides and flapped them, then stuck her tongue out again. Another ambulance screamed by.

"Well, I've thought about it a lot," she continued, "and I've thought about you, too, and what would be best for you."

Why was she bringing this up now? What had happened?

The car in front of them jerked forward an inch, then a hand appeared and yanked the little girl away from the window and down to the seat. A police car passed them, its siren blaring. Gus began whimpering and slid through the bucket seats onto Fin's lap. Fin could not look at Lady. But he blurted out, "You're best for me."

"It has been an adventure, hasn't it?"

The sun was red and glaring over the long line of cars. The

ambulance and police cars must have gotten where they were going—there was no sound of sirens now, though the lights still flashed, far ahead, beneath the fiery sun.

"I thought we were a family," Fin said. "Not an adventure. A family." The dog was panting, his breath hot. He licked Fin's hand. He looked up at Fin the way dogs do, full of sympathy, baffled. "I like things just the way they are. Exactly, perfectly the way they are . . ." Fin was babbling, he knew it, but he couldn't stop. "Nothing could be better in any way . . . I don't care how old you are. Everything is perfect."

"Really?" Lady said. She sounded surprised. She put her hand out and turned his head to face her. She looked so serious. "Thank you for saying that, Fin." She turned back to the road as the traffic inched forward. "I mean, I always hope you're happy. But how can anyone be sure of how anyone else feels?"

Fin never quite remembered what else she said. He hardly heard her. The sun was lower and the sky was streaked with lavender and orange. He remembered that. The blood rang in his ears. He remembered that. The fluff from the dog stuck to his lips as he leaned down to bury his face in Gus's heavy coat. He remembered all of that. He heard Lady say, "I vowed I would be married by twenty-five, and I am a girl of my word," and he sank lower in the seat. Which one would it be? It almost didn't matter at this point. It sounded as if she were paying a bill.

But then he heard her say, "Well, vows are made to be broken, I always say. So I have decided to give myself an extension."

Fin did not know the word "exultant" at that time. But if he had, he told me, that's how he would have felt. "An extension!"

"An extension. Of one year. Which is pushing it. But if you don't push it, what's the point, right?"

The Three Musketeers

Did you know Evelyn Waugh's first wife was also named Evelyn? Did you know the proofs of *Brideshead Revisited* were airdropped to Evelyn Waugh in a cave in Yugoslavia during World War II? Did you know Evelyn Waugh parted his hair on the left? Fin did. He knew a lot of things from reading the obituary page. Yugoslavia, for example. He had not really known of Yugoslavia's existence, much less that it was a place a British soldier might be stationed in World War II.

"But Yugoslavia does *not* actually exist," Biffi told him.

"But . . ."

"The Balkans," Biffi said. He shook his head sadly.

Another year had passed, and Lady, without too much fanfare, had given herself another extension on her deadline for matrimony. The three suitors now existed as an entity not unlike the Balkans, together, brooding, and suspicious. Biffi, Jack & Tyler, a trio of singers waiting to defect.

Biffi was both resigned and patient, as if he were back in Hungary waiting for the Russians to chase out the Germans, then waiting for someone, anyone, to please chase out the Russians. To Fin, he sometimes seemed to be besieging a walled city, the walled city of Lady, waiting and waiting until it ran out of food and water.

Jack was neither resigned nor patient. He was hearty and gung-ho. "He thinks I'm exotic," Lady said. "And I'm a way to shock his parents." He showed Lady off, which she had enjoyed at first. He liked to be with her in public, to be with her in the daytime when people could see her slender beauty in the sunlight. He played golf with her and tennis and took her riding and sailing and skiing.

"You make him sound like a gym class," Fin said. But he understood that Jack was a relief for Lady, a physical being who asked nothing more than to be physically near her.

And then there was Tyler. His attentions seemed almost like revenge, and maybe it was as simple as that, maybe that turned Lady on, his almost open hostility, the danger of Tyler, the threat of his somehow outsmarting Lady, after all these years.

"He wants to own her," Fin said.

"That's what all men want," Phoebe said.

"But what does Lady want?" he asked.

Phoebe chewed on a fingernail for a bit, then said, "Probably an orgasm."

Lady became obsessed with Leonard Bernstein that year. She met him at a party in September, and went to hear the New York Philharmonic as often as possible. Mahler, Schönberg, Copland. The Verdi *Requiem*. Jacqueline du Pré. She tried to take Fin to the Young People's Concerts on Sundays, but to his intense regret in later years, he refused, so Lady simply went to them alone. She knew everything about *The Magic Flute*.

Lady's Bernstein Period, not surprisingly, overlapped with her politics, and on May 29, 1966, Fin, who refused to go to the Young People's Concerts, happily joined Lady at her first sit-in.

It was in the lobby of Dow Chemical's sales office at Rockefeller Center. Fin wore a new corduroy jacket. One of the organizers, walking in an overly important way beside Lady, also wore a corduroy jacket. He wasn't a boyfriend, yet. Lady had met him at a teach-in where everyone sat on the floor in a circle.

"Blech," said Fin. "Sounds like my school."

Joel. He looked young, and his light brown hair stood out like an afro. Fin asked him his age. He was twenty-two, young enough to be a student, but he was actually a dropout, a political activist, he said. And a journalist. "Alternative stuff," he said vaguely.

"For *The Village Voice*?"

Joel shrugged a noncommittal shrug.

"Did you know Edward R. Murrow died last year?" Fin asked.

"No."

"Did you know he changed his name to Edward from Egbert in his sophomore year of college?"

"Are you a Fed or something?" Joel asked.

The sit-in was not very big. Fin had expected a huge crowd, but he counted twenty, twenty-one, including himself. There was a television camera, however, and reporters. He had counted a reporter as a demonstrator before he noticed the microphone. So, back to twenty.

The reporter, from a local news station, WPIX, put his microphone in front of Fin's face and asked, "What brings you here, son?" The camera was on a tripod operated by a large man behind it.

"I read about napalm," Fin said. The reporter's eyes lit up. He hadn't been expecting this. "It's liquid fire. It sticks to you."

Lady and Joel walked into the lobby and sat down on the shining marble floor. Lady patted the floor next to her, as if it were the sofa, and called, "Come on, Fin."

"What's your name, son?" the reporter asked.

"Fin Hadley."

The police came, huge policemen, and offered to let everyone leave. A few people did get up, but not Joel, not Lady, and not Fin.

"Just go limp," Lady said to Fin. "We're nonviolent," she said to the policeman who began to drag her away. "This is civil disobedience! Napalm kills!"

Fin waited to be dragged off himself, to let himself go limp as a policeman grabbed his arms and pulled him across the shiny floor. For a minute he thought it wouldn't happen, that he was too young, that he would be ignored.

"Napalm kills!" he yelled.

An annoyed-looking policeman dutifully came and dragged him to the door. There he realized that the policeman would also have to drag him down the steps and over the rough sidewalk. He turned his head, looking for Lady. He did not want to be dragged down the marble steps, bump, bump, bump, like Winnie-the-Pooh. He twisted around now, wildly. Where was Lady? Or even Joel?

"I'm with my sister," he called up to the policeman who held his arms.

"I don't care if you're with the Virgin Mary," the policeman said, and Fin realized that the look on his face was not boredom at all but rage, controlled, simmering rage.

Inside the police station Fin still did not see Lady. He was being separated from the others, the policeman behind the desk said, because of his age. Was it that policeman who led him to a cell that was clammy and cold? And locked the cell? Or was it another? Was it the one who asked him the names of his parents? He didn't know which policeman was which. He couldn't tell. They were all big and all gruff. He tried to explain, to tell them he couldn't call his mother or his father, that the only family he had was also dragged out of the Dow Chemical Building lobby. But that's when he began to cry.

"Goddamn Reds," the policeman said, and left him alone.

It was Biffi who came to bail out Lady and Fin.

"I have seen you on the television," Biffi said to Fin when they rode home in a cab. Biffi sat between Fin and Lady. "You were very brave. She?" he added, nodding sideways at Lady. "A fool."

"Fools rush in where angels fear to tread," Lady said, not in the least offended. "What an adventure!"

"Dilettante," Biffi muttered. "Crazy American. What if I was not there for extrication?"

"Have you ever been in jail?" Lady asked. Her eyes were glowing.

"We shall not talk of jail," Biffi said. "You are hungry?" he asked Fin.

"We stood up to Dow Chemical, to the police!" Lady said. "Who can think of food at a time like this?"

"A boy," said Biffi. He put his arm around Fin. "A boy from jail."

Lady leaned against Biffi from the other side. "You're sweet," she said. "In your obnoxious way."

"I'm not hungry, Biffi," Fin said. He felt his eyes closing. Stay awake. Keep your eyes open. If you let yourself fall asleep, all this will vanish. There will be no Lady resting her head on Biffi's shoulder. There will be no Biffi's shoulder for her to lean on. There will be no Biffi and Lady, quiet, together, like a couple, like a husband and wife. There will be no Fin. Like their child.

"I brought you a chocolate bar," Biffi said.

"Oh goody!" said Lady. "Three Musketeers."

Fin tore open the wrapper, suddenly very hungry. "I read the book," he said to Biffi.

"Better for your teeth," Lady said, which he knew meant she wanted a bite, the first bite.

"Lipstick?" he said.

"Nope. All worn off in the pokey."

"All for one and one for all, then." And he handed over the candy bar.

"Pokey," Biffi muttered, then spat out a barrage of enraged words that must have been Hungarian. They were, at any rate, not English.

Lady came back at him in Italian.

More Hungarian.

More Italian.

Lady did not understand Hungarian. Biffi did not understand Italian. Fin understood only that the spell was broken. They weren't the three musketeers. They weren't a family. They were a tower of Babel.

"I hate you both," he said when the taxi pulled up to the house. But they didn't even hear him.

Mirna called that night. Fin answered the phone in the kitchen while Biffi and Lady argued in the living room.

"You're a television star!" Mirna said.

"You saw?"

"Everyone saw!" She sounded happier than Fin had ever heard her. "Mazel tov, Fin! Today you have an FBI file! Today you are a man!"

"Hey!" Fin said, banging into the living room. "Mirna says I have an FBI file. Isn't that cool?"

Biffi looked sharply at Lady.

"Okay, okay," she said. "Okay, you're right, Biffi, okay?"

"No more arrests," Biffi said to Fin.

"But napalm is wrong. That's suppression of free speech," Fin said, though he was so relieved by this news that he could hardly stand up: no more sit-ins, no more policemen, no more jail.

"I am protecting you, the whole you, not just your talking," said Biffi.

"You're not my father," Fin said.

He ran up to his room. He waited. He slammed a foot against the wall, then again, looking with satisfaction at the black scuff marks on the white paint.

Still no one came.

No one came to punish him, to ground him for the week, to take away his TV, to whack him on the seat of the pants, to wash out his mouth with soap, to holler helplessly, to stamp feet or order him to apologize. To do something. Anything. No one came up to his room. Why would they? A father would have. A mother would have. But he had neither.

He kicked the wall again, the noise blunted by the crepe souls of his desert boots.

"What is wrong with you?" Lady asked the next morning. She had actually gotten up in time for breakfast. Or perhaps she had not slept. Her face was drawn and gray. "You insulted Biffi," she said.

"So do you. You insult everyone."

"Not when I need them."

"Fine teaching for the boy, Miss Lady," said Mabel, pushing a plate of scrambled eggs at Fin. "You pay no attention to what Miss Lady says, Fin. Not ever."

Lady put her face in her hands. "I'm sorry, Fin. Mabel's right. Mabel's always right. I'm a terrible guardian. And a terrible person. Biffi's right. Everyone's right. I'm wrong."

This was where Fin was supposed to say, *No, you're not. You're a wonderful guardian.* For an instant, he thought of agreeing with her. *You're selfish and irresponsible and immature,* he would say. *Not fit to be anybody's guardian. Not fit to be anybody's guardian but mine,* he added quickly, superstitiously.

"No, you're not, Lady," he said. "You're the best guardian."

Now she would look up at him and smile, tentatively.

She looked up from her hands. She smiled. Tentatively.

"You're nuts," he said. He smiled back.

"You don't hate me for getting you thrown in jail?"

"Nope."

"You don't hate Biffi for not wanting me to get you thrown in jail anymore?"

"Nope."

"No more sit-ins, though."

"I know. No more." No more policemen? No jail? Yeah, he could promise her that.

"For the time being," she added, to comfort him.

"Ever."

"I'm glad there's one adult in this kitchen," Mabel said. "Besides me."

That afternoon, after school, Fin called Biffi at his gallery.

"I'm sorry for what I said," Fin said.

"You said nothing but what was truth."

That's what I'm sorry about, Fin thought, but he said, "Don't be mad at Lady."

"No one can remain mad at Lady, can they?"

"Apparently not," Fin said, though he wished that sometimes, somehow, he could.

The suitors had become part of life. Like school. Like baseball. Like the movies that ran over and over on *Million Dollar Movie.* Like the chance of snow. That was certainly the way Lady seemed to feel. Sometimes she would make a big deal about how many places she still had to visit before she was "hooked up to the plow," that she still had to go to Japan and to India and to Africa, that she had to get away. She did rush around, that was true. Looking back, Fin sometimes said fondly that was all she did, that rushing was the substance of her activity rather than what happened in between, that she never really went anywhere.

So the trip with Biffi that summer was a big deal. A big deal signifying nothing, perhaps, but a big deal nevertheless. They went to a cottage in Wellfleet for two weeks. Lady took Fin with them, too. And Gus. Biffi, in retaliation, Fin thought, took his mother. Mrs. Deutsch had a big white paper bag on her lap in the car, where she sat in the tiny backseat with Fin and Gus. Grease showed through the bag in spots. Mrs. Deutsch kept opening the bag and looking in. Checking. Who could get into her paper bag to get whatever was in it out? No one. Yet she shot suspicious sideways glances, not just at Fin, but at the placid dog as well. Gus did once poke at the bag with his sharp nose, and Mrs. Deutsch let out a shrill cry. Sometimes, when she looked into the bag, she reached a hand in and rummaged around, a noisy operation, the paper bag rustling and crinkling, and what must have been other, smaller bags inside the big white bag also rustling and crinkling. When the bag was open and her hand had disappeared inside it, the smell of butter and sugar wafted from within, making Fin and Gus sniff the sweet air and stare at Mrs. Deutsch and her paper bag. She would furtively tear off a piece of whatever it was that smelled so deliciously of butter and sugar in the bag and jab it into her small, frowning mouth, lick the white powdered sugar from her fingers, close up the bag again, and clutch it, as if Fin or Gus or the man on the moon were trying to pry it out of her hands.

"What's in there, anyway?" Fin finally asked.

"Medicinal."

When they stopped at Howard Johnson's, she brought the bag into the restaurant with her. She held it on her lap while she ate fried clams.

"Did you make them or something?" Fin asked when they were back in the car and Mrs. Deutsch was once more rummaging in the bag. "The cookies?"

"They are digestives," she said. "For my digestion."

When they arrived at their cottage on a sand dune overlooking the beach, Fin stood looking out at the ocean. It was vast and gray, and the waves that crashed so insistently on the beach came from the other side of the world. He remembered standing on the deck of the *Cristoforo Columbo*, the blank foaming ocean everywhere, in every direction. He remembered his mother's hand, cool and smooth, resting on his on the railing. He remembered his father, one hand on Fin's head. "The English call whitecaps white horses," his father said. "They look like wild horses to me," his mother said. Wild horses, Fin had thought. Like Lady.

Mrs. Deutsch came up beside him and stood with him, watching the ocean from the tall, windy dune.

"Hmmph," she said. "In Hungary, *there* we had beaches."

The rented cottage had two bicycles, and Fin and Lady rode into town to buy fish to cook for dinner.

"I taught Lady to ride," Fin said to Mrs. Deutsch.

"In Hungary I ride with no hands holding," Mrs. Deutsch said. She grabbed Fin's bike from him, deposited her paper bag in the basket, and demonstrated. In her large red-skirted bathing suit she looked like an aging circus performer.

Each morning Mrs. Deutsch emerged from her room in the red bathing suit carrying her white paper bag. She spent the day on a beach chair reading Hungarian novels. When she wanted to take a "dip," she solemnly handed the bag to Fin to guard. When she returned from the water, she wrapped herself in a towel, said, "Thank God, thank God," as she poked in the paper bag, then fell asleep, the bag tightly grasped by both hands.

On the third day, Fin could stand it no longer. He had to know. What was in the bag? What cookies, what cakes, what pastries or doughnuts or Danish or petits fours could be so delicious, so precious?

He waited until Mrs. Deutsch was asleep, then asked Biffi, "What's with the bag? What does she have in there? Hash brownies?"

Biffi looked fondly at his sleeping mother. "My mother keeps her jewelry in the bag with the cookies," Biffi said. "The cookies are, I think, quite stale."

"Bad wine and grass"

Of course Fin could not really be kept away from politics. Even
the air was political, charged and blown about by the war, the
undeclared war, the illegal war. President Johnson had doubled
the draft. Thirty-five thousand called every month. The gov-
ernment increased the bombing. Marines were burning down
villages with Zippo lighters. You saw them do it on the evening
news. Channel 2. When the antiwar march happened, when
25,000 people marched down Broadway in the cool autumn
sunshine, Lady marched of course. So did Fin.

"We're marching with Women for Peace," Lady said. "People are bringing their toddlers, for God's sake. In strollers. And
his school is marching. The whole eighth grade . . ." She said
this to Biffi. "So don't say I'm being naïve."

"You leave me no choice, my darling."

"I can interpret that statement two ways," she said, "so I will
interpret it in the way that suits me best." She gave Biffi a hug.
"You're very sensible."

"I choose when there are my battles," he said. "That is my
charm."

Fin was sitting on the floor, listening as always, as he read *The New York Times*, spread out on the coffee table. Margaret Sanger's obituary.

"Margaret Sanger's mother died at forty-eight. And she'd already had eleven children," he said. "*Eleven*. No wonder Margaret Sanger invented the term 'birth control.'"

"Criminy Dutch," Lady said.

"Her father carved angels on tombstones."

"I should say so."

At the peace march, Fin and his class followed a huge papier-mâché airplane. Around them people dressed in black were wearing skull masks, banging on cans.

"We should have brought something to bang on," said Henry.

"Like your head," said James.

There were people everywhere, for blocks and blocks. You looked down Fifth Avenue and there were bobbing heads, thousands of bobbing heads. No cars. No buses. No taxis. Just people. No horns honking. No sirens. Just chanting, people chanting. The papier-mâché aircraft preceded them like a parade float.

The raw eggs thrown into the crowd didn't start until they got to Eighty-sixth Street. Fin and Henry James ducked them, laughing.

New York, and life itself that year, began to feel like a parade to Fin. When he'd first arrived in the city with Lady two years earlier, everything appeared exaggerated, like a circus. But he'd gotten used to the city and its people so quickly. New York became familiar. Take the bus across town, the subway uptown or downtown, streets that run west are odd numbered, east are even, one minute to walk one block. The Bronx was up, the Battery down, the Mets in Queens. The Village was home.

Now, however, that breathless feeling had come back, that city delirium, outlandish, raucous, giddy. Anything, *anything*, could happen, would happen, had just happened. It was a pageant. It was, Fin once told me in a voice suggesting there was no need for any further explication, New York in the sixties.

Looking back, you might think New York in the sixties was tailor-made for Lady. The language of the counterculture, "liberation," that word, on its own, should have welcomed Lady into its loose, flowing embrace. And there were so many possible liberations. There were Liberation Armies, for example, or, say, Sexual Liberation, now a cultural and political movement where once there'd been just Lady and her indiscretions. And, of course, there was the Liberated Woman. Lady had always been a Liberated Woman. In her fashion. But, in fact, in her fashion, Lady did not take to the sixties at all.

The idea of a commune, for instance. Communes struck Lady as barbarous. What was the point? she asked. Why would she live with other people, hell was other people, everyone knew that. Why would she eat undercooked lentils and sleep on a ratty mattress on the floor when she could sleep in her own house and eat lamb chops and baked potatoes? Why would she share in washing the dishes when she had a dishwasher? Not to mention a maid? She liked to wear flowers in her hair. But she did not like to serve the hippie men their coffee at political meetings. If that was communal, she wanted no part of it. She liked to have suitors, but she certainly did not like to share them. Why would she share a boyfriend? That was not freedom. That was slavery, or close enough.

Fin explained it to me this way: Lady grew up protecting

her independence, what she could find of it, cherishing every moment of freedom, fighting for it. She was not inclined simply to hand it over, not about to share it with the world at large.

But I wonder if it was more than that.

"I will miss you," Lady said as she tucked her Courrèges boots away in the closet. And she did miss them. For Lady, there was a nostalgia for those long-ago first glimmers of freedom, for the way freedom first looked, the way it first tasted.

"How is it," she said, "that the martini, which has served so many so well for so many years, is now unattainable when you go to a party? How is it that there is now only bad wine and grass?"

No, it was Fin who fell for the sixties.

"You cannot go to school barefoot," said Lady.

"You're so uptight."

"Good grief, Fin. You'll get tetanus."

"You are so straight."

"And you're an idiot. Put on your goddamn shoes."

Fin was astonished. Lady, his wild, untamed Lady, who had been so open to the world when the world had seemed so closed—now, now that the world was shaking off the oppression of the straight and the uptight, now when the world was beautiful and free, now Lady, that most beautiful and free spirit, had closed herself off with a vicious snap.

"She's an only child," said Phoebe. "That's why."

"I wish you wouldn't always say that. She has a brother. Me."

"But you're more like her kid. She's just trying to be a good substitute mother."

"That's fucked up."

Phoebe nodded sagely. In her book, which meant whichever of her parents' psychology books she had read most recently, most things were fucked up. Parents, certainly. Sisters, naturally. And a sister as a parent? Well, enough said.

"But," she said, "the most fucked-up thing is fucking."

Fin had developed, over the years, a fairly comfortable understanding of sex. There were the chickens in Connecticut, those unforgettable performances by the rooster.

"Sounds like rape to me," said Phoebe.

There were the Morgan horses at his neighbor's stable, stallions brought in specifically to inseminate the mares.

"Prostitution." Phoebe again.

There was Lady, who, Phoebe agreed, was as knowing and powerful and cruel as a goddess, as benevolent and natural and innocent as the birds and bees.

And there was Fin, who these days thought of little else. Sex. It was there in the warmth of the sun, in the touch of the rain. It was spring. It was eighth grade.

Sometimes in class he stared across the circle they still had to sit in for part of each day and watched the plaid pleated skirt of Karla directly across from him. Karla, whose brother was Mark, a boy in the grade below. Karla Mark, get it? The red diaper babies. Karla wore short skirts, as did all the girls, and sat with her legs to the side, bent like the sprite on Canada Dry bottles. Her pale knees, one resting lightly on the other, leading to her white thighs, one just before the other, and then the pleats, the crisp pleats parted slightly as the skirt continued on its way to cover up another pleat that Fin could only dream of. And so he did dream. Daydreams. Night dreams. All kinds of dreams.

Sometimes Fin and Karla would sit together in Earth Science. Fin could hardly breathe beside her. How could anyone breathe beside Karla? In eighth grade, how can anyone breathe at all?

Fin never mentioned Karla to Phoebe, or to anyone else. Not to Biffi, certainly not to Lady, not even to Henry James. It was a secret, one whose secrecy seemed vital, yet so utterly ordinary: he liked a girl. So what?

He didn't tell anyone, yet everyone seemed to know.

"You're an adolescent," Phoebe said. "Adolescents are nymphomaniacs because of their hormones."

"What about you?"

"I'm polymorphous perverse."

He made an unconscious decision to stop playing with his toy soldiers. He put them away in shoe boxes, wrapping the metal ones in cotton.

"Think you're all grown up now?" Mabel said. "No more toys?"

They were all in the kitchen, Mabel cleaning up after breakfast, Lady using markers to make an antiwar poster, Fin looking for tape to seal up the shoe boxes of soldiers.

"It's an antiwar thing," Lady said. "Philosophically. Right, Fin?"

"I don't think Fin's thinking much about philosophy these days," Mabel said, fixing him with a look, that Mabel look. "Unless girls are a philosophy."

"Lay off," said Fin.

"Really, Fin?" Lady said. "You have a girlfriend?"

"Lay *off*."

Summer came, the summer of 1967, and none too soon, to rescue him from Karla. She went to camp in the Berkshires. Fin wrote letters to her that he never sent. They said, "I'm so fucked up. But nothing gets me down." He had just read Richard Fariña's book *Been Down So Long It Looks Like Up to Me*. There were parts of it he didn't understand. There were parts of almost every book he read these days that he didn't understand, yet somehow sensed, as if they were in his dreams or were dreams themselves.

He appropriated Lady's guitar. Of course it was a Martin. He played on the front steps of the Charles Street brownstone, Gus at his side. He wasn't very good. Sometimes people would drop a coin in his guitar case.

"You're panhandling in front of your own house?" Lady said. "That's certainly sticking it to the Man." She laughed. "You crack me up, Finny."

"Hey," he said. "Peace, okay? I'm not hurting anyone."

She bent down, lifted his hair from his face, kissed him on the forehead. "Let's go away."

"You want to hitchhike to the Grand Canyon? That's what you said when I first came to live with you."

"I said a lot of things."

She sat down on the step beside him and lighted a cigarette. She flicked her hair away from her face. "Finino," she said. She plucked a guitar string. "Are you any good at this thing?"

"No. But we're starting a band. Fin's Henry James ExtravagAnts."

"Finino," she said again. It was as if she hadn't heard him. "Remember when we met? The day we met? In the piazzetta?"

He nodded. He would never forget that day: the warm embrace of the sun and the warm embrace of his strange, exotic sister; the glare of the sky and the glare of his angry father, the soft murmur of Italian all around him and the soft voice of his mother. It had all merged, soft-edged images, maybe, but at the same time clear, perfect, and vivid.

"Nine years," she said.

Nine years? She must have been so young. He'd never thought about it, how young she had been. Why would he? Lady was ageless, young then, young now, young forever, forever the same. He, of course, had changed in nine years. Nine years ago he was a tiny little boy in a sailor suit; now he was taller than Lady, now he played guitar, now his hair hung down over his face. He had changed. He had grown. He had grown up. But Lady . . . Had she changed, or grown, or grown up? He had never considered the possibility. She was the norm, the glowing, unpredictable, unstoppable norm.

"What have I done in nine years, Fin? *Niente.*"

"The way to do is to be. That's from the *Tao Te Ching.*"

"That's all very well for you. You're still young." Lady was twenty-seven. "Can you imagine what the world would be like if everyone decided that the way to do was to be?"

"Peaceful."

"Maybe." She stood up. "Unless you tried being where someone else wanted to be being."

"So profound," Fin said. "Anyway, you've done a lot."

"Like what?"

Like what? Like be Lady. Wasn't that enough? It was enough for Fin. Lady was everywhere for him. She didn't have to be anything.

"I don't know. Everything. So where should we go?"

"Remember our deal? You were going to find me a husband, Fin. What happened?"

"You don't really need to get married anymore. The world has changed."

"Has it? Don't girls get married?"

"Anyway, you don't really want to get married. You never did."

"Is that right?"

"I guess it is, Lady. Or you would have."

She tapped a foot. Fin remembered how her pale nail polish had seemed so exotic. Now her nails were natural. She was not one to cling to passé fashion. Mourn it, yes. Wear it? No.

"You don't want to get married. Not now. Not ever. Just admit it, Lady. Go with it."

"I just never thought I'd be twenty-seven and still not married. I haven't found the right man, okay, I get that. But what if I never find him? Ever? It would be horrible. Oh, you don't understand, Finny," she said softly. "How could you?"

If he really admitted to himself that Lady would never marry Biffi, then, yes, he thought he understood. There simply wasn't anyone else who was good enough for her. Lady was beautiful and charming and rich, all the things that should have made her an easy match. But to Fin's mind, there could be no easy match for Lady. She was too beautiful, too charming. Too quick. Too generous. And too rich to need to get married. But he couldn't say that. So he played the first few chords of "Sloop John B." *I wanna go home . . . Let me go home . . . Well I feel so broke up . . .*

Lady stubbed her cigarette out on the step. "I hope this dirty war is over soon, Finny. If you grow up . . ."

"What do you mean *if*?"

". . . and then get drafted," Lady said, "we'll have to move. Where should we move to?"

"Hitchhiking to the Grand Canyon won't cut it then, huh?"

"When did you develop this passion for the Grand Canyon? Jesus Christ, Fin, we're talking about Vietnam."

"You want to move to Vietnam?"

"Ha ha."

Fin played the first few chords of "Mr. Tambourine Man." "I used to think that you were half a person because you were my half-sister," he said.

"Which half?"

"Bottom. Patent-leather shoes. And white socks."

"Did you really? That's sweet. Why are children so literal-minded, I wonder." She picked the cigarette stub off the step and threw it into the open guitar case.

"Hey!" Fin said.

"Don't litter."

He saluted her.

"Not funny, Fin. Not funny at all."

The Italian Word for Hedgehog

Maybe the suitors each had a timer and it had been ticking away and the autumn of 1967 set off the fuses and the fuses were crackling, the flames moving along like the flames in a cartoon, three teardrop-shaped flames sizzling and getting closer and closer to three sticks of dynamite. Maybe time itself had changed and three years became even longer than it really was, an eternity, to them, to Lady. Maybe their clothes had turned into costumes. Maybe Jack wore bell-bottoms striped and starred like the American flag. Maybe Tyler wore a peace medallion. Maybe even Biffi wore a suede vest and sideburns. Maybe the Beatles gave up drugs for the Maharishi, but maybe the smell of marijuana in the house on Charles Street got thicker and thicker. Maybe Jack started dropping acid. Maybe Tyler took too much speed.

Lady didn't like any of it. Fin sometimes pictured them, Jack, Tyler, and Biffi, sitting on the sofa, one, two, three, ducks in the carnival. Going round and round on a conveyor belt, as they always had with Lady, each blast from the air gun missing, missing, missing, until . . .

"If you drop acid, or anything else for that matter, I will know," Lady said to Fin. "And I will kill you."

"Don't you want me to expand my mind?"

"I will know," she repeated. "And I will kill you."

Fin almost believed her.

"You're such a drag sometimes," Jack said.

"I've seen what I've seen."

And what she had seen was too many friends left dazed by too many drugs.

"You're really quite prudish," Tyler told her. "Capriciously prudish. A mercurial drag."

Capricious? Caprice was Lady's perfume, a trace of temperament that told you she was in the room or just had been or was skipping down the stairs toward the doorway. Lady loved the word "capricious." She said it came from the Italian word for head and the Italian word for hedgehog. Unless it came from the Italian word for goat. Capricious. It reminded her of Capri. "Mercurial"? She loved that word, too. "Like a god," she said.

Was she simply bored with them, like a god? Is that why she ended up doing what she did? Or was it simple, active cruelty? Fin explained it to himself later as an act of desperation, the desperation of someone capricious, someone mercurial, someone so capricious and mercurial that the capricious and mercurial times were squeezing her, dimming her, making her feel she was disappearing in the smoke and hallucinations. Of course, he explained it to himself later as many things, some of them angry, but most of them extraordinarily kind.

It started that year leading up to her twenty-eighth birthday. It was almost as if the suitors sensed something, as if she'd given off some signal, a chemical, like a bee or an ant: the end is nigh, fellas.

It rained heavily for days. The sky was low, dark, a uniform iron gray.

"I've never met anyone like you," Jack said to Lady, holding her hand in his. "You're so different, so fascinating. You're . . ."

Fin insists that Jack then said, "You're . . . out of sight."

The cold rain continued, and Tyler started bringing Lady little gifts, Mexican silver earrings, things like that, things she liked, lovely, not extravagant. He knew how to play it. "There is something piquant about the pursuit of your sister," he said to Fin. "Don't you think?"

"Something peculiar, anyway."

"One man's rejection is another man's invitation. Remember that, son."

Then, on what seemed like the fortieth night of the fortieth day of rain, Biffi Deutsch, age thirty-one, birthplace Budapest, which he pronounced as if it were spelled Budapesht, announced he had enlisted.

"Don't be absurd," Lady said.

"I am absurd. That is my charm."

"You did not enlist. You're too old."

"Apparently I am not."

"Jesus H. Christ, quit joking around, Biffi."

"I am in the United States Air Force. And that is that, with no jokes."

At his tone, which was serious, and a little angry, Lady sat down. "Shit," she said. "Shit." Then: "Come on, Biffi. You didn't. It's a rotten joke to play on me."

And me, Fin thought. But he said nothing. He was lying on the floor behind the couch reading the paper. Woody Guthrie had died. Nine years in a nursing home. Dying for nine years. Fin felt he himself had barely been living for nine years. The obit said Guthrie said he knew his voice did not sound "like dew dripping off the petals of the morning violets." But it does, Fin thought. Though he had never seen dew dripping off the petals of the morning violets. He wondered if Biffi had seen dew dripping off the petals of morning violets. Or heard it.

"But you're a pacifist," Lady was saying.

"No. You are a pacifist. I have never chosen to argue about it with you. That's all."

"But you're not even American."

"I am American. I am a citizen, and a very proud, grateful one."

"You know what I mean. Oh God, everyone is trying to get out of the draft and you enlist?"

Woody Guthrie said, "I had rather sound like the ashcans of the early morning, like the cabdrivers cursing at one another, like the cowhands whooping, and like the lone wolf barking." And you did, Fin thought. Like ashcans, cabdrivers, cowhands, barking wolves. Like Walt Whitman, too. Was that what Biffi thought he would be fighting for? For Woody Guthrie, for Walt Whitman? Was that what he was proud of?

"You don't understand," Biffi said.

No, Fin thought. No, I don't, either. But why don't I? You have been my friend for three years, my pretend father, my idol. And I know nothing about you. Maybe because I never asked. Fin stood up from behind the couch. "Hello," he said. "Please don't go to Vietnam."

Biffi threw his head back and groaned.

"Just don't go. Just don't."

"See?" Lady said. "You can't do it. Think of Fin. That's what you always say to me."

"Think of ashcans in the early morning," Fin said. "Think of morning violets." Think of me, he meant. Think of Fin, think of me.

"Do you give him LSD?" Biffi said, turning on Lady. They

were all standing now, a triangle, a circle, a shapeless shape of three.

"How dare you?" Lady said. "You . . . you . . . warmonger."

The house rang with arguments for the next few days.

"This is something I have to do," Biffi would say.

"No, you *don't*," Lady would cry out miserably. "Of course you don't. That's the point. You weren't drafted. You can still get out of it. You can get a doctor, a shrink . . . to say you're crazy. Which you fucking are, you crazy motherfucking bastard."

The house rang with arguments. And declarations of undying love.

"I wish you to marry me," Biffi said. "I love you, Lady."

"You want me to be a widow. I see. Fuck you."

"I've waited for you. Because I love you."

"I said no before. Do you think I'll say yes now? And have you go off and die in the jungle?"

"Yes. I think you will say yes."

Fin could hear them. Who couldn't? They hollered. They stamped up and down stairs. They threw dishes. They made love.

How could Biffi leave Fin alone? How could he? What difference did it make if Biffi got Lady to marry him? He still wouldn't be around. They still wouldn't be a family.

"Don't you care about us?" Fin asked him. "Don't you care about Lady and me?"

"More than anything in the world."

"Then why are you going? You'll have to kill people. Real people. For a stupid domino theory."

Biffi began to talk about Hitler and Czechoslovakia.

"It's not the same," Fin said. "China and Vietnam are traditional enemies. Everyone knows that."

"You're fourteen years old. Do you study history in that foolish school? Maybe one week you have studied World War II.

I *lived* World War II, do you understand? One country falls, then the next. It will stop here, you think. Surely it will stop here, on this border. No? Not on this border? Well then—on the next border. We are sure of that. But then that border is no more a border. It is a doorstep. Your doorstep . . ."

"It's a *civil war.*"

Now they were yelling. Biffi and Fin, not Biffi and Lady. Now Fin was running up the stairs, not Lady. Now Biffi was slamming the front door. Again.

But still Biffi Deutsch was enlisted in the United States Air Force.

No amount of yelling changed that. No door slamming. Nothing.

One night when Lady sat glumly in the living room listening to Billie Holiday, cursing Biffi every once in a while, and drinking her third martini, mixed by an equally glum Fin, Tyler Morrison arrived. Fin opened the door.

"Salutations," said Tyler.

"Uncle Tyler!" Lady called from the living room. "Fancy meeting you here."

"I have homework," Fin said, and he started up the stairs.

"Uncle Tyler, you're not enlisting in the United States Air Force, are you?" She was clearly drunk. Drunk and scared. Fin heard it in her voice.

Fin sat on the top step, the way he used to when he was little. He hated it, these days, when Lady drank too much, which was a lot in the last week, since Biffi's patriotic, idiotic announcement. Usually Fin hid out upstairs and watched television. But now he sat there on the top step. How could he leave her alone with just Billie Holiday and Uncle Tyler? Anything could happen.

"No," Uncle Tyler said. "I'm not enlisting."

"You're still Uncle Tyler? Not Uncle Sam?"

"Yes, babe," Uncle Tyler said. "Still me. The one and only."

Just one of him. You had to be grateful for small things.

"I'd like to stay that way," Uncle Tyler continued. "In one piece, that is. No one wants to be a soldier. Not in this war."

"Unless you're a fucking Hungarian."

"Well, no one's ever mistaken me for a Hungarian," said Uncle Tyler. "God, she's depressing." And Billie Holiday was switched off. Fin heard ice cubes dropped into the shaker. Tyler still acted as if he owned the place. "You're out of vermouth? What kind of a gin joint is this?"

"Shut up, Tyler," Lady said. "You're interrupting my wallowing."

"You mean I'm cheering you up?"

Lady gave a short laugh.

"You see?" Tyler said. "I am cheering you up." A pause, then: "That's all I want to do, all I've ever wanted to do."

"Sit down, you lousy hypocrite."

Another short silence, then the smell of pot, then coughing. Then Tyler: "I'm still here, right? All these years. And we've been through so much together. All I want to do now, Lady, is make you happy."

Fin thought, *You?* Make Lady happy? What a joke.

"What a joke," Lady said.

Fin smiled. He knew Lady. He knew her so well.

"It's no joke, Lady. I'm asking you to marry me."

"Again? We've been through this." She noisily inhaled, waited, continued in her hoarse exhale voice, "So many times. I don't even know why you'd want to."

"Lady." Something in Tyler's voice changed now, too. But it wasn't smoke. It was desperation. Or sounded like it. "I'm begging you."

Fin the eavesdropper, Fin the spy felt sick. He did not want to hear Uncle Ty open his heart to Lady. He didn't want to think Ty had a heart to open.

"Hey. Calm down. Tyler, Jeez Louise, what's wrong?"

"Forget it."

"What are you on?" she asked harshly.

"You have to marry me. You have to."

"Okay," Lady said. "Okay, just sit quietly, Ty. I'm right here . . . I'll get you through this."

"I got drafted, goddamn it."

Uncle Ty, man of principled action: Marry me to get me out of the draft. Perfect.

"You got fucking drafted? You got *drafted*?"

"You have to marry me, Lady. Okay? Get it? You have to. We can start a family right away . . ."

She has a family, Fin almost shouted. He thought wildly that he should stomp down the stairs, interrupt them, ask if anyone had seen his notebook or his protractor, anything to make Lady stop and think. She was so impulsive. She was such a contrarian. She was nuts. And she hated the war. So much. She talked about it all the time. She went to a peace vigil every Sunday. She made Fin come, too. "Karma," she said. "You need to build up good antiwar karma so you don't get drafted." They would stand in the cold or the heat or the rain or the wind. Newspaper would swirl around their feet. They did not speak. It was a silent peace vigil. It was excruciatingly boring, but Fin didn't mind. It had to be done, he understood that. Not just for his own karma, which, really, why not? And not just so they wouldn't have to move to Canada. But because the war was wrong and too many people were dying for no reason. And now Tyler, the odious Uncle Tyler, was supposed to go to Vietnam and get killed. What would Lady do about it? Would she marry him, someone she had known forever, someone she had almost married once before, would she do that to save him from the draft? It seemed horribly possible. Fin knew her so well—he'd just had that thought—but nobody knew Lady, knew what she would do, not really. Not even him.

"At my age, married, pregnant wife . . . You *owe* me," Tyler said.

You *owe* me?

Tyler began to sob.

"Stop it, Tyler," Lady said. "Immediately. Godfrey fucking Daniels. You're not going to Vietnam. No way. So just stop it."

"You mean . . ."

"That I'll marry you?"

Fin put his head in his hands. Not possible. This could not really be happening. To have gotten so far, and then, poof, the end of life, the beginning of everything he had forgotten to be afraid of . . .

"Don't be absurd," Lady said. "I'm not marrying you. And you're not going to Vietnam. You're a lawyer, Ty. You'll find a way out. Everyone does. Except poor people. And black people."

"*You're* my way out."

"Thanks."

"My way out, my way in, you're everything, Lady. I've been in love with you since you were eighteen years old."

"You knocked me up and agreed to marry me. That's not love."

You knocked me up . . .

"Not for you, maybe," Ty was saying. "But it was for me. It was love."

You're the child Lady never has to have.

I took care of it, she'd said on the boat.

And Fin knew, suddenly and with certainty; and he knew that he'd always known without realizing it. Lady had been pregnant. Knocked up. She took care of it, took care of being knocked up, knocked up by Tyler. Fin felt ill. Lady and Tyler. They had almost had a child, that was the bond between them. They were tied by what had almost happened, what had never happened.

He stood up as quietly as he could.

"Fin!" Lady called, before he could take one step. "Fin! Get down here."

He scrambled down the stairs. Gus, who had been asleep in the kitchen, heard him and ran into the living room barking.

"The whole damn menagerie," said Uncle Tyler.

Fin could have made Gus stop. He could have grabbed his collar, petted him, just said, *Gus, quiet.* But the loud shrill noise was a relief.

Ty looked awful, angry and sheepish both. Lady sat in the lounge chair, her long legs folded beneath her. She wore a Russian peasant shirt, embroidered around the collar, and tight bell-bottomed jeans. She had sunglasses on, though it was eight o'clock at night and the room was dim. Perched there, thin and fragile in her sunglasses, she reminded Fin of the picture he'd seen before he met Lady: Lady on the beach in her bathing suit and sunglasses, legs folded beneath her, Lady at eighteen. Left her groom at the altar. Got rid of her baby.

What Fin remembered all his life about this moment, what he never forgot, was a flash of something that felt like electricity: a painful flash of someone else's pain. Lady's pain. He couldn't say anything. Gus barked and circled and nudged him and barked more.

"He's herding you," Lady said with a smile.

"Lunatic asylum," Tyler muttered. "Even the dog is nuts."

"This morning Fin and I were talking about his grandparents' house," she said to Ty loudly, over the incessant barking. "We thought we could drive up there again, just to check up on things."

"The cows," Ty said wearily. "The everlasting cows."

"It's okay," Fin said. "We don't have to."

At the sound of Fin's voice, Gus was suddenly quiet. He sat beside Fin and looked up at him.

"Go see your cows," Tyler said. "What's it to me? Tell them I said hello."

"I'm sorry," Fin said. It burst out of him, sounded odd, strangled.

Lady said, "For what? Sorry for what?"

She reached out, took his hand. Lowered her sunglasses, gave Fin her gentlest gaze. "What for, Finino?"

For the child you didn't have to have. For being the child you never have to have. For not being the child you didn't have.

"I don't know," he said. "Nothing, I guess."

April Fools' Day

If you're the child someone never has to have, do you have to be an especially good one? Fin thought this late at night, a record playing softly on his stereo, Joan Baez or Joni Mitchell or Son House or Skip James. *You know, I laid down last night*, Skip James sang, *and I thought to take me some rest; / But my mind got to rambling, / Like a wild geese from the west.* This was also when he thought about his mother. This was the time he missed her, and when he missed her, he felt close to her. He could almost talk to her. Sometimes he dreamed about her, nothing special, but she would be there, sitting in a chair or walking down the road, while something else was happening around her, and he would say, "Mommy! I didn't realize you were still alive. I'm so happy to see you. I've missed you so much!" And she would hug him. When he woke up, he would feel as though he had visited her, or she had visited him, and he would go about his business refreshed. They didn't happen often, these visits. Sometimes he tried to make them happen. He would concentrate on his mother, willing her to appear in his dreams. Then his mind would get rambling. Like wild geese from the west.

In the daytime, school; in the evening, suitors, feet up on

the coffee table, reading the paper, discussing what to put on the record player, the ice clinking in their whiskey glasses.

"It's like Bizarro World. Sometimes they play cards. Biffi drinks, Jack is tripping, Tyler's doing speed. It's biblical," Fin said to Phoebe. "They're just there, all three of them. Together. Like a cloud of locusts."

"Those are mixed metaphors."

"Similes."

"Luckily, Lady has gumption."

Phoebe thought a lot of people had gumption that week. It was a word that had three consonants in a row. "What if you were French and had to learn how to pronounce 'gumption'?" she said. "Goom-puh-tuh-ee-ow-nuh."

Did Lady have goom-puh-tuh-ee-ow-nuh? She was quick on her feet, sure. She could dance like Muhammad Ali. She could dance and quip and defend herself against the ropes. But why was she in the ring at all? Fin had been dispatched as an eleven-year-old to find her a suitable husband. He had seen for some time now that such a thing did not exist. Not for Lady. She could fight them off too well.

"Why doesn't she just tell them she does not love them and they should go away and leave her alone?"

"Because then," Phoebe said, "she'd be alone."

Fin told himself that Lady was trying to find love and freedom, both together, in her own eccentric way, and he had no right to say a word. He tried not to say a word. He tried hard. But the deadpan melodrama taking place in the living room never stopped, never let up, and when he found Lady alone one afternoon, before the suitors drifted in to take their places on the uncomfortable lounge chairs, he could not help himself. He said, "When normal, sane people refuse to marry other normal, sane people, they stop seeing each other."

"How would you know?" Lady asked.

"I read books."

"All I want is to be left alone," Lady said.

"No, you don't. That's what you say. You always say you want freedom, you want to be alone, you want to get away."

Lady was emptying ashtrays. "Slobs," she said.

"Then you surround yourself with men you don't love, and it's like you keep them on a leash. But that means you're stuck on the other end of the leash."

"Please don't lecture me, Fin. I'm so tired of people telling me what I want."

"You're scared of being on your own."

"Seriously, Fin. Shut up."

But Fin was just getting going. He followed her from the coffee table to the side table down the steps to the kitchen, then to the garbage can outside, where she emptied the ashes.

"You *want* to be tied down or you'll be by yourself, and then you think you'll just float away. *That's* pathetic, Lady. That's what's pathetic. Not being single. Not being twenty-seven. But that."

Lady slammed the lid on the garbage. "You're just like everyone else, you know that? Just exactly like everybody else." She said it in a normal tone of voice; she turned back to the kitchen and went inside at her normal pace, all of which infuriated Fin. Didn't she hear him? Didn't she get what was happening? Didn't she want to be free at all?

"And you never go anywhere, either," he yelled after her. "You're a coward. And a fake. And a . . . an old maid to boot!"

Then he took a walk, the kind of walk he had taken when he first came to the Village. It was odd, walking along the

185

narrow streets with Gus. He tried to retrace his steps, to find that aimless anxious curiosity, the sense that the closed-in streets were a new world, an endless one. But they were just streets now, streets filled with other kids, older kids drawn to Greenwich Village from all kinds of places, looking for whatever they were looking for and looking scruffy and a little stunned. They stared at the dog, the great white-ruffed collie prancing past, and then they glanced at Fin. Not that long ago, Fin had been one of them, a kid from somewhere. Now he was just another New Yorker.

He took a walk the next day and the next, just to get out of the house where the suitors were drinking up Lady's liquor, eating her crackers and cheese and potato chips. He walked farther and farther, to the Bowery, to the East River, to Chinatown, to Wall Street. Lady was just the same, he thought. Not paying any attention to what he said. The days were getting longer, you could see the sun set over the river, slowly, excruciatingly slowly, hovering in the sky, turning it orange, a burning orange, threatening never to set, like Lady with her suitors. And then, suddenly, the sky would turn gray, the sun would disappear, just like that. Just like Lady.

She disappeared on her twenty-eighth birthday, April 1, 1968. I haven't mentioned her birthday was April Fools' Day, have I? Well, it was. And she was nowhere to be found.

Fin was in his room with Henry James that day. A lazy Monday afternoon. They were listening to the Mothers of Invention and getting high. Henry and James no longer looked alike. Henry had grown tall, and James had not. But they were always together, and the nickname stuck. They got hungry and clattered down the stairs.

"I know what you're up to," Mabel said. "And it's nothing good."

Fin looked in the freezer. Pound cake. "Are we saving this?" he asked Mabel.

"Help yourselves," Mabel said. "Eat Miss Lady out of house and home."

Fin was already slicing through the cake. "Where is Lady, anyway?"

"Probably burning her draft card," Mabel said.

James started laughing, then Henry, then Fin. They couldn't stop.

Mabel might have cracked a smile, Fin wasn't sure. The part he did remember was going out with Henry James, walking around the Village, playing on a swing set in a school playground, walking them to the subway, coming home and knocking on Lady's bedroom door.

No answer.

He wanted to play her a new song he'd learned on the guitar. The Carter Family's "Single Girl, Married Girl." There was a verse in which the single girl stays in bed till one, while the married girl has to get up with the sun. Lady would like that. He wasn't sure about the verses with the annoying, noisy baby who interfered with the joy of living—maybe she would realize how lucky she was to have skipped the baby part and to have gotten a kid when he was already eleven years old and knew how to dress himself and eat without dribbling and who went to the toilet on his own, but maybe the song would just make her sad. There was a part of Fin that was still trying to please Lady, the same part that had tried so hard to please her when he first came to live with her. Of course, everyone tried to please Lady. There was that way she had of being so openly delighted when you succeeded, of looking so overwhelmingly happy. Joy—that was the word. She would smile her wide, horsey smile of joy. If you gave her a raspberry, the plumpest, reddest raspberry from the Jefferson Market. Or if you made her a cup of tea when she was sick with a cold, and you poured whiskey in it, and floated a slice of lemon on top. Of if you thanked her for a book. Or if you sang her a song.

Fin knocked on her door. But Lady didn't answer.

Where was she? She should be home. They were having fried chicken, Mabel said. Mabel said Lady especially wanted fried chicken for her birthday. Fin had left his present for her on her bed. She must have seen it by now.

"Lady," he called, knocking again.

Okay. She wasn't home yet.

No big deal.

He went up to his room and . . . and what? Daydreamed, he guessed. Because there he was, sitting on the edge of the bed, and the clock said forty-five minutes had passed.

He went downstairs to the main floor. No Lady in the living room. He went down to the kitchen. "Lady come home yet?" he asked Mabel.

Mabel shook her head.

"Maybe she's staying out tonight."

Mabel shook her head again. She held up a chicken leg she'd been rinsing. "She'll be here for this."

Fin went back upstairs. He was reading *Manchild in the Promised Land*, occasionally taking time off to read *Treasure Island*. He found them oddly similar. A boy in a world of selfish, crazy, violent, colorful adults.

Back upstairs to Lady's room, because what if she'd been asleep before? He knocked again. No answer again. "Lady," he said, his voice sounding odd to him.

What was he worried about? He didn't know. Just an emptiness in the house, a hollowness. Because what if she was lying in her room? Dying? Or dead. He used to think that sometimes when he was little, think that she had died and left him, the way everyone else had. He would get up out of bed sometimes, to check on her. She didn't know, she slept like the dead, that's what she said. *Like* the dead was okay, he used to think. Dead was not. He would stand by her bed and try to hear her breathing. He would stand there for what seemed like an hour, worrying. And then, one night, he couldn't help it; he called her name, "Lady! Lady!" and she sat up and gathered him in her arms. Another time he opened the door and there was someone in bed with her and he never opened the door again. Just stood outside, the way Gus sometimes did.

"Lady!" he called now, and pushed open the door. Maybe someone would be in bed with her. Maybe she would be dead on the floor.

She wasn't dead on the floor. There wasn't anyone at all in the bed. The room was empty. The last light slanted through the window, rich and yellow. The bed was smooth, Lady's lavender velvet bedspread undisturbed. Except for one thing. An envelope leaning against the pillows. A pale blue envelope. You couldn't see it, but it had Lady's name and address engraved on the back. Fin knew, because that box of pale blue envelopes and pale blue stationery was what he had given Lady for her birthday. On the front of the envelope "FIN" was written in big capital letters. In Lady's rich purple ink. Fin had given her that, too. For Christmas. She used a fountain pen that had been her mother's. It was silver, engraved. Sometimes she wore it on a long silver chain around her neck. Fin opened the envelope, pulling out a piece of the pale blue stationery. "Lady Hadley" said the top of the sheet of thick blue paper. "Lady Hadley" in beautiful script that Fin had picked out. "Gone to Capri," said the bottom of the sheet of paper. In Lady's thin, tilty purple script. "Gone to Capri."

"Mabel," he cried. "Mabel, Mabel . . ."

She ran up the stairs from the kitchen. She read the note and made soft disapproving sounds.

Fin followed her into the kitchen. The summer sun was even lower now, blocked by the brownstones across the street. The kitchen was dim. Wax paper lay across the table, a pile of flour on it.

"She ran away," Mabel said. She absentmindedly sprinkled some pepper on the flour. "She ran away from home. Now, why did she do that? Miss Lady is not eighteen years old."

Yes, she is, Fin thought. "She didn't really run away," he said. "Did she?"

Mabel looked at him across the table. Yes, said her look. And we both know it. "She'll be back," she said.

Lady must have gone on a ship; she would never fly, flying terrified her. Eight days on a ship. Even if she went and turned around and came back, that would be sixteen days, and she wasn't going to turn around and come back. She would take a ferry to the isle of Capri and sit in the piazzetta, she would smoke a cigarette and drink a coffee, she would smile at an Italian woman and call out to her in Italian. He could picture it so vividly. Lady. The sun. The buildings washed by the sun. Lady lit by the sun. The sky alive with the sun. Only one thing was missing. He was missing. Fin was missing, a little boy running into her arms.

"What do we do?" he said.

"What do we do," Mabel repeated softly, a chant, no question in her voice, and so no answer. "What do we do . . ."

"She ran away from the suitors," Fin said. She ran away from me, he thought.

Mabel washed her hands and dialed Biffi's number. "She asked me to make fried chicken. Then she left," she said into the phone. "She didn't come back. She left a note. It says she's gone off to Capri in Italy. Just like the last time . . ."

Fin sat at the table and watched Mabel cook the chicken, watched her roll it in flour, pour corn oil into the heavy black skillet, place the pieces of chicken in it. He listened to the squeak and sizzle of the pieces of chicken frying.

"Don't you worry," she murmured with each movement. "I'm here. I'm not going anywhere. I'm here . . ."

By the time Biffi got there, the chicken was done, brown and crispy, lying, piece by piece, on paper towel spread across a platter. Fried chicken was the meal Lady and Fin liked best of all the meals Mabel cooked. Fin and Mabel were sitting at the table, the platter of chicken between them. "No one's going to eat you tonight," Mabel said to the chicken. "No appetite for you tonight."

Poor chicken, Fin thought. You died for nothing.

"This is unbelievable," Biffi said. "Even for Lady."

"It's my fault," Fin said. He had lectured her. He told her she never went anywhere. He said he was sick of her, that she was a coward and an old maid.

"Certainly not," said Biffi.

"Then it's your fault. Why couldn't you just let things be the way they were?"

Biffi spent the night, on the couch, as if he and Lady were married and had had a fight.

The next morning Biffi was still sprawled on his back on the couch in the living room, a glass of what looked like Scotch on the coffee table beside him.

"Hello," Fin said.

Biffi turned his eyes from the ceiling to look at Fin.

He lifted the glass in an unenthusiastic salute.

"Where is She now, do you think?" Fin asked. Sometimes they liked to refer to Lady as She with a capital S. They both said it in conspiratorial tones, raising one eyebrow. "Which ship? Won't She send a telegram or something?"

"Life is bitter, Fin. Remember that always."

Fin said, "Why are you here? Don't you have to go fight an unjust war or something?"

"That is beneath you, Fin."

That was when the doorbell rang. Fin ran to answer it, because maybe she'd come back, without her keys, which would be just like Lady.

"Salutations."

It was Tyler.

"She's not here," Fin said. "She ran away."

"I know," he said. He pushed past Fin.

"Salutations, brother," he said to Biffi.

Biffi said nothing.

"I come bearing tidings from the runaway."

"Why did she get in touch with you?" Fin said. "It makes no sense."

"Ah," Biffi said with a sigh. "Sense." He shook his head. He reeked of Scotch.

Tyler took a telegram out of his pocket and read: "'Sorry. Not good at goodbye. Pay bills.'"

"That's it?" Fin asked.

"No. Sadly. It goes on: 'Take Fin to see farm. Will send for Fin end of June.'"

Biffi stood up. "If telegrams are arriving, I will go home for mine."

"She sent me one for you, too," Tyler said.

"To you? For me? She is infuriating." She could never remember Biffi's address.

Tyler reached in his jacket for the square yellow telegram.

Fin watched him remove it from his inside pocket, watched him hand it to Biffi, but it all seemed unreal.

"What about Gus?" he said. A sudden panic.

"No telegram for Gus."

"I mean, when I go there, when she sends for me. Does Gus go on the plane?"

Tyler shrugged.

Mabel had come upstairs, and Tyler gave her the first telegram. She muttered what might have been "Lord have mercy," but Fin hardly heard her. He hardly heard Biffi reading the second telegram.

" 'Stay alive. For me.' "

"Did I get one? Did Mabel get one?" Fin asked.

"Stay alive for me? That is very dramatic. This is all very dramatic of her," Biffi said, crumpling his telegram.

Gus sensed something was up and moved uneasily among them, giving someone a poke now and then to get them in line.

"I don't want to go to the farm with you," Fin said to Tyler. "I want Lady to come home." He knelt next to the dog and laid his head against Gus's soft ear.

Mabel knelt down beside Fin and put her arms around him. "You're a good boy, you hear me? I told Miss Lady she was lucky to find you."

"You never told me that."

"It was none of your business. But now it is."

"She can't make me go to the farm with Tyler. She can't."

Biffi was saying, "What if I choose not to stay alive? Eh? That would show her some things or two."

"No argument from me," said Tyler. To Fin or to Biffi? It was unclear.

When Jack arrived, no one was really surprised. He had gotten a yellow telegram, too. "Where did she go? She just wrote, 'Don't forget me. But let me go.' "

"She's having a nervous breakdown," Fin said. "Can't you see? We can't just let her go off like this."

Mabel said, "Am I to understand that you gentlemen are staying for dinner?"

Yes, she was to understand that. They stayed, and they returned, night after night, for seven nights, until the first telegram from Capri arrived.

"Don't try to find me. I need to breathe."

"She wants you to go after her," Phoebe said to Fin. "That's why she said not to. She wants someone to rescue her, like you and your father and mother did. It's a psychological manifestation."

"Of what?"

"How should I know? I'm not a mind reader."

The suitors continued to hang around. They arrived, all three, at about six, settled themselves in the living room, and read their papers and argued amiably, as if they were in an old-fashioned men's club.

"Well, my father says not to worry," Tyler was saying. "He knows a shrink who can get me out. People like us don't have to go—Lady was right."

"Lady was wrong," Biffi said, puffing on his pipe. "People like us ought to go."

"Shorty, make us a pitcher of martinis, would you?" Jack said to Fin.

"No. I owe martini fealty to only one master. And she is gone."

"Christ, you're a pain in the ass. Since the minute I met you, you've been nothing but a pain in my ass."

"Then my work has been successful." Fin bowed.

"Fresh little brat, isn't he?"

Tyler said, "He's part of the package, Jack. Better make your peace with the kid."

"Yeah? Well, when I was a kid, kids went to boarding school."

"You're not a kid anymore," Fin said. "And this is my house, and I think you should all get out of my house."

"No one's going anywhere, sport," said Tyler.

And indeed no one did. The suitors ate at the house on Charles Street. They drank at the house on Charles Street. And if they drank enough, they frequently slept at the house on Charles Street. Sometimes Fin sat with them. He wasn't sure which was worse: the anger he felt at himself for forcing Lady to run away or the anger he felt at the suitors for forcing her to run away.

"I didn't mean this to happen," Fin said while they all sat at the dining-room table. You're a fake, he had said. You're a hypocrite. You're an old maid. How could he have said those things? He'd driven her away.

Mabel had made meat loaf and mashed potatoes and string beans. The meat loaf was enormous and sat there on its platter like a hunched animal.

"It's not your fault," Biffi said. He reached for the knife to cut the meat loaf, but Tyler grabbed it first.

"Well, it's not your fault, that's for sure," Tyler said. "You're leaving town. She didn't need to get away from you. She needed to get away from me. I was the one putting so much pressure on her. But if I could just see her, talk to her . . ."

"You?" Jack said. "She already ran away from you once. No, it was me. It's all my fault. I drove her to this."

Mabel had come into the room with a bowl of salad. She slammed it on the table. Leaves of lettuce flew into the air, then landed safely back in the bowl. "No wonder she ran away."

The three men looked a little startled. Then Biffi said, "You are upset, Mabel. So are we all. We all miss Lady."

"Just continue your discussion, all about what you need, what you did, never a thought to that poor girl, what she needs. You just eat your dinners at her dinner table and feel sorry for yourselves. Nothing's changed. You just go right ahead."

"Should we fire her?" Tyler said when she'd gone.

"She doesn't work for you," Fin said. "So you can't."

And they continued eating and quarreling in comfortable acrimony.

On the day before Biffi had to leave, he arrived at the house earlier than the others, and he had his mother with him.

"I'm being sent to Crete," he said.

"Not Vietnam?"

"No. My language skills prefer me to Crete."

"No wonder we're losing the war."

"You are too young to be so cynical, but I forgive you. My mother is coming to stay with you. I have arranged everything. She will look after you until you leave to be with your sister."

Mrs. Deutsch gripped a white paper bag in her tiny hand. Fin wondered if it was the same paper bag as the one she'd had in Wellfleet. The pastries must be really stale now. Two cases of champagne were delivered minutes after her arrival.

"A going-away toast," she said, "to my son, who should know better," and she swallowed a glass of warm champagne.

"We will drink champagne and toast my Biffi every day, yes?" said Mrs. Deutsch. "You will read to me Colette. Such days! A fête, every day a fête." Then she began to cry.

Biffi put his arms around his little mother.

"Take care of her, please," he said to Fin.

"Where's your uniform?" Fin said.

Biffi shrugged and said, "Soon enough."

"Too soon," wailed Mrs. Deutsch. "Too soon."

Biffi spoke to her in Hungarian, then hugged Fin. "You will look after each other," he said. He said it as a question.

Fin said, "Good luck."

Biffi held out his hand. Fin grasped it, shook hands, and found, when he pulled his hand back, a wad of twenty-dollar bills there.

"Whoa."

"For emergencies."

After Biffi had gone, Fin took Mrs. Deutsch up to his room. He had a small safe, a toy really, that Mirna had given him as a twelfth-birthday present. He kept his stash of grass there when he had any, but it was empty at the moment. He convinced Mrs. Deutsch to lock her paper bag of "medicinals" there.

"See?" he said, as if he were talking to a little kid. "I'm putting my money there. So you can put your paper bag there, too. For safekeeping."

She closed the little door with a sigh of satisfaction and turned the red combination lock. "Now," she said, "if only my son could be as safe."

She went back to the living room to crochet and drink champagne and cry.

Fin sat on his bed and tried to ignore the weight of the emptiness he sensed everywhere in the house. Lady was gone. Biffi was gone. He looked out the window at the gardens of his neighbors, strangers. A cat walked delicately across a brick wall. There were three robins poking for worms in the dirt. The sky was a flat powdery blue. He wondered what the sky was like in Capri right at this moment, in Crete, in Vietnam. He went downstairs and found Mabel and asked her if she knew Biffi had left his mother with them.

"Yes," she said. "Not quite what I was expecting. But then nothing ever is."

Mirna called that night.

"She's not here," Fin said. "She ran away."

"Very funny."

"She did. On a ship. To Capri. She left a note."

"Oy."

"Yup."

"Are you . . . okay?" Mirna said in her Mirna voice.

"No."

Mirna was silent a moment. "Oy," she said again. "Fin, you'll come stay with me. Until Lady comes home. She'll come home soon. I have a couch. It pulls out."

Stay with Mirna? Good grief. But he was touched that she would ask. She hated people in her apartment. They cluttered it up, she said. With themselves. "It's okay," he said. "Mrs. Deutsch is staying here. Biffi brought her. We are babysitting for each other. And Mabel's here. Except she has to go home every night because she has a family. Did you know she has a family? She never mentioned it before. She has a sister with diabetes and two cats. And her son and his wife live two blocks away from her and they have two babies, a girl and a boy. I never knew any of that until Lady ran away. So I'm glad Lady ran away. Because now I know Mabel better. She's a grandmother. Do you know I didn't even know her last name? It's Sparks."

He hung up.

"Mabel," he said, finding her in the kitchen, "Mirna invited me to stay with her. But I said no thank you."

"I'm thinking of throwing Miss Lady across my knee when she comes back."

"You could come to Italy when she sends for me. Then you wouldn't have to wait as long. Except you have a whole family here."

"That's the truth."

"Lady is my family."

"That's the sad truth."

The sad truth was everywhere that spring, an enormous sad truth, bigger than Fin's. It filled the days and the nights and the street and the country and the world. Martin Luther King was assassinated. There were half a million U.S. troops in Vietnam.

Mrs. Deutsch was miserable, her son having gone off in the

service of what she called a second-tier imperial nation. Fin was miserable, too, his sister having gone off the deep end, and they suited each other just fine. They sat upstairs after dinner watching television, something Lady would never have done. They both liked *Bonanza*.

Downstairs, lurking, were the two remaining suitors.

It occurred to Fin that Biffi had assigned his mother to babysitting duty not so she could look after Fin or so that Fin could look after her, but so she could look after his own marital interests.

Sometimes Fin was so angry at Lady that he had to literally walk it off. An hour, two, three hours' walk in the lengthening afternoons. He would compose angry letters to Lady in his head. You left me with a crabby, senile Hungarian lush, a superannuated high school prom king, and a rat-pack impersonator. How could you?

Did he use those words? Not then, not striding through the streets in a fury. He used those words later, years later, when he tried to explain how angry he'd been and how, after taking one of these walks of wrath, he would think of a horse, a wild horse, a mustang, no, a thoroughbred, prancing, eyes rolled back, nostrils flared, backing away, its head high, and that vision of that horse would make him think of Lady and of her suitors and of her ward, him, and of life itself, and he would think, Of course she ran away, what else could she possibly do?

He did write to her. Real letters. He told her what was happening in school, which was not much. He told her that he still went to the silent peace vigils. He told her about Tyler and Jack inhabiting her house on Charles Street, drinking her Scotch. He told her Mrs. Deutsch was babysitting, that she still had her paper bag of jewelry, that she had arrived with two cases of champagne, which she'd almost polished off already. He told her the wisteria was blooming. He told her to come home.

The *Odyssey*

First shalt thou reach the Sirens; they the hearts
Enchant of all who on their coast arrive.

The copy of the *Odyssey* arrived two weeks before school ended, two weeks before the telegram summoning Fin to Capri. "The Sirens lived here," Lady wrote in a note tucked into the book. "On Capri." Where she'd found it, an English translation, in Italy, she did not say. But it arrived on a Tuesday and was waiting for him in the living room when he got home from school.

"A classic," said Mrs. Deutsch. "By János Arany."

"It's by Homer, I think, Mrs. Deutsch."

"In Hungarian, it is by János Arany."

"So he's, like, the translator?"

"I read it in Hungarian. Therefore it is by János Arany."

Fin liked Mrs. Deutsch. Her occasional bursts of gaiety and underlying melancholy reminded him of Biffi. He missed Biffi terribly, almost as much as he missed Lady. Mrs. Deutsch liked to check the safe each night before she went to bed. Fin would open it and extract the bag of jewels and old, rock-hard cookies, and her delight at finding them there, just as she left them, surprised Fin every time. The sigh she gave, a soft puff of air, as if she'd been punched, lightly; the smile, small and secret, the relief in her eyes were the same every night, and every night Fin felt strangely protective of her, paternal, strong, and tender.

"János Arany was a great poet," she continued. "Shakespeare is the János Arany of English."

"I guess you miss Hungary."

"No," she said. She shook her head. "No. I miss the past."

Tyler took Fin to Connecticut, as requested by Lady. The dog came, too. He was going to stay with Mr. Cornelius, the music teacher, while Fin was away.

"Turned out not to be such a bad idea, holding on to your Connecticut property," Tyler said. "Real estate keeps going up, sport."

"Are you referring to my ancestral home? And all the chattel therein?"

"Oh brother."

"When you say 'brother,' are you referring to my blood tie to Lady Hadley?"

After that there was silence in the car for an hour or so. Then, from Tyler: "What have you got against me? Exactly?"

Fin thought for a minute. "I'm not sure, actually."

"Just chemistry, huh?"

"I guess."

"You excited about going to Capri?"

Fin thought about that for a minute, too.

"It would be better if Lady just came back," he said.

"We agree on something, then."

Fin tried to read the *Odyssey*, knowing it would somehow annoy Tyler, but he immediately felt carsick and closed the book. It annoyed Tyler, anyway—he gave a dismissive grunt—and Fin was content.

Fin stared in front of him, waiting for the carsickness to pass. Why *did* he hate Tyler? Because he wore an ascot? Yes. Because he was in control of everything Fin had? Yes. Because he wanted to be in control of Lady? Yes, that most of all.

"No one can control Lady," Fin said aloud.

Tyler emitted his small, sarcastic laugh. "Even Lady can't control Lady."

"She's free," Fin said. "That's all."

"Yeah," Tyler said. "Right. Free as a bird." Again that laugh. Then: "A vulture."

"So why do you stick around? If she's such a vulture?"

"I like getting my eyes pecked out. Don't you?"

"Ha ha."

Silence for a while. Not real silence, the roar of the road was loud enough, but human silence. And in the silence, Tyler seemed almost human, too, unhappy and human. Fin shook off the sensation. Don't go soft on Tyler now, after all these years, he told himself. Do not fall for this pretense of humanity. But then, in a voice that was, indeed, soft, he found himself asking, "Why do you stick around, really?"

Now it was Tyler who took a while to respond. "I don't know exactly," he said at last. He gave Fin a quick smile, then turned back to the road. "Chemistry?" he said. "Bad, bad chemistry."

They stopped at a Carrols and had cheeseburgers and French fries.

"One for the cur?" Tyler asked, and Gus got to have his own hamburger, which made Fin almost like Tyler. The car smelled of hamburger grease.

"She's just so damn inconsistent," Tyler said when they got back on the thruway.

"That is her charm," Fin imitated Biffi's voice and immediately felt disloyal.

"Now he's an odd one," Tyler said. "How are you doing with the mother?"

"We watch TV. She taught Mabel to make something disgusting with sour cream." He didn't mention the paper bag of jewels and stale cookies.

"She makes me nervous, prowling around all night," Tyler said.

"Maybe you make her nervous," Fin said. "Hanging around all night."

"Touché, kid."

And there was silence again.

Tyler drove fast, faster even than Lady. He didn't slow down when they turned off the thruway, either. Slow down! Fin thought, but he wouldn't give Tyler the satisfaction of saying it. Slow down! I'm sorry I said you hang out all the time at our house, even though you do, I'm sorry, I'm sorry, just slow down. Instead, Fin gripped the door handle. They were going to hit a deer, they would squash a rabbit, the car would skid into an oak tree and flatten like an accordion, like a car in a cartoon.

The car stopped in the familiar driveway, a sudden jerky stop that stirred the dust.

There was the house, newly painted. There was the barn, still peeling dark red paint. He heard a cow.

"Calling your name," Tyler said.

Fin wondered, suddenly, for the first time in all the years that he'd known Tyler, what it was like to be Tyler. Not what it was like to be with Tyler, not what it was like to watch Tyler with Lady or Mabel or Biffi or Jack. But what it was like to be Tyler Morrison, not married, jokey and sarcastic and dapper in a way that was a little old-fashioned, a man who had to drive a fifteen-year-old boy to a farm in Connecticut because the woman who had left him at the altar a decade ago asked him to, and had not even asked nicely, a man stuck in a car with a fifteen-year-old boy who hated him and said so.

He turned and looked at Tyler. Tyler was wearing driving

gloves. Fin felt suddenly and deeply sorry for Tyler. He was natty. He was rich. He was in a dirt driveway with Fin.

"Really," Fin said softly. "Really, *why*?"

Tyler knew what he was talking about. He shrugged. "Really? I don't know, Fin."

Fin thought it might have been the first time Tyler had called him by name. Before that it had always been "kid" or "sport" or the dreaded "son."

"Not money, because you have enough money, right?" Fin said.

Tyler laughed. "No one ever has enough money. Didn't Lady teach you the facts of life? But no, not money."

"I used to think it was money."

"Yeah, you would. But no. No, it's like you get an idea in your head . . . no, it's more like you get an idea in your heart."

Fin must have made some movement, or expression. He didn't mean to. But he was surprised. He couldn't have been more surprised. Tyler, the odious Uncle Tyler, was being so serious, so earnest. So eloquent, to Fin's mind. An idea in your heart. Of course. That's what Lady was for him, too. But he must have moved or twitched or something, because Tyler said, "Laugh all you want. I don't care."

"No, I'm not," Fin said. "I'm not."

"It all used to seem so important, so urgent." Tyler pulled the keys out of the ignition. "Now I've had it. So go ahead. Laugh your head off. The joke's on me. This last little caper . . . I surrender." He held his hands up, as if someone had a gun to his back. The way he had the day Fin met him. I surrender, he had said then. He had surrendered to Lady. Now his car keys jingled in his hand. "I surrender, Lady. You go your way, I go mine. No more begging, no more hanging around for me. The spell is broken."

The spell, Lady's siren spell, was broken. Tyler no longer needed to lash himself to the mast, to stuff his ears with beeswax. That night, Tyler dropped Fin off at the house on Charles Street and did not come in. Fin climbed into bed and read about the Sirens. The spell of the Sirens, of *the mellifluous siren song*. The island of the Sirens, Capri, where he was going, where all around the bones of men lie, accumulated, *now putrid, and the skins mould'ring away*.

But mould'ring or not, Tyler was there the next morning. He sat at the kitchen table with Jack reading the Sunday paper. Mrs. Deutsch had made them fried eggs. She put paprika on the eggs. She put paprika on everything.

"Telegram from Lady," Tyler said. He handed it to Fin.

The telegram said Fin should fly to Rome, then take the train to Naples, then take the ferry to Capri.

"Is she going to meet me? In Rome? Or at least in Naples?" Fin asked.

"You're a big shot," Tyler said. "What do you care?"

Jack laughed.

"Not like in the war," Mrs. Deutsch said. "Peacetime easy peasy."

"No, really," Fin said.

"Really, wise guy," Jack said.

Fin sat on the steps and missed the dog. If he could just have put his face against Gus's silky ears. The dog never did much, no rescuing people from wells, not even any tricks, but he was always there, his breathing was always there, his tail sweeping the air, the click of his nails on the wood floor, his nose pushing and herding, the way he looked at you, hopeful, as though you could actually make something happen in the world. Maybe that was the way Lady felt about the suitors. But she had run away from the suitors, and he would never run away from Gus. Maybe that was the way the suitors felt about Lady.

Phoebe came down the steps of her house. She wore a flowered cotton dress, black, with gaudy red roses, long and smocked like the dresses pioneers wore in the movies. She was barefoot. Her hair was long now and she wore it in a braid. She crossed the street, her bare feet slapping. She had tried to get her parents to send her to a commune in Haight-Ashbury instead of camp. They had declined. They compromised on a teen tour through Europe.

"When do you leave?" she asked. She sat down on the step below him.

"Thursday." School ended Wednesday. "When do you go?"

"Saturday. The other girls will probably be so straight. I could run away and come see you in Capri."

"Yeah."

"Hitch a ride."

"Yeah."

They sat gloomily. Phoebe said, "Bummer."

Fin said, "Yeah."

Phoebe said, "Is that all you can say?"

Fin said, "Yeah."

Sometimes he wanted to touch Phoebe. But not very often. Sometimes, like now, she touched him. She grabbed his leg and put her head on his knee. He stroked her hair.

"Maybe I'll lose my virginity," she said. "Maybe I'll fall in love and lose my virginity."

"Your parents thought of that already. That's why it's all girls."

"True. But maybe I'll meet someone."

"Who? The bus driver?"

"The incredibly gorgeous bus driver."

"Ralph Kramden."

"Shut up, Fin."

"In the bushes with Ralph Kramden."

Now she stood up, grabbed his hand, and dragged him over to her house. Up the stairs, into her room. Onto the bed.

They made out for an hour or so.

Then Phoebe jumped up.

"What?" Fin said.

"We're not in love. We love each other, but we're not in love."

At that moment Fin didn't really care if they were in love or had just met or were sworn enemies. "I don't know," he said.

"Yes, you do."

He told her she was beautiful, which on that day she was.

"I know," she said.

"What if the bus driver is ugly? And old?"

"I like older men. It's a complex."

This was so like Phoebe, the Phoebe he rarely thought of touching, that Fin came to his senses.

"You can drink wine in Europe," she said. "They don't have alcoholics because children drink wine. You have to wear long sleeves in churches. In Italy you say 'please' when you mean 'excuse me.'"

"I'll keep that in mind," he said.

Helen Keller died. Her father had been a Confederate soldier. He found out about the Perkins School for the Blind in a book by Charles Dickens.

Robert Kennedy was shot. The world was coming apart.

On the plane, Fin was in the window seat. He looked at the clouds and the sky and was suddenly filled with happiness. He was on his way to see Lady. The world was coming apart, he reminded himself. Lady had abandoned him. Bobby Kennedy was dead. Martin Luther King was dead. His mother had loved John F. Kennedy and he was dead and she was dead. But still the clouds billowed like an infinite sea below and the sky darkened and the stars came out.

Beside him sat a woman who put on eyeshades and took a pill as soon as she sat down. The stewardess wore a little armylike hat and a pin on her collar with gold letters: TWA. Fin couldn't remember what he ate, couldn't remember much about the plane except the hat and the pin and the sleeping passenger in the eyeshades. He remembered climbing over the sleeping woman as quietly as he could to go to the bathroom. He remembered crawling back into his seat, again without waking her. He remembered wondering where she was going after they landed in Rome and if she spoke English. He thought of his first, and only other, flight, with his mother and father. It seemed so long ago. It was so long ago. Almost ten years. And here he was, going to find Lady again. He remembered wondering if she would run away again nine and a half years into the future. He would be twenty-four and a half and he would be flying across the Atlantic Ocean looking for Lady. And then nine and a half years after that. And nine and a half years after that, until he was an old man and Lady was a very old woman, still running away. He remembered thinking those things, he told me, and he wished, so many years later, that they could have been true.

On the train, Fin clutched his guitar case and sat on his backpack. The train was crowded with people so foreign he could have been in a dream. Kerchiefs and crumpled hats, cardboard suitcases spread on laps, cheese and bread unwrapped from butcher paper, smiles from a wrinkled face, suspicious glances from others. He had walked past each compartment, his guitar bumping into the doors ridiculously, his eyes cast down, until he settled on the floor in the area near the toilet. When the conductor came, Fin's heart pounded. What if his ticket was wrong?

What if the conductor made him sit in a compartment with people who would stare at him? But the conductor smiled, took his ticket, and moved on. Fin bought a sandwich through the open window when they stopped somewhere, he no longer remembers where, only the sandwich itself, fragrant, greasy salami on a round, hard roll. He slept then. When they reached Naples, he checked his money and took a taxi to the ferry, the ancient city slipping past him in a humid, chaotic blur. Soon he would see Lady. What would he say to her? Would he ask her how she could have abandoned him like that, with no warning, no discussion, no explanation? No. He would say nothing about it. He would be happy to see her. They would swim off a boat and visit the Blue Grotto.

And then they would go home to New York.

Enchanted

"*Questo è* Michelangelo," Lady said. She presented the man as if he were a Michelangelo, a sublime marble monument in a city, as if he were the city itself, an actual city, a great city. As if he were Rome. As if, like Rome, he had existed for thousands of years, as if, like Rome, he were an empire, as if he straddled the world. "*Questo è* Michelangelo."

Michelangelo was not as obviously good-looking as any of Lady's usual suitors. Foreign-looking, absolutely. No one could have mistaken him for an American. His nose took up a lot of his face. Large, a little bony, a foreign nose, not sharp, not bulbous, not pug or hooked or aquiline. Not American. His mouth was a little sulky. Sometimes he pushed his lips out, just a little, when he was thinking. When he dismissed an idea, his lips pushed out a little more, a quick puff, a kiss of disdain. He was dark, tanned, with dark wavy hair combed back, away from his face. But it was his eyes that caught your attention. That's what Lady said, and Fin had to agree. His eyes were as blue as the blue water; Lady was right. His eyes were sad and steady, but most of all, they were blue, each time he looked at you, blue. Blue again. As if they got bluer.

"Michelangelo! Finino!"

Fin couldn't tell which made Lady more excited, more nervous—that Fin was meeting Michelangelo or that Michelangelo was meeting Fin.

They took the tram up the steep hillside, his guitar case like an extra person, a dwarf squeezed in among the others. Why had he brought it? Lady smiled at him, beamed at him, you'd have to say. He felt as out of place as the guitar case. But taller.

They emerged in a street lined on one side by shops and cafés, on the other by the Bay of Naples. Fin lowered his backpack.

"Mommy and Daddy and I took a taxi," he said. A surrey with the fringe on top, he remembered. Then, suddenly ashamed of the words "Mommy" and "Daddy," he turned away from Lady and Michelangelo and stared out at the water. The ferry was already making its way back to Naples.

"This is where Fin and I met," he heard Lady say to Michelangelo. "This island."

"The island is enchanted," said Michelangelo. His accent was heavy and rather beautiful. "Everything that happens here. Enchanted."

What a phony, Fin thought. He turned back, expecting to see Lady rolling her eyes. But she had slipped her arm around Michelangelo's waist and was looking at him in a manner that Fin, in spite of himself, thought of as indeed enchanted. She seemed womanly, suddenly, to Fin—a woman enchanted. Not the sophisticated New York girl who had run away from home.

I guess you're one of the beautiful people now, Fin wrote in a letter. She never answered his letters, not in the sense you usually think of when you say "answer." There was never a response. There would be, instead, new, unrelated bursts of communication, brief, sporadic: a telegram to Tyler or the copy of the *Odyssey* or, twice, a postcard. *I guess you're one of the beautiful people*

211

now. She hadn't responded to that conjecture, but looking at her now in the blazing light, looking at her bronzed and grinning beside this man in a loose white shirt and sandals, he knew she had changed. She looked somehow ripe. She looked delicious. She looked calm. She looked, it took him a minute to realize this, happy.

They stopped at a café.

"It's the same one," Lady said.

The heat and the dirt and the fatigue of his train ride vanished. Lady was sipping a cappuccino. Nothing had changed. The chairs were the same. The tables. The umbrellas. Lady smiled at him and she was just as beautiful. If she had pulled him onto her lap and given him a teaspoonful of milky coffee, he would not have been surprised. He felt again that confused affinity, as if she'd been another species, but one he'd known all his life.

He smiled back at her.

She was so pleased with herself, with her café, her island, her new Italian boyfriend; she was so obviously pleased to be sharing it all with Fin, to be sharing this place, to be sharing the past. How could he say, *Lady, you ran away like a thief in the night, you left me alone with three morose men and an addled old lady.* And Mabel, of course. How could he say, *You scared me?* How could he not?

"Mabel says hello," he said.

"I asked her to come, you know."

"She has a family," he said.

"Who is Mabel?" asked Michelangelo.

"A member of the family," Lady said.

Fin looked away. Lady sounded like Scarlett O'Hara. "She has her own family," he said. "She is our maid," he said to Michelangelo. "Our Negro maid. I don't think she would have felt comfortable here, actually. Lady never mentioned Mabel to you? She's the one who took care of me when Lady vanished."

"Okay, Fin. I know it was sudden, I know I was wrong, but can we talk about this later?"

"Also, there were the three boyfriends. They sort of moved in."

"Enough, Fin."

"Yeah, but then one of them had to go be in the air force, so he moved his old mother in to keep his place warm. A lot happens, I guess, when you disappear to enchanted islands."

Michelangelo said, "Families have many complicateds."

Lady kicked Fin's leg. "You're foul," she said. Then she kicked Michelangelo. "You, too."

Fin kicked her back.

"Foul!" she said, laughing.

"I have many complicateds," Fin said. He felt better now. Unburdened. "Many, many complicateds."

"Just as I say," said Michelangelo.

Lady opened her bag and pulled a book out. "Here. It's about lesbians on Capri. That ought to shut you up."

Walking behind Michelangelo and Lady, Fin tried to ignore his backpack digging into his shoulders. His guitar case weighed three hundred pounds. More. He was so tired and hot that the sun seemed to obscure the world rather than reveal it. He watched Lady slip her hand into Michelangelo's. Michelangelo's hand slipped out again as he lifted his Leica and clicked. At what? Fin saw nothing but the glare and the dark shadows.

"Michelangelo is a photographer," Lady said. "A professional photographer," she added. "An artist."

"I desired to make films," Michelangelo said. "But I am not cut up for it."

"You're a terrific photographer. He's terrific," she said to Fin.

"This is our lives," Michelangelo said in his melancholy Old

World voice. "We cannot fight them." Then he put his arm around Lady and kissed the top of her head, the way Lady sometimes kissed the top of Fin's head. "Not all the time, eh?"

Lady, the fighter, said, "Why not?" But she pushed her head closer against him and walked like that, tilted and protected, like a tree growing into a windy hillside, and added, "On the other hand, why?"

Lady Hadley was in love. She had fallen in love for the first time in her life. And it was not lyrical, it was not the familiar refrain of a song. It was, Fin saw at once, desperate and deep. Lady could not be in the room with Michelangelo without looking at him. And she could not look at him without smiling, a small personal smile. On the beach, the miniature beach at the Marina Piccola, she sat on a towel, her knees bent, her arms clasping her legs, and she gazed at Michelangelo's back as he lay in the sun, facedown. What did she see there on that long, narrow torso? On the smooth tanned skin? Her future? Looking back on those days in the sun, Fin hoped not. He hoped she saw inscribed on Michelangelo's back only her sunny present, the gentle waves lapping the shore in the background.

Every radio in every bar and café seemed to play the same crooning singer singing the same songs that summer. *L'amore vieni, l'amore va.* Love comes and love goes. That was the kind of Italian Fin learned on his stay in Capri: song lyrics. Love comes and love goes. *Ascoltami, perdonami,* listen to me, forgive me. *Con te ogni istante era felicità.* With you every instant was happiness.

A summer language of song lyrics. *Perchè no?* Fin said, looking back at that summer long ago. Capri was a musical, lyrical island, the island of the Sirens.

———

Michelangelo carried his cameras with him everywhere. A Leica hanging from his shoulder, a Rolleiflex from a strap around his neck. He was never at rest, not at a party, not sitting in the piazzetta having a coffee, not on the little boat they sometimes took out, Michelangelo and Lady and Fin, beneath the blue-and-white-striped canopy, letting themselves bathe in the shaded heat before bathing in the turquoise sea. As soon as they climbed back aboard the boat, Michelangelo picked up the Leica and was gone. He was right there, dripping wet, but he was gone. He took pictures of Lady, of the salt water beaded on the graceful slope of her shoulder, of her hand on the varnished wood, of her face turned toward the canopy and the sun that filtered through it, but he was not with her, not with her shoulder or her hand or her face or the boat or the sun. He took pictures of Fin, too. From behind, mostly. Fin wore cut-off jeans to swim in. Michelangelo wore a small, tight European bathing suit, almost a bikini bottom, and Fin often found himself looking away in embarrassment.

"What are your interests?" he asked Michelangelo. It was habit. It was required. But he already knew.

"What I see," said Michelangelo.

Michelangelo was in Capri for the summer, a long two-month holiday interrupted by occasional shoots that took him away for two or three days. For work, he shot models posing against rocks dressed in the kind of flowing Pucci pajamas Lady sometimes wore in Capri. For his vacation, he was more likely to shoot, simply, the rocks.

Lady was full of praise for him, planning gallery shows in New York.

When I go back to the city, she would say at first. When she went back to the city, she would speak to Biffi's friend Leo about a show.

As soon as I go back to the city, she began to say after a few weeks.

Someday, she said a few weeks after that. *Someday we'll get you a show in New York.*

Fin wondered if she would ever really go back. Or would she stay here on this fragrant, rocky island?

So shalt thou, raptur'd, hear the Sirens' song.
But if thou supplicate to be released,
Or give such order, then, with added chords
Let thy companions bind thee still the more.

Lady had turned Homer inside out. She was a Siren lured by the Sirens. She was bound not to the mast of a passing ship but to the island itself.

"Don't you miss New York?" Fin asked. "New York is an island, too."

They sat in the piazzetta at the Caffè Tiberio. They drank Campari and soda, which Fin pretended to like and by the end of the summer did. The sun was low in the sky. The bell on the clock tower rang.

"Are you serious?" Lady asked him.

No. He wasn't, not really. He could see that Lady did not miss New York. He could see that Lady missed nothing, nothing was lacking, she was full, full of life and full of this place. "But . . ." he said.

"But nothing." She lifted a camera from her lap and aimed it at Fin. "But nothing, Finino." Click. He still has that picture. A sunburned teenage boy in an unbuttoned oxford shirt, his hair in his eyes, his expression imploring.

A few days later, Michelangelo, standing on the terrace with a glass of white wine, in the rosy light of the setting sun, waved

Fin over. "Come," he said. The sunset rested on white walls of the neighboring houses, a soft blush. "Beautiful, no?"

"Yes."

"You have nostalgia for New York, I think."

Fin looked at him in surprise. He had never talked to Michelangelo about being homesick. Lady must have told him. "A little," he said. "Sure."

"It's difficult to be in another country's life."

Fin liked that: in another country's life. "And not its real life, either," he said.

Michelangelo smiled. "No," he said. "Nothing here is real. All is dreaming."

Then Lady appeared, barefoot in a white cotton shift. She caught the pink light and glowed. Michelangelo held open his arm and Lady nestled against him. "Lady, darling," he said. He closed his arm around her gently, kissed her head.

Then they were all three quiet. The sound of laughter from a boat below them. The buzz of a mosquito. A gull. Fin noticed again the stillness, the calm stillness of Lady when she was with this quiet Italian man. That was real. Michelangelo gave her something, his arm around her shoulders gave her something. The gentle color around them faded to slate, and Fin realized that Michelangelo gave Lady what no one had ever thought to give her, what no one realized she needed. Not protection or guidance or lectures or even ardent, worshipful love. But shelter. As passive and unquestioning and miraculous as a blue cave.

Phoebe sent Fin a letter care of American Express. She was the only girl in the teen tour from New York. The other girls were from the Midwest. How had her parents come up with this trip? On the other hand, they all drank a lot of wine. The bus driver was at least forty years old and had a nose like W. C. Fields, but the counselor was in her twenties and she and Phoebe hung out a lot and talked about Marcuse. Chartres was beautiful. No wonder the masses were opiated. She hoped he was having a good time. Peace and love and pasta, Phoebe.

Fin wrote back immediately. He told her he was incredibly tan. He told her Lady was in love with an Italian photographer and he would probably have to live on Capri for the rest of his life, which would be like living on Fire Island for your whole life except much prettier and with better food.

He said nothing about the way he really felt, because he wasn't sure how he really felt. To see Lady happy—that was something. It was as if there were two suns on Capri, the bright, gaudy one in the sky and the other sun, the joyous one emanating from his sister.

"*Bella*," said the pharmacist, smiling as Lady left his shop with the Italian version of Sea & Ski. "Here," he said, touching the place where the heart beats. "*Bella* here. She is *bella*, your sister." This was the sentiment of the waiters, the porters, the chefs who came out from their hot kitchens to greet her, the men and women in every shop selling sandals and espadrilles and salami and Pucci pajama pants. At first Fin assumed it was because Lady threw money around. What merchants wouldn't respond with smiles to such a generous American customer? It was the way of the world, the fate of the American tourist everywhere. But it was more than that. Lady seemed somehow to belong on Capri. The shady narrow streets, the sunny little piazzas, even the chairlift to the top of Mount Solaro—she was so at home. She knew everyone's name. In back streets, where tourists did not usually venture, she would greet an old woman in a kerchief by name.

"How do you know her?" Fin asked.

"I get around."

Or she'd wave to a fisherman who told her where he'd brought his catch, which restaurant, what to order. She knew the elderly English botanist. The taxi drivers called out to her as they drove by.

Fin was used to people noticing Lady. He was used to Lady noticing everyone around her. But in New York, all that noticing had to do with strangers. In Capri, Lady was suddenly, completely, among friends.

A happy, radiant Lady? He was as proud as a parent.

But if Lady belonged on the rocky seductive island, Fin wasn't so sure about himself. He missed the dog. It was ridiculous, but he did. He missed his friends. He missed American radio stations. He missed Biffi, though that was weak of him. He missed Mabel, perhaps most of all.

Dear Mabel, he wrote.

This is a very strange place. There are high cliffs and you can jump off them into the water, which is bluer than any water I've ever seen. There are caves you can row a boat into. Which are also blue. The streets are so narrow you can almost touch the buildings on both sides at once. You will be happy to know there are very few kids my age, hardly any kids at all, so I'm sure all the houses are calm and unchaotic. I miss New York. It is very quiet here. No baseball. No politics, either. Well, maybe Italian politics, but how would I know? Lady is unrepentant. Are you surprised? It doesn't really matter, though. She has a new boyfriend, but he is different than the others. He is very protective of her. Like a big tree. He's Italian. I hope your sister is feeling better. And your children and grandchildren are all happy and having a fun summer. I hope it is not too hot in New York. There are no movies here. All the visitors are very rich. I don't know about the people who live here all the time. Unless the rich visitors pay a lot for everything. Sometimes, there is no water to take a shower. Like every day. You have to wait. I wonder why the rich people don't mind. Probably because it's so beautiful. Maybe they think they're roughing it. Well, I'm going to the post office to buy stamps to mail this. But I just realized I don't have your address. So I can't send this. I don't have your address because of racism. I know you don't like to talk about it because you have too much dignity to discuss it with me, an ignorant white person whose sister employs you to do EVERYTHING. But it's true.

Love, Fin

He never sent the letter, but he kept it, a thin blue sheet of air-mail stationery folded into the size of an envelope. "Mabel Sparks" was written on the front. "Address Unknown Because of the Legacy of Slavery in the United States of America." Fin showed it to me once with a rather rueful smile.

"I meant well," he said. "Foolish but not a fool, as Mabel would say."

Lady always hoped to see Graham Greene at the Caffè Tiberio, but if she did, she didn't recognize him. He, the Capri resident best known, was unknown to her. Jackie Kennedy and Caroline and John-John did walk by one day, though, followed by several photographers, Michelangelo among them. Lady, to Fin's acute embarrassment, waved gaily and threw earnest kisses at the children. Fin turned his face to the ground and suffered. Now Michelangelo was off on a shoot for a couple of days, and Fin and Lady sat, just the two of them, at their usual table. Fin leaned back and linked his hands behind his head. "I wish I liked coffee," he said. "It smells so good." He drank Coke every morning, a sweet, syrupy Coke that tasted much better than the Coke at home.

"Let's take a walk together today," Lady said.

"I have letters to write," he said.

"Ha! You sound like a Henry James character. How are your friends Henry James, anyway? What are they doing this summer?"

"Camp. Junior counselors."

"Eh?" she said, jutting her chin out, the sides of her mouth down. "A lake in the Poconos? Camp Capri is preferable, no?"

Lady slipped into Italian cadences more and more, even when speaking English. Especially when speaking English, Fin sometimes thought.

"Yup," he said. "The best." Lady had rented a small boat, and Fin often took it out in the morning, alone, motoring around the island, the cliffs sheer and towering beside him, through rocky arches, the water as green as jade as it disappeared into the curve of one grotto, as blue as the sky as it disappeared into another. He dropped anchor at different spots, slipped into the cool sea, and thought. Sometimes he thought of Odysseus and the briny, broad-backed sea, sometimes of Mabel and her family and how unfair it was that he was floating on his back in paradise while she was hot and discriminated against in Harlem.

"I wish the *International Herald Tribune* came in the morning," he said.

"Well, it doesn't, so let's take a walk."

"I wish the *International Herald Tribune* had a decent obituary page."

"Poor Fin. You want to walk in the cemetery instead? The one for non-Catholics? The guest cemetery. For guests who never leave."

Yes, he did want to walk with Lady in the cemetery. And he would like to have Lady all to himself, for once. She was pretty preoccupied these days. Sometimes with Michelangelo. More and more with taking pictures.

"I like being alone behind the lens," she had announced. "I've never liked being alone before. I feel so"—she hesitated, gave a discomfited smile, and said—"well, liberated."

Fin sometimes wondered why she had even bothered sending for him, but he knew. She needed him. "You're my family," she'd said. "You're my brother. We are in this thing together." *This thing.* That was Lady's way of saying the Past, the Present, the Future: Life. "We're stuck with each other," he answered, and he meant the same thing. "Blood is thicker than water," Michelangelo had added, and Lady had laughed and asked how he knew that expression and did it have a counterpart in Italian, but of course it must be biblical, and she and Michelangelo began babbling in Italian. Fin wondered then if Michelangelo saw himself as water and not quite as thick as Lady seemed to hope. He liked Michelangelo, who treated Fin with casual good humor, who wasn't annoyed by Fin, threatened by Fin, or drawn to Fin, who maintained an easy, friendly distance. All of which made Fin suspicious. Maybe it was just the language barrier: Michelangelo's English was careful and often off. But Fin didn't really think it was Michelangelo's erratic English or his own nonexistent Italian. It was something else, something about Michelangelo, a man whose interests were what he saw, who wanted very little from the people around him. But Lady was besotted with Michelangelo, so besotted that she couldn't see he was not besotted with her. Fin did try to tell her, but she smiled at him in an uncharacteristically condescending way and then reassured him that no matter what happened between her and Michelangelo, she would always love Fin and always take care of him. Which he knew was a pile of crap. Not that she would always love him—he believed that. But take care of him? That was a joke. To say that to him after leaving him in New York with all her discarded lovers? After sending for him as if he were one of them? He had gotten from New York to Capri by himself; he could take care of himself, which was lucky, because he had to.

So did he want to take a walk with Lady that day when Michelangelo was away? Yes, of course he did. But he wouldn't give her the satisfaction of knowing how much. "I have to wait for the paper to check the box scores," he said.

"How are the Mets doing this year?"

"Battling for ninth place."

"So you're not missing anything," she said. She finished her coffee. "So," she said. "Walk or no walk?" She reached over and smoothed his tousled hair, the way she used to when he was little. He pushed her hand away, but she simply took hold of his and put it to her lips. "Come on, come on, come on," she said, standing up, grabbing two rolls from the basket and shoving them into her pocketbook.

"Okay, okay," he said. "*Perchè no*, right?"

He usually walked in the afternoon, after lunch, sometimes for hours. He would scramble up steep paths or stroll beneath the shade of palm trees, then find himself, suddenly, on an outcropping of gray rock facing the ancient city of Naples across the bay, or Ischia across a different bay, and feeling as if his heart were expanding, were limitless. Even when he looked back on that summer in Capri from the distance of many years, he would remember that expansive feeling, remember it palpably. It was the feeling of freedom, he said, the smell of it, the sound of it, the clarity of a vision of freedom. Freedom from the absence of his parents. Freedom from the puzzle of Lady. Freedom from everything and everyone he knew, which meant, most transcendent of all, freedom from himself.

Sharing a walk with Lady . . . not quite the same thing. But Lady gave him a big smile, and Fin thought, Okay, it will be another thing, a Lady morning full of Lady pronouncements and quotes from Homer and energetic chatting with whoever we meet, and he smiled, a big smile, couldn't help himself. As usual.

"What?" Lady asked.

"You're nuts," he said.

She held her arms out, the way she had when he was a five-year-old in a sailor suit. The arms weren't held out for Fin to jump into this time. They weren't held out for Michelangelo, either, or for anyone. They were spread out in simple joy.

"I love it here," she said. "I just do."

He loved it here, too, the place where he and Lady first met, a craggy paradise overflowing with flowers and tourists during the day, with music and parties and wine at night. Here they were, the same two people under the same sun, under the same moon, the same stars.

"Thank you," he said.

"For what?"

"You know." And he looked at her, and she did know.

It had happened more than once: Fin would be sullen and solitary, angry at Lady, angry at himself for caring, for expecting anything from her. Then, as if she read his thoughts, she would lavish attention on him, and everything would seem normal, if anything could be normal on an island that even Roman emperors, rulers of most of the known world, had chosen as an escape from that world, as a garden of peace and beauty.

But nothing could be normal there. Was it normal to look up casually and see Mount Vesuvius, the subject of so many paintings, so many postcards, the protagonist of so many ancient tales and tragedies? Was it normal to swim through caves of emerald green water? To float on your back and gaze up at tall arches of stone? The stars that summer were shooting stars. Stars shooting across a jasmine-scented sky. The night was the color of the darkest plums. The plums were the color of night.

And Michelangelo was there beneath the tender night sky

walking along the Via Tragara with Lady, a man as self-contained as the island, as serene. They stopped to look beyond a stand of pines at the sliver of moon that hung above the water. Lady put her hand out for Fin's. Michelangelo stood beside her, as he always stood beside her, reassuring, almost paternal. Fin realized it was the first time Fin had ever seen Lady with a man who needed nothing from her. She had always seemed so strong to Fin, a creature of unfettered will. Now he saw the effort it had taken to be so unfettered, kicking off all those chains. It was not always easy to find a chain to kick. She had to be so alert, so attentive. But on Capri, no one needed chains. After all, it was an island. There was no place to run, and so no fetters to undo. Freedom, of sorts. Freedom for Lady, anyway. Freedom from all that freedom shit.

When Michelangelo went off on a shoot the first time, Fin assumed that Lady would be lonely and would want to spend every minute with him. He assumed it and he welcomed it, and they did take out the little boat once or twice, sit on the beach one morning, walk for miles along winding streets on another afternoon, along dirt paths clinging to the slope, along ancient steps, the slanted sun keeping them company.

But Lady wasn't lonely. Lady wanted to take photographs. Alone. Each time Michelangelo was away for a few days, they slipped into the same routine. After breakfast, they would go their separate ways, then meet up again for lunch. It is difficult to tell exactly where Lady went. I've seen her photographs from that time, and they are abstract and close up. There is no context, no clue, just shape and texture and light. It's also difficult to know exactly where Fin went. He certainly didn't know. He followed streets that wound their way between buildings closing in on either side, streets that had steps, that sometimes climbed steeply uphill, sometimes down, alleys that were dark, shaded, clammy, and then suddenly burst out into the sunlight on the side of a sheer cliff, the sky enormous overhead, the water sparkling below. He walked along dirt paths, past tumbled-down houses and flustered chickens and curious goats. Sometimes a path ran along the sea, high above it. Sometimes a path led to Roman ruins, the palace of a great Roman emperor, now an immense rocky blueprint scattered with wildflowers. He walked up the snaking road from the Marina Piccola to the Gardens of Augustus. He walked up and down the seven hundred ancient steps to Anacapri. He walked with tourists, past tourists, beyond tourists. Purple bougainvillea spilled over pitted stucco walls; cats sprawled in the sun, lifting their heads slightly to watch him pass, flicking their lazy tails.

Ragazzo triste, sang a deep-voiced woman. *Ragazzo triste come me*. Why did it sound like a Sonny and Cher song? Because it was a Sonny and Cher song with new lyrics. And so Fin learned to say *a sad boy* in Italian. *A sad boy like me*. He learned to say *Sometimes I cry and don't know why* in Italian. He learned to say *Hey hey hey* in Italian: *Hey hey hey*.

"I think your Italian is brilliant," Lady said. "You can ask for food and talk about love. That's all anyone needs in Capri."

That was all Lady needed. She looked so comfortable, scrambling across gray rocks in her white pants, her dark blue T-shirt, her sandals made for her by the man in the shoe store the size of a closet.

When they did walk together, Lady did not chatter as Fin had feared. She could easily have been Gus, the perfect walking companion, if Gus could hum "Lucy in the Sky with Diamonds."

"I met a girl who wants help with her English," he said on one of these walks.

Lady's hair was pulled back, her face, what you could see of it surrounding her huge sunglasses, a little pink with exertion. Fin stopped to give her a chance to catch her breath. The heat was blazing and acute, burning off the softer, uncertain morning air.

"I'm sorry, Fin," she said. "I just don't have time for that right now."

"From *me*." She was a beautiful girl from Florence. He'd met her on the beach.

Lady raised an eyebrow.

"She's sixteen," he said, as if that could lower the eyebrow.

"An older woman, eh?"

"Her name is Donatella," he said stolidly. "She's sixteen," he said again. "From Florence."

Fin and Donatella had spoken in English. When Fin tried to think of something in Italian, all he could come up with was *Dobbiamo stare insieme*, we must be together, which he did not say aloud.

At first Fin delivered his lessons on the beach, naming common things around them, a chair, a basket, an apple, a bottle of water. He asked Donatella what music she liked and they spoke haltingly of the Beatles. Her English was very much like his Italian. "It's so fine," she said, when he asked her what she thought of the weather. "It's sunshine." *It's the word "love,"* they both thought.

"Girl"

Two weeks passed, and Fin saw less and less of Lady. They still
had breakfast together, with Michelangelo when he was not on
a shoot, but they rarely met for lunch. Fin ate sandwiches with
Donatella on the beach or joined her mother and father and
two sisters at a restaurant. Lady ate an orange, somewhere on her
rambles, then went back to taking pictures. She spent her afternoons in the darkroom; Fin spent his swimming, waiting for
Donatella and her family to return from their postprandial naps.
He took Donatella out on the boat, too, always with at least one
of her sisters, one a little older and happy to look the other way,
the other younger and an avid, observant pest. Then he and
Donatella would part for dinner, and Fin would join Lady and
Michelangelo for white anchovies, octopus, wine, lemon cake,
but his mind was not there, and neither was Lady's or Michelangelo's, and the dinners were quiet, pleasantly distant. Sometimes Donatella joined them, or they joined Donatella's family.
Fin explained that President Johnson was an evil man. He tried
to translate *Hey, hey, LBJ, how many kids have you killed today?*
He talked about segregation and voting rights. But how do you
explain the burning of draft cards in a language you don't

know? Donatella's parents were Communists who understood a little English, so they nodded their heads complacently no matter how radical Fin tried to be, but when he turned to them to ask for help in making himself clear to their daughter, they lifted their shoulders, held their hands out palms up, jutted their chins out, and made a small noise that sounded like the beginning of a word that started with the letter *b*. Lady was not much help, either.

"Why talk about the war *here*? *Now?* Look—fireworks! Someone must be getting married."

And, yes, in the deep night sky there were thunderclaps of golden flowers, soaring rockets of green and red that exploded and arced and drifted through dun-colored smoke toward the water, lighting up fishing boats and yachts. Yes, there were fireworks decorating the sky, but still he could not understand how Lady could let politics fall away from her so easily, like a scarf left behind somewhere. There was still bigotry and segregation and poverty. There was still a war.

"There is a war going on," he said. "There's still a war going on."

"There's always a war going on, Fin. Why did the Greeks have a god of war? Because we need one."

"You've converted? To paganism?"

And Lady laughed and said, "I didn't have to convert. I just had to look around me. The gods are everywhere on this island."

"Oh brother," Fin said.

"You have brother?" Donatella asked proudly. "I have two sister."

Sometimes during these bumpy attempts at conversation, anger would rise up inside Fin, his ears would ring, his face would turn red.

"When you get mad, you look just like Hugo Hadley," Lady said lightly.

"Like father like son," he answered, and Lady looked hurt, as if it were Fin who was being cold and disloyal.

Then his thoughts would turn to Charles Street and the house left behind. Mabel would be going there once, twice a week to check on things, to clean the city grime that crept inexplicably into a shut-up house. He imagined her opening the door to the smell of pipe tobacco and cigarette smoke. He imagined them there, the suitors, even Biffi, still waiting. He imagined them there when Lady and Fin got back, just where she had left them. If Lady and Fin ever got back.

It was hard for Fin to talk to Lady these days, about anything, almost as hard as talking to Donatella, but especially about New York, about going back to New York, where they belonged. Lady never took a hint, for one thing. On principle, she said. *Just come right out and say it*, she would say. *Don't expect me to do the work for you.* Which he hated. There were times when he hated Lady, period, hated little things about her, the way she smoked, say, with her head thrown back as she exhaled. It was a little phony, anyone could see that. Why couldn't she be more natural? He even mentioned it once. Lady said, of course, typical Lady, "I'm naturally phony." She made him laugh when she said things like that, and he would be left wondering why on earth he'd been so mad at her in the first place.

After dinner, the "young people," Fin and Donatella and her older sister, went to one of the discotheques. Naturally the little sister did not come. She went back to the hotel with her parents. But Lady did not join them, either.

She did not consider herself one of the young people.

When had that happened?

At some level Fin did not care. The air smelled of lavender. The stars were enormous, vibrant, scattered and clustered across the darkness of the sky. All he cared about was dancing to strange corny Italian rock. All he cared about was watching

Donatella move. All he cared about was standing so close to her he could feel the sweat of her arm on the sweat of his arm. Outside, in the dark street, he would hold her against him and kiss her, and she would run her hands up his back, inside his shirt, and he would run his hands up her back inside her shirt, and even the Emperor Tiberius, who was supposed to have lived such a licentious and depraved life on the island, could not have experienced anything close to the glorious agony of Fin Hadley.

Donatella learned more and more English.

Lady took more and more photographs.

Michelangelo had a friend on Capri, a fellow photographer with a darkroom, and there he'd taught Lady how to develop pictures. He'd offered to teach Fin, too, but Fin could not imagine spending even one minute in the small stuffy room when he could be swimming or climbing. Lady's photographs did not impress him, either. They were grainy and sad, shadows of the meticulous pictures Michelangelo took. At first, anyway. But that changed. While Michelangelo was away and Fin was entwined in the arms of his English student as much as possible, that changed.

If you walked to the right of the church, down a steep, narrow street, then turned right at the shrine to the Virgin Mary, you would come to the house Lady and Fin lived in. You would open a green door and walk down a long path. Above, an arcade of trellised lemons hung down, colossal lemons, and the sudden change from the glare of the street to the dappled shade was almost shocking. There was a garden and a terrace and steps to the small, cool white house. And from the windows upstairs, you could see beyond the other cool, shaded white villas to the sea. Fin's room was not much wider than the window at the end of it that faced the blue sky and the bluer water. Lady's room, downstairs, was a little bigger. She hung her prints all over the blank white walls. And slowly, as the weeks passed, the photographs seemed to find their feet. That's what Lady called it: finding their feet.

"They look better," Fin said. "They really look better. But why?" They were still black-and-white photographs of rocks, of the trunk of a tree, of the shadowy whites of a plaster wall.

"They've found their feet," Lady said.

Fin lay on his back on the little deck that formed the bow of the boat. His hands were behind his head. Donatella was beside him. Behind them, Donatella's sister listened to a portable radio. "Girl" in Italian. Ahh, gii-irl. He tried to translate the song back to English for Donatella, but instead of *"She's the kind of girl you want so much / It makes you sorry,"* the Italian seemed to mean something about the sea telling a story. Maybe. He wasn't at all sure.

"She's the kind of girl you want so much it makes you sorry," he sang, hoping Donatella would not understand. Or hoping that she would. The suitors would understand, and Fin thought that perhaps now at last he understood the suitors. Hopelessness is not the end of desire, it's not the end of need. And so? Hopelessness is not the end of hope.

"Ahh, gii-irl," Donatella's sister sang from the back of the boat.

Donatella rolled over on top of him.

"Tomorrow," she sang to the tune of "Yesterday."

"Yesterday," he corrected.

"No," she said. She shook her head and her hair flicked across his chest. "Tomorrow we go."

"Where?"

"Firenze," she said. She pointed vaguely in the direction of the mainland. "Home."

Goodbye, Donatella. Fin remembered the last sight of her, a small figure in a yellow dress pulling farther and farther away, away from the enchanted island on a ferry. He could not remember her older sister's name. He could not remember her younger sister's name. He could not remember Donatella's last name. But that vision of a girl shrinking on the wide horizon he always remembered.

He mourned in his room. He tried to read *Extraordinary Women*, the book about lesbians on Capri, though he knew Lady had given it to him just for effect. But it required too much concentration. Some of it was in Latin, some in Greek, and there was, as far as he could tell, absolutely no sex. Just squabbles.

"It does have one of the most satisfying endings in literature," Lady said. "But, yeah, maybe when you're older."

"Not everything is about age."

"I know, Fin. And I know you're sad. Even if you're just fifteen."

"Gee, thanks."

Lady sighed. "That didn't come out right. Nothing I say to you these days comes out right."

No argument from Fin.

"But you have to get out of the house, Finny. You want to go out on the boat?"

"Not really."

"Anacapri? Ruins?"

"No thanks."

"Okay. We could go shopping."

Fin made a face. How many pairs of sandals could Lady buy? How many scarves and floppy pajama pants?

"Beach?" she said.

He shook his head. No. Of course he couldn't go to the beach. The beach without Donatella? "I'm fine."

"Right." She took hold of his shirtsleeve and gave him a pull. "Then we'll walk."

"You're always pulling me," he said.

She pushed him instead.

"Great." But he went with her. She packed two oranges and a bottle of water in his backpack and threw it at him.

"*Andiamo*, Mary Sunshine," she said.

He led her on a particularly steep path down to the water, an almost invisible path, straight down to a little cave on the stony shore. Fin had discovered it on one of his rambles. If Fin had been little, this would have been his pirate cave. But he was not little. If he hadn't been so down, it would have been his own nymphaeum, the caves the Romans decorated with statues and tiles, places where they worshipped or swam or cavorted. But he was down. So down.

Lady sat on a damp, flat rock and peeled her orange. The scent of orange mingled with the briny sea smells.

"You didn't take any pictures," he said. "Not one."

And it was unlike Lady to go at someone else's pace, not to stop to pet every stray dog, every mangy cat, to talk to old men in baggy suits who bent precariously over their canes.

"Not in the mood." She turned to look at her camera perched on the rock beside her, as if she had never seen a camera before. "Just not in the photography mood."

What kind of mood was she in? A quiet one, anyway. Fin ate his orange in the shade of the little cave and listened to the gulls, and all the irritation and annoyance and indignity that came along with Lady seemed far away. Even his broken heart, as he secretly described it to himself, lifted. He felt oddly sheltered here, protected. Beyond was the Bay of Naples, an expanse of deep, rich blue, and beyond that Mount Vesuvius. The

volcano looked down on them, so far off, so benign when
viewed from this spot, cushioned by the water between them;
so benign when viewed from this moment, cushioned by the
centuries of quiet, a dormant volcano, sleeping.

He looked at Lady. She, too, gazed out at the water and the
distant mainland.

They've found their feet, Lady said about her photographs.
But it was Lady who had found her feet, Fin thought. It was
Lady who looked better than she ever had. It was Lady who
smiled her smile with a new warmth, who could sit still, for
hours, calm and still in the fading evening light.

It was Lady who was pregnant.

"I'm pregnant," Lady said.

He hadn't heard her right. "Huh?" he said. "What?"

"Pregnant," Lady said. "I'm going to have a child."

But I'm your child, he thought.

I'm your child. Everyone knows that.

I'm your child, he almost said.

"Oh," he said. "Wow."

"I wanted to tell you. To tell you first."

"Oh," he said again.

"I haven't even told Michelangelo."

"Oh. No? Oh."

Lady put her hand out, and he took it. There was orange
pith in her fingernails. She was perfumed with orange.

He didn't know what to say. Or think.

"No more Uncle Tylers or Uncle Jacks," she said.

"No more Biffi?"

She shook her head.

"Oh. Of course not." But he could see Biffi and Tyler and
Jack, could see them camped in the house, the ice in their glasses
making a cheery jingle, the low murmur of male voices. He
realized he would miss them. He would miss his enemies Tyler

and Jack. He would miss his friend Biffi. But she was done with the uncles, done with the suitors, done with them all. And in some way done with Fin.

"I'm out of a job," he said.

"No more lemon sorting?"

"Well, anyway, I approve. Except for his bathing suits. Aren't you supposed to be vomiting or something?"

He smiled and tried to joke around. But he remembered Mrs. Holbright at the dinner table a few years ago. *She really does like to bat them around a bit.* Like a cat with mice, bat them around while they're alive. "It's so easy for you," he said.

"What is?"

"To cut people off."

Lady didn't say anything.

"Just like that. To leave them. Leave them behind. When you can't walk, run, right? Run away and leave the mess you made behind."

"Oh," she said quietly. Then: "I'm sorry, Fin. I told you I was a lousy guardian."

"Thanks for the breaking-news bulletin."

"But things will be different now."

"I'll say."

"We'll have a real home. You and me and Michelangelo and the baby. We'll be a family."

"We are a family," Fin said. "At least we were."

"You're not happy for me?"

Fin picked at a stone embedded in the hard, wet sand.

"Yeah, I am."

He was. He was angry, he was worried, he was horribly, stabbingly jealous. And he was happy for her. She would have a baby, a bald, big-headed, screeching, lumpy, gluey baby. And she would have a husband. A taciturn Italian husband. Every-

thing she wanted. Everything she had secretly wanted all this
time.

He realized that Lady had never asked him to call Michelangelo "Uncle Michelangelo."

"So no Uncle Michelangelo, I guess," he said as they walked
back up toward Capri town.

"Just Uncle Fin. You're the only uncle now."

"Yeah. I guess I am," he said. "Uncle Fin. Weird."

"And Papa Michelangelo."

It turned out, however, that Michelangelo did not really
want to be Papa Michelangelo. It also turned out that Michelangelo already was Papa Michelangelo to several boys and girls
who lived with their mother, his wife, in Milan.

"You're married?"

"Separated. For many years."

"But then . . ."

"We can't get a divorce, Lady. This is Italy. Not New York."

"I don't care," Lady told him. "As long as I have you."

Uncomfortable silence.

"I *forgive* you," she said.

"I did not ask forgiveness, Lady."

"I just want to live here for the rest of my life with you and
our child."

"But I don't live here, Lady. I live in Milan. I can't just move
to this island, this fantasy place."

Then Lady would move to Milan with him.

"You can't do that."

"I don't mind. I do mind, actually, but we can come here for
part of the year, can't we? The rest of the time we'll squeeze in
with you in your bachelor pad."

"Lady, I live with my mother. I have children almost grown.
It is all wrong."

"Well," she said, mimicking Joe E. Brown in *Some Like It Hot*, "nobody's perfect."

Fin did not hear this discussion. It was relayed to him by Lady. She sat on the tile floor of her bedroom, crying. At first, Fin thought she was retching, vomiting, the sound was so coarse and so pained. But it was sobbing, a kind of sobbing he had never heard from Lady. Or from anyone else, for that matter.

Lady had never eaten much. Now she stopped eating altogether. She was queasy from the pregnancy, and she seemed to be in a kind of shock.

"Let's go home, Lady," Fin said.

"This is home."

"We'll go home, and Mabel will cook us fried chicken."

Lady ran out of the room. He heard her throwing up.

"Okay," he yelled. "We'll go home, and we'll fast."

She came back into the little living room looking pale and haggard. She lay down on the old couch, a hard, high-backed thing upholstered in faded blue brocade, her feet in Fin's lap. He massaged them, first the left, then the right. Her feet were swollen. Her hands were swollen. Her eyes were swollen from crying. Fin leaned toward her belly, put his ear to it.

"The baby says it wants to go home to be born in New York."

Lady gave a feeble laugh.

"The baby says the doctors here are all Italian and don't know how to say anything it understands. The baby says you should try to stop crying. It gives the baby a big headache. And the baby says it's hungry and wants a piece of bread, at least. And the baby says . . ."

"Okay, okay."

They sat in the garden at a wrought-iron table. Lady took a small bite of bread.

"The baby says, It's about time, it's famished."

"Tell the baby to lay off for a bit."

"The baby says to tell you, What, are you crazy? Babies never lay off."

Michelangelo came and sat with Lady for hours, holding her hand.

"Come with me to New York," she said.

"I am already a father. I have already children. I live my life in Milan."

"And me?"

"I will never desert you, Lady. But I cannot give up everything of my life for you, either."

Their conversations were repeated every day, throughout the day; their words looped around, tangled up, knotted themselves, came out the same every time.

"I'm sorry," Michelangelo said to Fin each time he arrived at the house.

"I know," Fin said.

"It does no good."

"No."

Fin never mentioned the baby Lady had never had. Neither did Lady. But that information was there, unspoken, unacknowledged, between them.

"Will you write to Tyler?" Lady said.

"Me?"

"And Jack. And Biffi, of course."

"Don't you think it would be better coming from you, Lady?"

Lady shook her head. No.

Fin nodded his head. Yes.

They stared at each other through the bright humidity of late morning.

"The baby says, Pull yourself together. The baby says, How the hell are you going to take care of it? You're a basket case."

"The baby said I was a basket case?"

"Direct quotation."

Lady began to cry again, this time quietly. "Smart baby," she said.

That was the day Fin sent a telegram to Biffi. *Lady pregnant. Complete mess*, he wrote. *Doesn't eat. Even drink. Don't know what to do.*

Michelangelo had gone to Morocco on a shoot.

"He'll be back in a week," said Lady. "But it doesn't really matter anymore. It's duty, his duty. I don't believe in duty. I believe in love."

It all made sense, if you were Lady. You believed in love, so you toyed with those who loved you, trying it out, trying out their love to see if it turned into your own. Then you fell in love at last, except the one you loved was not the one who loved you; you left the ones who loved you behind, moaning and beating their breasts, and now the one you loved was going to leave behind the one who loved him. You believed in love the way others believed in a god, an all-powerful god, a god who was destructive, indiscriminate. The god of war.

Lady had waited all her life to fall in love. And now the god of love made her suffer for his sins.

"No more than I deserve, I suppose," she said.

Fin was sympathetic and exasperated. And, when Biffi showed up, relieved.

"I'll give you a tour"

Fin saw Biffi in the piazzetta. He just appeared there one morning. No letter, no telegram, no warning, just Biffi sitting at a table by himself, sitting there smoking his pipe. His hair was short, but he was not in uniform. Was that legal? When he caught sight of Fin, he gave a desultory wave. "You look surprised," he said.

"Well, yeah."

"But relieved."

"God, yeah."

Fin sat down in the chair next to Biffi. They both faced the square, both with their legs stretched out in front of them, crossed at the ankles.

"You're taller," Biffi said.

"You're not."

Biffi gave a short laugh. "No. Not taller. Just the same. Same old Biffi Deutsch."

"Biffi Spumoni Deutsch."

Another short laugh.

"Thank you for coming," Fin said.

"I told them someone died. I'm at the funeral. Do you know

what service life is like? It is softball games. That is a form of baseball with a bigger ball. Softball games and basketball games. That is another form of baseball with an even bigger ball."

"Better than killing people in a jungle. Or being killed. So you translate stuff? From what language to what language? What stuff?"

"It is confidential."

"Yeah? Hey, you're a spy."

Biffi modestly nodded in agreement. "For now."

Fin took Biffi out on the boat. They motored past the Faraglioni, the three rocky stacks poking up dramatically from the calm blue water. "I'll give you a tour," Fin said with some pride. "But also, you never know where she'll turn up. She stalks around. She's so erratic. I guess she's always been erratic, but in ways you kind of expected. But now she's like, I don't know, like someone else." He had turned the boat around and sailed along the coast until they reached Monte Tiberio. "She stopped smoking. She stopped drinking. Because of the baby. But she also stopped eating. She's spooky. She wears a big straw hat."

Fin cut the motor and dropped the little anchor. He pointed up to the top of the cliffs. "Villa Jovis. Tiberius built it. He built twelve palaces."

Biffi closed his eyes. Leaned forward, his head on his bent knees. "It seems so long ago."

"What does?"

"Lady."

"It's been a month. Two months."

"A long time ago and a long way away." He sat up and put his arm around Fin's shoulders. "Tell me," he said.

So Fin told him, told him about Michelangelo, about his photographs and his darkroom and Lady's plans to get a gallery show for him in New York and how that plan dimmed the lon-

ger Lady stayed on the island and then vanished completely
when she started to take her own pictures. He paused. Should
he tell Biffi how happy she had been? How serene? How she
had danced with Michelangelo, spinning and spinning, when
there was no music but their laughter?

"What?" Biffi asked. "Tell me."

"She was different. From New York, I mean."

Then, dancing around, Lady and Michelangelo tripped over
the champagne bottle on the ground and it rattled along the
tiles and a cat howled somewhere and Fin started laughing and
Lady reached down and pulled off a sandal and threw it at Fin.
He could tell that part. That was recognizable. But the other?
The sleepy, enchanted romantic face turned to Michelangelo?

"You're worried for me?" Biffi said when he paused again.
"No, no, I must know what is the situation. Say, go on, say
what you mean."

"Well, she was kind of happy, I guess."

"In what way happy?"

"Quiet happy. Not insisting on being happy. Just softly
happy."

Biffi let his hand fall into the water. Little splashes. It reminded Fin of Suetonius and the little fishes.

"Did you ever read Suetonius?" he asked Biffi.

"Naturally."

"Remember the little fishes? Tiberius? In Capri?"

Biffi colored. "Has this man bothered you, Fin?"

"No. Gross. Just, do you think it's true? Little boys under-
water? Swimming between his legs? Doing that to Tiberius?
And then he threw people from a cliff. That cliff." He pointed.
"Michelangelo said it's not true. That Tiberius was a great war-
rior and ruler."

"Why did you read Suetonius? You read Latin now?"

"No. Lady gave me a translation."

Biffi said a few things in Hungarian. Unless it was Greek. Fin had no idea.

"Your mother is nice," Fin said when the diatribe had finished. "Except she thinks the *Odyssey* and the *Iliad* were written by a Hungarian."

"Talk to me more about Lady. No more diversions. My mother is peculiar. Suetonius is outrageous. Talk to me about Lady."

Fin told him then. Told him how Lady had sent for him, how he had found his way from Rome to Capri, how delicious the sandwich was, the greasy salami sandwich he'd bought through the train window. He told Biffi about Donatella, too. He said, "I know I'm only fifteen," and Biffi said, "Pah! Old enough to love and old enough to suffer." Fin told Biffi about the walk to the cave and Lady's announcement. "She was so happy," he said. "She was so happy for a week, happy to sit still and just look at the sky. It was weird. Really weird." Biffi did not look angry the way Fin expected him to. He looked wistful. A little smile, his fingers flicking the water. "Go on," he said. And Fin told him about Lady crumpled on the floor sobbing. It went on for over a week, the sobbing, then she put on her enormous straw hat and enormous sunglasses and began haunting the island like a spook.

"She is angry at this man?"

"No. She's just sad."

"She knows? That you wired to me?"

"Good grief, no."

Biffi smiled. "Good grief," he said.

"She told me to write to you and Tyler and Jack and tell you all what happened, but when she finds out I asked you to come rescue her, and me, she'll kill me. She'll throw me off Monte Tiberio. And you."

They went back to the house, walked beneath the lemons

hanging in heavy dignity, up the worn steps into the living room. Fin called Lady's name. No answer. He kicked off his sneakers, flopped onto the stiff-backed sofa. The tiles were cool under his feet.

"Who knows," he said. "She could be anywhere."

He poured Biffi some wine and himself some water. "I only drink wine at dinner," he said.

"Do you?" Biffi asked. "In Iraklion it is all beer or ouzo. And hamburgers," he added brightly.

It was then that Lady entered. "Entered" is perhaps too strong a word. Fin told me that she would just appear in that period, an apparition. She would not be in the room, and then, with no transition, she was there.

She stood and stared at Biffi in obvious confusion. "Biffi!" she said, her voice warm. "Did you desert? You poor man. But you're safe here. Everyone is safe here."

He stood up and walked toward her. "Lady," he said, "Jesus." He put his hand on her cheek. Her face in the shadows of the straw hat was gaunt, haunted. There were dark circles under her eyes. Biffi had not been prepared. She was still beautiful, but in a fevered way, her eyes too large, her cheekbones too sharp, her smile a grimace.

Now she was self-conscious. She backed away from Biffi, gave Fin a quick, savage look.

"You told him to come?" she said.

"No, no, the boy didn't know," Biffi said.

Lady had not even heard him. "You did, didn't you, Fin? You traitor." She took off her hat. She was barefoot. "Well, what difference does it make? You're here," she said to Biffi. "What shall we do with you?"

"You went out barefoot?" Fin said. "Are you crazy?" He was sorry the minute he said it, because he thought, Yes, she is crazy. She's gone completely crazy. "I mean, you always tell me not to."

Lady looked down at her feet. "Oh," she said. "I guess I forgot."

"Lady, sit down. I want to talk to you," Biffi said.

"I won't give it up," she said. "I'm a big girl now. I am having this baby."

"You sound like *As the World Turns*," Fin said.

"Shut up, Fin."

"Lady, just sit down," Biffi said. "Please."

Lady sat cross-legged on the floor.

"Take a walk," Biffi said to Fin.

"I don't feel like taking a walk."

"My god, Fin, I came from Iraklion to talk to your sister. Go away. Please."

Fin walked upstairs with as much dignity as he could. At the bend in the stairs he stopped. He listened. It went on for an hour or so. Lady wept and Biffi comforted her. Lady said she was a fool, and Biffi said it turned out she was human, after all. Lady said she would always love Michelangelo, and Biffi said, Yes, she would. Lady calmed down and asked him about being in the air force. Biffi said it was more American on an air force base in Crete than it was in Times Square. "What am I going to do?" Lady asked. "Marry me and be happy," Biffi said. "You just ruined everything about this visit," Lady said. "I know," said Biffi. "I would like to marry you, though." Lady said, "We're both fools," and Biffi agreed.

They went to dinner at a fish place overlooking the Marina Piccola. The waves lapped at the small beach. The moon rose, a crescent. Lady looked a little more like herself. She was animated. She stood up and danced to the music playing on the radio in the kitchen. They could barely hear it, just enough for Lady to dance.

"Thank you," she said to Fin. "Thank you for getting Biffi here."

"You're welcome."

"Because now I see what to do. You were right all along, Finino mio."

Fin held his glass up. "To me!" He was giddy, carried along on the giddiness of Lady.

"It was there in front of me all the time."

"To you!" said Fin.

"All that worry about lemons. What a lot of bother for nothing."

Biffi held his glass up. "To lemons."

"To the god of lemons," Fin said.

"Thank you for understanding me," she said to Biffi. "For understanding everything about me. For forgiving everything about me."

"It is because I love everything about you."

"Me, too," Fin said. "So, when's the wedding?"

Biffi and Lady stared at him.

"No wedding, Fin," said Biffi. "Have you not been listening?"

"But she said I was right."

"And so you are," said Lady. "Why should I marry anyone? I have plenty of money. I have you," she said to Fin. "I have my dearest friend, Biffi. And I have you," she said, tenderly addressing her belly. "I have everything now. Thank you, Michelangelo. I would wither and die married to anyone. Wouldn't I, Biffi?"

"Quite possibly."

"Thank you. You came here and you reminded me why I ran away."

Biffi sighed. Gave a small smile.

Fin looked at them in horror. "So you're free? Is that it?"

"Oh good grief, no. I'll never be free, not with a baby. Why would I want to be?"

She took Biffi's hand and led him down the steep steps to the darkness of the beach, pulling off his shirt as they went. Fin could just make them out as they dived naked into the water.

Biffi left the next day. Fin walked him to the ferry.

"She is so alive, your sister," Biffi said. "She makes the sun come up each day, you know. Though even she cannot prevent it from falling down again at night."

"What the hell happened? Is she really okay?"

"For now," Biffi said. "I think so. I am like a glass of cold water. Splash! In the face." He laughed.

"She really is crazy."

"A little."

"What about you?"

"I'm crazy, too."

"Not what I meant."

"I am to be fine. I am to be Melvyn Douglas."

"Who?"

"In *Mr. Blandings* American movie. Do you know nothing about your culture?"

"I know Homer wasn't American. Or Hungarian."

"Then you will go a long way in this world."

They shook hands.

"Don't shoot anyone," Fin said. "And don't let anyone shoot you."

"Not on Crete. No."

Fin hugged him. "I don't want you to go," he said.

"My dear friend," Biffi said, kissing his head.

That Baby

They came home on a boat. It was a rough crossing, but if it had been calm as a pond, Lady would have been sick. She and Fin shared a cabin, and at night Fin, on the top bunk, could hear her retching in the bathroom.

During the day, she put a good face on it. "I'm putting a good face on it," she said. "Do you know why?"

"For my sake?"

"No. Don't be silly. I'm putting a good face on it because I don't want the baby to be sad."

They stood at the rail in the wind. There was a fine, misty rain. Lady breathed deeply. She smiled. "Won't everyone be surprised?"

"A lot of people won't approve, I guess, yeah."

"No, I mean, won't they be surprised at me? Being so happy?"

Fin was certainly surprised. You're pregnant! he wanted to say. You have no husband. You are in the family way, wearing your apron high. The man you love went back to Milan to his wife and children. You're knocked up, like the eighteen-year-old girl you used to be, going back to New York to face the world as an unwed mother. "Are you happy?"

A soft film of rain rested on her pale face. She smiled. Pushed his wet hair off his forehead. "Yes," she said. "Yes, yes, yes!" They walked a little. "And no." Then the wind picked up. "But yes." The deck got too slippery to walk on. "But I can't go inside." Lady looked green. "Ever again."

There were deck chairs sheltered by an overhang. They pulled wool blankets around their legs. Lady said, "'If equal affection cannot be / Let the more loving one be me.'" Auden: the poem about the stars who do not give a damn. Fin felt a stab of love and pity and jealousy.

A steward offered them steaming cups of beef bouillon. Lady waved him violently away.

She said, "You know, nausea means it's settling in nicely."

"Breakfast?"

"The baby, you idiot. I've never felt this sick in my life, so it must be a very comfortable baby." She smiled. "I'm very lucky."

Lucky? She was violently sick to her stomach, vomiting all day long, carrying a love child, once known as bastard, and an Italian one, to boot. The man she loved, the one man with whom she'd ever fallen in love, was left behind on a noisy dock in Naples.

They told each other they would meet every summer in Capri.

"It's better this way," Lady said to Fin. A little unconvincingly. "Capri is where we exist, nowhere else."

"You think he'll change his mind? Come to New York?"

"Never."

"Miss you so much he wants you to move to Milan?"

She hesitated before she said, "No. I guess not."

The hesitation reminded him of something. Her tone. The resignation. The absence of resignation in the dreamy timbre of her voice. The unconscious shrug. The rueful smile. And then he realized: Lady had become one of them, one of the suitors.

"It's very romantic," she'd said to Michelangelo on the dock.

"You are an extraordinary woman," Michelangelo said to Lady.

She's dying inside, Fin thought.

That was true. But there was the other truth, the new one: Lady was alive, inside and out. Ever since Biffi's visit, since their impromptu naked plunge into the bay, she had come slowly back to life, cleansed, born again, like a fish, flapping desperately on the shore suddenly restored to its watery home. Or a Siren. Sometimes Sirens were mermaids, weren't they? Mostly they were birds with women's faces. Not very appealing. Not at all like Lady. And yet, like Lady, the chicken-legged ladies lured so many sailors to their ruin.

No accounting for taste.

No accounting for anything.

"Next summer," Michelangelo said to Fin, slapping his shoulder, kissing his cheeks.

Fin picked up his backpack and his guitar case and headed toward the ship. He had not played his guitar once. He turned to see Lady and Michelangelo in a passionate embrace. He watched as they backed away from each other, each lifting a camera and taking the other's picture.

"So you don't think he's a cad?" Fin had asked as they stood on the deck and waved.

"I suppose he is."

"Jesus, Lady."

She laughed. "Who are you more jealous of?" she asked gently. "Michelangelo or the baby?"

Not an easy question. Which room would the baby take over with its spit rags and diaper pail? And whose fault was that if not Michelangelo's? "I'm not jealous."

"You will always be first in the hearts of your countrymen."

"No, I won't. Anyway, I'm not jealous. I'm concerned. For you."

"Well, I do have you, Fin."

"What are you going to do with it? The baby, I mean. I mean, I know you'll take good care of it, but do you even know how to take care of it?"

"I love Michelangelo," she said.

"Okay, okay," he said.

"Anyway, who knows what will happen with him? In the future? Right?"

Fin said nothing.

"And whoever this baby turns out to be, it will know its father. Every summer."

"Yeah, but . . ."

"And the rest of the time, we'll do big things, the baby and I. Things I could never do if I were a hausfrau in Milan, right? First, we'll go to Japan."

"By boat?"

"Shut up, Fin."

"Japan, huh?"

"The baby," she said with a happy sigh, "will love Japan."

When they got back to the house on Charles Street, there were no suitors waiting for Lady, as Fin had imagined there might be. Biffi was not there. He was still a spy in Crete. Tyler had unsurprisingly managed to get out of the draft without benefit of a wife and had quit his law firm, leaving the Hadley business behind him. He was engaged to the daughter of the head of his new firm and was thinking about taking a stab at politics. That's what his former law partner told Lady. Tyler himself never spoke to Lady again. Jack, too, was out of the picture. He had met a girl dressed in orange robes tapping a tambourine and disappeared for many years.

"So the coast is clear," Lady said.

"You're sort of ruthless," Fin said. He was thinking of his talk with Tyler in Connecticut. Actually, he was thinking of all the suitors.

"Yeah, well, kill or be killed. Love or be loved." She squared her shoulders and stood almost at attention. "This is a new life, Finny. My real life."

"Maybe that's how Tyler felt about your old life. That it was his real life. Or even Jack. I know Biffi did."

"Well, they were wrong. Jesus, Fin, what is it with you? You were mad at me when they were around. Now you're mad at me because they're not."

What *was* wrong with him? Lady may have been ruthless, but she was also brave. It's hard to imagine now, Fin told me, but being unmarried, raising a baby by yourself in those days—it wasn't done. It was still a scandal, and Lady knew it. She knew who would drop her, who would drift away. Just about everybody. "I'm sorry," he said. He hugged her. He kissed her on top of her head. He was so much taller than she was now. She smiled, then began to cry.

"Everything will be okay," he said.

"You told me that when you were a little boy."

"And I was right. I'm really sorry, Lady. Don't cry. I don't like it when people disappear, I guess."

"Well, I'll never disappear," Lady said.

But that was a lie.

They did not go to Japan that first year, though Lady did return to Capri for the month of August.

She flew.

"Eight days versus eight hours. The baby says, Fly. The baby says, Don't be such a baby."

"I'm glad someone responsible is making the decisions," said Fin.

Lady and Michelangelo rented the house with the green door at the gate, with the gigantic lemons hanging from thick, twisted vines above, with the sunset blushing on the walls.

Fin didn't want to go.

"You're such an only child," Phoebe said. "No offense."

"Have you ever lived with a baby?"

"I said no offense."

They sat in a classroom in their new school. The New Flower School stopped at the eighth grade, so both Fin and Phoebe had moved on, both to a somewhat more conventional and demanding school on the Upper West Side. When Fin first got there in the fall, a rattled guidance counselor had called Lady in.

"At the request of the algebra teacher, we've given Fin a few tests, and I'm afraid he has developed a psychological block that prevents him from retrieving even the basic mathematical information he has learned."

"Oh no, not at all," Lady said. She bounced the baby and cooed at it. "He hasn't blocked anything. How could he? He hasn't learned anything to block."

Fin stayed after school four times a week to be tutored. So did Phoebe. She was a year ahead of him, but so was her mathematical information block. The tutor spent twenty minutes or so explaining something, then left them to do problems together.

"Work in groups," the tutor would say as she exited. "Form your groups."

Fin and Phoebe were the only ones being tutored. They were already sitting next to each other. Fin shuffled through the book and opened and closed his binder, hoping that would indicate grouping. Phoebe just threw her head back and sighed loudly.

"You know that baby is not my sibling, anyway," Fin continued.

That baby.

Fin was scared of that baby. He told me it looked like a possum, a baby possum, wrinkled and hairless. "You looked like a possum," he said. "A baby possum." He twisted up his face in disgust. "You were wrinkly and you had no hair."

But Lady thought I was beautiful. "She used to hold you and stare at you and make unconscious noises. She sounded like a mourning dove. She said your name over and over. When you cried, she sang and put you on her shoulder and walked in circles."

"That's what all mothers do," I said.

"But she was Lady. It was like watching a ballet."

I was born in May, a few days after the anniversary of Lydia Hadley's death.

"So it was a little hard to concentrate," Fin said. "Plus you were so ugly."

"Maybe you could have said to yourself that your mother would have found joy in the beginning of a new life."

"That's what Lady said."

"What did you say?"

"I didn't say much in those days." He was thinking of death, not life, of all the deaths when he was so young, of his mother, not my mother, of his father, not my father, of himself, not me.

"I'm sorry," he said. "I was a little messed up that year."

"Nineteen-sixty-nine? So was everyone else, by all accounts."

"Not you. Not Lady. She was the happiest person in the world. She was deliriously happy. Lady Hadley boarding an airplane? Do you know how much strength you gave her?"

Maybe it took someone so completely dependent on her to

give Lady real independence. That's what Fin thought, anyway. Or maybe he just said that to make me feel important. He liked to make me feel important. And loved.

"Lady took you everywhere from the minute you were born. People didn't do that in those days. She took you to restaurants and movies. She took you to peace rallies in your perambulator, a giant baby carriage with a camera case strapped to it. She took you to SDS meetings. There was so much urgency to Lady. It was contagious."

At the SDS meetings, she took pictures of boys sitting on the floor, narrow shoulders hunched forward, of men with beards, their heads held contemplatively to one side, of pretty girls with long shiny hair standing at the edges. Lady didn't like the edges, though.

Fin said Lady probably would have taken me to Woodstock if she hadn't already made plans to see Michelangelo in Capri in August. "So you must always respect decadence," he told me, more than once.

"It's not really decadent to take a baby to see her father instead of going to a hippie rock festival."

"On Capri everything is decadent, and for that we must be grateful. At Woodstock, you could have been trampled in the mud."

Fin did not go to Woodstock, either, which broke his heart. In July he worked in the storeroom of a shoe store and went to concerts at night. He saw everyone. Everyone. He saw Janis Joplin. He saw Cream. He saw Jefferson Airplane, the Grateful Dead, Jimi Hendrix, Ravi Shankar, B.B. King, Chuck Berry. He saw everyone. There were concerts at the Fillmore East. At the Cafe Wha? At high school gyms. He smoked grass and listened to music. And he went to Shea Stadium, where the Mets were, miraculously, winning.

It was a giddy time, especially looking back at the music and the clothes, the things people like to look back at. But there was something menacing, too. Not just the war, though that was there, always, an accompaniment, like a soft drumbeat, to everything that went on, especially as he got older and closer to draft age. But there was also, often, something more immediately foreboding. At peace rallies, there were police on horseback, high above you, with shining black boots digging into frothing sides, the horses skittering nervously, the police stern and staring. There were kids on the street, runaways, dirty and strung out and homeless. Maybe if you lived out of town and you came to the Village to buy some jeans or get a poster of the Doors, maybe the gritty kids with cracked fingernails and glazed eyes looked like children of the revolution or flower children. To Fin, who lived among them, they looked beleaguered and desperate and sad. Which is how he felt that year. He was sixteen. He wrote songs about it. But he never sang them.

"So you see why I didn't pay much attention to you," he told me.

"The world was coming apart."

"Well, I thought so, anyway."

Lady tried to help him. She offered to ride bikes again, but he was too old for that now. She asked Mabel for advice.

"They get like this," Mabel said.

"Boys?"

"Don't tell me you didn't get like this."

"Yes, but I was so unhappy."

Mabel said, "Sometimes you play dumb. Sometimes you are dumb." Then they bathed the little baby in its bathinette, and Fin, that difficult dark cloud hovering unaccountably in paradise, was momentarily forgotten.

"What the hell is a bathinette?" I asked Fin. "You made that up."

"Someone did."

Lady wouldn't leave Fin home alone when she went to Capri, which was why he did not get to go to Woodstock. He refused to go with us to Capri, so he spent August on a bicycle trip with Henry James.

"Through the Alps?" Phoebe said. "That's kind of hilly, don't you think?" She was working at a camp for disadvantaged children. "They bus them in so we advantaged rich white teenagers have something to do," she said. But really she loved it. The children taught her how to dance, and she seduced the director, who was twenty-four.

The beginning of Fin's trip was spent in a motel outside a provincial city he cannot remember the name of. One of the kids had strep throat, so they all had to sit around for almost a week playing gin rummy until he got better. When they set off, it was raining, a steady drizzle that followed them up and down mountains. After two weeks, Fin convinced Henry James to jump ship, and they took a train, with their bicycles, to Greece.

"I have a friend in Iraklion," he said, and they descended, three sunburned sixteen-year-old boys with enormous calf muscles, on the air force base.

Inside the base it was dusty and orderly, outside the base it was dusty and disorderly. "You will stay outside the base," Biffi said. He took them to a small restaurant and watched, laughing, as they ate.

"Do you have any idea what it is you're eating?"

"Who cares? We haven't had anything but sandwiches since, like, New York," Fin said.

"It could be goat," Biffi said.

"Who cares?"

They continued to shovel whatever the stew was into their mouths.

"When do you get out of here?" Henry said when they were finished. He took a sip of the Greek wine, which looked like olive oil.

"Another year."

"Maybe the war will be over by then."

"In two years we'll be in the lottery," James said.

Fin pointed at Biffi. "See?" he said.

"I didn't start the war."

"No, but you perpetuated it."

"I did what I thought was right. But it has not done anyone any good," Biffi said sadly. "Poor Czechoslovakia."

There was confused silence. None of the three boys paid attention to any news unless it was about Vietnam.

"Well, at least we got rid of Johnson," Fin said. "But everything else in the world is pretty fucked up."

There was some murmuring and clinking of squat heavy glasses. Henry and James went off to sleep at the student hostel.

"Good night, sir," they both said politely. "And thank you for a lovely dinner."

Biffi looked at Fin in surprise.

"They're from very good homes."

"Oh." Biffi saluted them.

"The baby looks like a dead baby possum that fell out of a tree," Fin said when they had gone.

"How unpleasant."

"Lady loves it. She is actually in love with it, I would have to say."

"Do you mind?"

Fin shrugged. "It has nothing to do with me."

"So cynical, Fin. It is just a baby."

"A baby possum."

"It will grow up."

"Into a possum."

Biffi laughed. "So she is happy? Really happy? This breaks my heart with joy."

"How can you spy and translate when you can't even speak English? I still don't understand that."

"One of the many mysteries of world domination."

Now Fin laughed. "I miss you," he said. "The house is like, I don't know, a Christmas manger."

"Straw? Virgins?"

"It's so fucking blessed. Everything is joyous and blessed. You know, there are people dying all over the world, but at our house, it's peace and joy."

"Would you rather have dying?"

"You know what I mean. It's so . . . hypocritical."

"What a rigid ideology you have. No joy?"

Fin drank some more wine. Which tasted surprisingly like dirt. Sweet dirt.

"Youth is idiotic," Biffi said.

"Thanks."

"I miss you, too, you know."

The moon was high in the sky. Some wobbly airmen passed by. Fin ate something smothered in honey that James had left on his plate. "Good," he said. "I'm glad." He was glad someone missed him. "If no one misses you, you don't really exist."

"Then you exist very much."

"And you never had to kill anybody."

"Not directly."

"Shit," Fin said. "Really?"

"I don't know. Which makes it worse, in a way."

It was when I was born that Mabel finally agreed to stop calling Lady "Miss Lady."

"I mean, what will the baby think? Growing up and hearing you talk like that, Mabel?"

Mabel pondered that. "I've always said it to be ironical," she said. "But babies don't need anything more ironical than life dishes out, that's true." And she stopped. She called my mother "Lady." I called my mother "Lady," too. It sounded so pretty to me. When I was very little, I called Mabel "Maybe," though she was as certain a part of my life as anyone.

I haven't told you my name yet.

"What's its name?" Fin asked when my mother and I got home from the hospital. It could have been anything, Fin thought. Anything awful. Lady had refused to discuss it. She was hiding it from him, which meant it was a crazy hippie name like Coriander or Tundra. What's its name? he remembers asking with the superiority and contempt he tried so hard to cultivate in those days.

Lady said, "Lydia."

Lady named me Lydia.

"That was my mother's name," Fin said.

"I know."

For one moment, just a moment, Fin bristled, thought, It's a bribe. So I will like the baby. Then he looked at Lady holding the small, silent thing wrapped in a white blanket, and he knew it was not a bribe, it was an act of love, pure and simple.

I think it was Gus who finally changed Fin's mind about me. Gus loved me. He loved to lick my sticky cheeks. He watched Lady, followed her, as she carried me around the house. He slept by my cradle. He ran to get Lady when I woke from a nap, ran to her and pushed his nose into her hand and whined and barked like Lassie. Fin swears he rocked the cradle when I cried, but I don't believe him.

And then sometimes Fin would hold me, hold me out to Gus as an offering, and Gus would lick my feet and I would laugh.

"When you laughed, you didn't look so possumy," Fin said.

I've seen pictures of myself when I was a baby. Hundreds of them, actually. Once I was born, Lady was much more interested in taking photographs of me than of rocks and blank walls. I didn't look at all like a possum. I was a very pretty baby, I think. I had round cheeks, not narrow possum cheeks. I had no teeth, not long yellow possum teeth. I had blue eyes, my father's beautiful blue eyes, not red pinprick possum eyes. And Gus loved me. And Mabel loved me. And Lady loved me. Lady, my mother, loved me. Finally, Fin loved me, too.

"You used to sit in a corner with your toys and talk to them. You never stopped talking. You were so charming. You were so intent. A little bossy."

"What did I say?"

"I have no idea. But your toys were very attentive. They never seemed at all bored."

"It's a beautiful name," Mabel said that day when we first got home from the hospital.

Fin nodded. He couldn't speak.

"You're lucky to have such a pretty name," Mabel cooed at the baby.

"Wow," Fin said at last.

"Lydia," Lady said very softly.

And that's when Gus licked my face for the first time and Mabel and Lady shooed him away and Fin's resolve began to falter.

"That's when we became a family," he told me. "Right then. I just didn't know it yet."

Fin started to love me gradually. But from deep within his cramped, personal teenage misery and his big, apocalyptic, six-ties teenage misery, he started to love me.

"Where has everyone got to?"

The first few years of my life are not as clear to me as they were to Fin, of course. Fin says Lady sang mildly obscene ditties to quiet me down. *Oh, I used to work in Chicago, in a department store . . .* That kind of thing. I remember the Central Park Zoo, riding on Fin's shoulders. He smelled like Neutrogena soap. Lady smelled like L'Air du Temps, Fin said. Mabel smelled like me, Ivory soap. Fin would swing me around by my arms until I got dizzy. Then we would lie on the floor next to each other and watch the room spin. He unpacked his toy soldiers on my second birthday and let me play with them. Little men from long ago. Then he packed them up again. I ate my dinner early, but as soon as I could sit, Fin says, I sat at the table in my pajamas and watched Fin and Lady eat theirs. Sometimes I retreated to the floor beneath the table. Gus would lie beside me and look at me with his serious brown eyes. Sometimes, when they were done eating, Lady and Fin would join us. Fin told me we would sit underneath the table, the four of us, Gus and I both wriggling with joy, and Mabel would come in and say, "Where has everyone got to?" The trick was not to laugh.

I know we finally did go to Japan, because Fin told me. He

says I was the tallest person there. Ha ha. I know we never went to India. It was planned for when I was four. But we did go to Australia. And we did go to the Grand Canyon. Sometimes I think I remember seeing a kangaroo, which would obviously be in Australia, but since my memory of the kangaroo is in black and white and it is wearing boxing gloves, it was probably from a movie or a rerun of an episode of *The Gale Storm Show*. I was only one and a half.

In the summers, Lady and I went to Capri. In 1970, when Fin and Henry were traveling through Europe on a Eurail pass (James had moved to Boston with his family and fallen out of touch), they came to see us. They started out in London and made their way slowly to Rome, then took the train down to Naples.

"A little different when you're seventeen than when you're fifteen," Fin told me. He sat in a compartment, Henry across from him. A woman patting her face with eau de cologne sat beside Fin. Next to Henry was an elderly, florid man slicing and offering cheeses and apples and salamis. "He'd been a prisoner of war," Fin said. "War always ends with people sharing apples, I guess. Eventually."

Fin looked for Donatella on the beach, but he never saw her there. They stayed for a few days. I was just starting to walk, I'm told. I was a baby on a beautiful island with my mother and father. "I think she still hoped you all would live together someday, permanently, you and Michelangelo and her." But even without that, Lady came back from that summer happy, Fin said. "We all wanted peace and love," he said. And in her uneven, scrappy way, my mother seemed to have found it.

And then it was Fin's senior year of high school. So much of what happened in those years has been reconstructed for me by Fin, it's sometimes hard to tell which are my memories and which are his. The place on my mother's shoulder that fit against my cheek. The pressure of her hand, cool and light and reassuring, when she held mine. I remember black patent-leather shoes with seed pearls in the shape of a flower. I remember driving in the car, curled up in the back with Gus. I remember cows, big and black and white, with tails like whips swatting flies. I remember my mother reading: *You must never go down to the end of the town without consulting me.* I remember being happy. At least I think I do, thanks to Fin.

And then came July 4, 1971. The air was sweet with summer. The windows were down and the freshness of citrus and jasmine traveled with us in the little car. Hunched brittle pines, stars heavy in the sky, too bright, too big, too many, too close to be real, four people squeezed into the Fiat 500, Lady and Michelangelo in front, Fin in back, his hands emerging from the sunroof, palms forward, me on the seat next to him, watching, I'm told. I don't remember this part. Any of it. But I know the story as well as I know my name.

Fin had arrived in Capri that day. He'd just graduated from high school. He was eighteen. I was two. Lady was driving, fast, as fast as she always drove. We had gone to Anacapri to celebrate, to celebrate everything—the Fourth of July, Fin's graduation, Fin's acceptance to Columbia, Fin's arrival. Lady had borrowed the car from a friend and that was part of the celebration—driving. My mother loved to drive. There was only one real road in Capri, and she drove up that narrow, twisting lane to the restaurant and now down the narrow, twisting lane, fast. It was the perfect night. Fin was so happy. We were all happy. The car careened around each curve, hugging the steep cliffs that soared beside them. I was clapping my hands.

Then Fin remembers lights, headlights, a wall of rock, sheer, rising up blank and immediate. Then looking up at the starry sky. The scented breeze. The delicate perfume of lavender. The mineral smell of blood. Someone cradling his head. Someone telling him not to worry, but not in English. Not in Italian. Still, somehow he knew. But who was it? Not Lady. Not Michelangelo. Where was Lady? Where was Michelangelo? Where was I? He remembers the ambulance, a tiny ambulance. He remembers the lights, the European siren, that World War II movie siren.

And then nothing.

I remember nothing. And then nothing. And then Fin.

I remember him sitting beside me holding my hand. In a hospital. A hospital the size of a thriving veterinary service, he told me later, years later. He had a cast on his arm and black stitches like Frankenstein's monster on his forehead.

I cried for Lady. "I want my Lady."

"I'm here," Fin said. He had been there all night, sitting, waiting for me to wake up. Before that, he had been in a hospital bed, too. He'd woken up in a room with several beds, but at that point he didn't know he was in a hospital. He didn't know where he was. He saw two handsome older men in white linen suits standing beside him. You have blood on your jacket, he tried to say to the one who looked vaguely familiar, but nothing came out, and he went back to sleep, or whatever you call the drugged, shocked unconsciousness after an accident. When he opened his eyes again, there was a nun standing beside him. Oh no, he thought. I have died and heaven is Catholic and I'm in big trouble. But he was alive, and the nun told him in halting English that he had been in a car accident.

"Who were the men in the white suits?" he asked. "Who was the man with blood on him?" Because what if the men were angels and the nun was lying and Fin was dead and heaven was Catholic?

"They found you," she said.

Fin wanted the men to come back. He didn't want to be in a room that looked like a World War I ward with a nun in a black habit, her face round and smooth, her nun hat lifting off her head like starched plumage.

"French," the nun said. "They waited until they saw you were doing well. Now they go back to France."

"Am I doing well?"

"Oh yes."

He had a sudden, sinking thud of a thought. "The others?" he said. "How are the others?"

"Everything is fine," said the nun, and Fin knew everything was not fine. Everything was far from fine.

When he woke up the next time, a doctor was there with the nun. Fin felt stitches on his forehead, the long welts and furrows of stitches.

"How are the others?" Fin said. "You have to tell me."

"Everything is fine," the doctor said.

And Fin was sure we were all dead.

He was wrong. I was alive.

When they let him get up, he came to my room. I had been thrown from the car. You flew, Fin told me when I woke up. You landed on a cushion of fragrant lavender. Like a little bird in a nest.

"Did you fly?"

"Just a little," Fin said. "But I had a rough landing. See?" He held out his arm in its thick white cast. "We're a little broken, you and I. We have to put ourselves back together."

I asked for Lady. I remember, in little jagged bits, how thoroughly, utterly, she was not there.

I was bruised, but that was all. Flung from the car into a pillow of lavender, just as Fin said. Through the open window I had
flown. Fin had been flung against the door and broken his arm.
Lady and Michelangelo had gone through the windshield. The
two Frenchmen in their white linen suits found us. One drove
on to get help. The other held Fin's head. The Frenchman didn't
even know I was there at first. Then I mewed like a kitten, that's
what he told the doctor, and he found me in my lavender nest.

We left the hospital the next day and went back to the green
door that led to the garden that led to the small white villa. Fin
carried me on his shoulders, and I rested a foot on his cast. I
could touch the great, rough lemons overhead. It was then, as
we walked beneath the lemons, that Fin told me that Lady and
Michelangelo had been killed.

My mother is buried in the Cimitero Acattolico, the tiny
Protestant cemetery on Capri. She would have liked that, I
think. Fin was sure of it. Especially when Gracie Fields moved
in eight years later. Capri was where Lady felt most at home,
where she fell in love. It is an enchanted place, and that's all
Lady really wanted, isn't it? To be enchanted, finally, after enchanting everyone else.

Biffi was at the funeral. He flew over right away, and Mabel
came with him. She wore a black hat with feathers that she let
me blow in every direction.

My father was buried in Milan. I've never followed up on
that part of my family, thinking he would not have wanted me
to. But Fin and I went back to Capri almost every year. We
stayed in the house with the green gate. We walked in the Cimitero Acattolico. We talked about Lady.

For a long time I didn't really understand that my parents
were dead. I understood only that they were not there. And I

understood that Fin was. That he would always be there. He took me home to New York, and he was there, holding my hand or putting me on his lap, telling me stories about my mother or giving me sips from a spoon of milky cappuccino. He carried me under his arm, he put me on his shoulders, he fed me and bathed me, he took me to my first day of school, he pushed me on the swings. And when I had nightmares, which I did for years, nightmares of drowning, he rocked me back to sleep singing soft Italian songs, pop songs about love. He taught me to ride a bicycle. A navy blue one with three speeds.

We visited the cows, of course. Darlington and Daisy were his mother's favorites. His mother's name was Lydia, too, just like mine. Did I know that?

I did know that. I knew Fin's father was my grandfather and Fin's mother was not my grandmother. But most of all, I knew Fin was my guardian.

"A guardian means I shelter you," he said. "And get you coffee ice-cream sodas."

Which he did.

"I had a guardian, too," he said.

"You were lucky, too," I said.

And Fin laughed and kissed me on the head and said, yes, he was lucky, too.

Epilogue

Fin is turning sixty this year. My guardian, Uncle Fin, though, understandably, he never wanted me to call him that.

Imagine being an eighteen-year-old boy suddenly responsible for a two-year-old? Well, Mabel was there, thank goodness, holding my hand in the stony alleys of Capri, on the ferry, up the stairs to the airplane. She was there in the house on Charles Street. She said, *Thank the Lord you're a girl, boys are nothing but trouble, except some boys, of course.* Then she'd laugh and say, *Who am I talking about, Lyddie?* And I'd say, *Finnie!* And she'd say, *No! Gus!* And I'd say, *Finnie!*

We also had Biffi, and thank goodness for him, too. Biffi was there in Capri, arranging everything, smoking his pipe, making me dolls from pipe cleaners and attaching them to the buttons on my blouse. He was there in New York. He was there whenever Fin needed anything, whenever I needed anything. I used to call Biffi "my Biffi," the way you might say "my grandfather." I don't see how Fin would have gotten through college without Biffi. And Biffi has always been the one I could go to when I wanted something Fin wouldn't let me have. My first car, for instance. It wasn't the money—I had saved enough to

25

pay for that hunk of junk. It was that Fin never wanted me in a car at all, ever, even taxis. I can't really blame him. But there are places in the world without buses or subways, and I went to college in one of them. Biffi had a series of girlfriends over the years, all of them artists, one odder than the next. Sometimes I went to see their shows. They painted themselves with dots or slept in glass cases. But when they were off duty, as Biffi put it, they would do ordinary things like take me to the Bronx Zoo.

Sometimes I wonder what my life would have been like if my mother and father hadn't died in that car accident, of course I do. Fin smiles that Lady smile of his and says it would have been wonderful. It would have been full of fun and freedom. It would have been full of books. It would have been an adventure. And then I say, *My life has been wonderful. It has been full of fun and freedom. And books. And isn't everyone's life an adventure?* And then he tells me one of his stories about Lady. He's been telling stories about Lady since I can remember. The stories are full of love. *I try to keep out the ironical*, he says. *Children have no need of the ironical. Mabel said that.* I miss Mabel. She retired when I went to college, moved into a condo in Virginia with her sister. They're both about a hundred and one. They send birthday cards for each of my kids every year. Mabel even signs them "Maybe."

Children have no need of the ironical? I don't know. Maybe that's exactly what they need. Is it ironical that, when I got married, Fin gave me the house on Charles Street and moved back to his grandparents' house in Connecticut? Is it ironical that I even got married?

Fin never did. He lives with a beautiful woman named Debbie. She was very much a part of my growing up, she was part of my family, but she and Fin have never married. I have a feeling, and not a happy feeling, that his refusal to marry has been some kind of homage to Lady, but maybe I'm wrong.

Maybe Debbie didn't want to get married, some sixties residue, perhaps. For a while they said that they could not in good conscience get married until their gay friends were able to. Then the laws started changing and Phoebe and all the rest of their gay friends started getting married, and still Fin and Debbie did not. Maybe they're waiting until they're twenty-five. Ha ha. Sometimes Fin says, *How can I marry someone named Debbie, of all things? The name of a commercial cupcake.* And then Debbie says, *How can I marry a man named Fin? Named on a whim? Not even Huckleberry Finn, but French for 'the end.'*

To which I say, *But it wasn't the end at all, was it?*

Acknowledgments

I would like to thank Antonio Monda and Davide Azzolini and everyone involved with *Le Conversazioni* for introducing me to the enchanted isle of Capri; Sarah Crichton for her battered red diary; Jennifer Crichton for her memory; Nat Hentoff for *Jazz Country*; Mara Nierman for her colorful education; Vicki Tolar Collins for long-ago Iráklion; Paul Berman for the romance of little ways; and Gabriella Platania for her kindness, coffee, and lemon-scented garden.

Discussion Questions

1. In Fin and Lady's world, what constitutes good parenting? What special wisdom do Fin and Lady share, despite their youth?

2. If you were to become the guardian of a young person in your family, who would be the best fit? What sort of life would you try to make for him or her?

3. How are Fin and Lady influenced by the memory of Hugo and Lydia? How is the siblings' relationship affected by the fact that they have different mothers?

4. Which of Lady's suitors were you rooting for? Was Fin an asset to Lady as she pursued love? What did her suitors teach him about the ideal man?

5. What are the similarities and differences between Tyler, Biffi, and Jack? How does each of them uniquely influence Lady's life?

6. How does the 1960s time period affect the story line? Why is it appropriate for this tale to be set against a backdrop of social change in the face of tragedy?

7. What were your theories about who the narrator was? Is the narrator a sign of a new chapter for Fin, or is history repeating itself?

8. Discuss the irony of the names Lady and Fin ("end"). Do their names affect their sense of self?

9. What is Michelangelo's appeal, in Lady's eyes? How is he different from the other important men in her life, including her father?

10. Discuss Fin's friendships with Phoebe and Donatella. What does he discover when he tries to find a love of his own?

11. What does Fin's letter to Mabel, written from Capri (pages 219–20), reflect about this transitional time in his life?

12. On page 183, in the opening scene of the chapter "April Fool's Day," Fin asks himself, "If you're the child someone never has to have, do you have to be an especially good one?" How would you respond to him? How is his life shaped by missing his mother?

13. Discuss the book's three major locales—rural Connecticut, Greenwich Village, and Capri—and the ways in which they reflect the shifting personalities of the characters. Which

locale would you prefer to call home? What does Fin and Lady's globe-trotting say about the meaning of home?

14. Cathleen Schine often creates characters who triumph in unconventional ways. Do Fin and Lady possess any of the traits you enjoyed in Schine's previous novels?